THE FORMER FAKE BOYFRIEND

SWEET SOUTHERN
BOOK 2

MAYA JEAN

Alpha read by Emory Winters

Beta read by Sage, Lexi, Devin, and Donatella

Edited by L.C. Valentine

Proofread by Judy's Proofreading

Cover by Black Jazz Design

❋ Created with Vellum

For all the eldest children,
You're seen and loved by all that know you.

PLAYLIST

- Yellowstone Theme - Andrew Crawford
- Breathe - Faith Hill
- More of you - Chris Stapleton
- Cowboy Take Me Away - Cameron Hawthorn
- Found Your Love - Bailey Zimmerman
- Neon Moon (with Kacey Musgraves) - Brooks and Dunn
- To a T - Ryan Hurd
- Unchained Melody - The Unrighteous Brothers
- The Trouble with Wanting - Joy Williams
- Love is a Wild Thing - Kacey Musgraves
- Lonely Cowboy - Kaleo
- H.O.L.Y. - Florida Georgia Line
- Tennessee Whiskey - Chris Stapleton
- Two - Sleeping At Last
- Midnight Moon - Paper Kites
- Murmur of Yearning - Thomas Csorba
- Can't Help Falling in Love - Kacey Musgraves
- Space and Time - S.G. Goodman

- Ride Out in the Country - Yola
- When You Say Nothing at All - Allison Krauss
- I Like to be Me When I'm With You - Drew Holcomb
- Best Shot - Jimmie Allen
- Wanted - Hunter Hayes
- Give In To Me - Garrett Hedlund and Leighton Meester
- Cover Me Up - Zac Brown Band
- Front Porch - Joy Williams
- Millionaire - Chris Stapleton
- It's Your Love - Tim McGraw and Faith Hill
- Bless the Broken Road - Rascal Flatts
- Heaven Is - Kacey Musgraves
- Grow Old with Me - Sunny Sweeney
- Forever and For Always - Shania Twain

Spotify

CONTENT AND TRIGGER WARNINGS

- Death of a parent from cancer (off page)
- Grief over the loss of a parent
- Neglectful parents
- Parents in prison
- Sex work (Trevor continues sex work after first meeting Beau)
- Brief mention of drug use by a minor
- Brief mention of an MC experiencing and not enjoying rough sex
- MC utilizing sex work as a form of self harm
- Eldest child syndrome

AUTHOR'S NOTE

I like to paint grief as I personally know it. I hope by now that my readers know this about me. All that to say that Beau and Trevor make certain decisions that are *true* to them. I'm sorry if you disagree with those decisions, but please keep in mind that I write what the characters tell me, not what is always palatable to readers. With that note, I hope you enjoy their story, because they took me to hell and back to write it.

CHAPTER ONE
BEAU

Lonely seems to be my default state. Maybe a little ironic considering I'm constantly surrounded by family. But somehow the loneliest I feel is in a room full of loved ones. Looking back to childhood, that odd feeling of loneliness was present even then. I'm always an outsider looking in. Just an onlooker to everyone else's life.

One hundred bucks that no one would ever think I feel that way. Strong Beau. Reliable Beau. Perfect son Beau. Former high school quarterback star Beau. The one that gets called when a friend needs help moving. The one that steps up to run the farm when the elder family members start dropping like flies.

Sometimes I ache to be the one that gets cared for. The person that someone else makes sacrifices for to make happy. But people take one look at my six-foot-five frame, my easy nature, and assume that I am *never* in need of anything. Someone that takes up as much room as me could never need to be cared for, to be loved gently. My entire life has been a cycle of helping everybody else, without anyone thinking of me. Why would it change now?

The truck rumbles beneath me as I head down the familiar gravel road that leads to my parents' property. It's not far from mine, we all live within ten minutes of each other. My cousin Colby even lives right across the street from me. A fifteen-minute walk in country terms.

A few months ago, I took over running the family farm, Clay Road Farms. The farm has been in business for over a hundred years. Providing fresh produce to the region along with seasonal U-pick of strawberries, blueberries, peaches, and our renowned sunflowers. The land is my safe place. Growing up here, running free on soil that belongs to me, to my ancestors, rooted me to this land in a way I can never explain. Rooted me to my family.

Which is why everything about what's happening to us now is so emotionally crippling. At least for me.

Pulling into the long driveway, I park just outside my parents' large farmhouse, right behind my sister's beat-up green truck. For a few moments I sit quietly, taking it all in, with all the weight of a bomb sitting on my chest. Just months until it all explodes. I blink back tears of frustration, of sorrow, then take my hat off to run my hands through my still-sweaty hair. Days start early and end late at the farm, leaving me beyond exhausted most days. Fatigued to the very bone.

And now my dad.

After steeling myself, I climb out of the truck to head into the house. Heart viciously pounding against my ribs, I quietly push the front door open. Everything about the house is the same as always. Warmth and love and a million different memories that are impossible to narrow down to a handful of favorites. So many memories that bring me wild amounts of joy, stacked right on top of each other, but new ones that bring immense grief filter through and infiltrate the happiest moments of my life.

The sound of Andy's harsh sobs echo around the house, pulling me out of my reverie. Andy crying has always broken my tender heart, making me want to burn the world down to stop her tears. A big brother's job, my mama always said. Andy doesn't cry much now that she's an adult, but when she does, the need to fix it is almost insurmountable. The fact I can't fix it this time tears my heart apart with awful grief.

"Daddy, please." Andy's whispered plea is so full of pain that it almost brings me to my knees. But I hold firm and continue into the living room.

Andy and my dad sit together on the large sectional, her head resting on his chest, tears soaking through his shirt. Mom looks on from the kitchen, a mug of tea in her trembling hand. They were supposed to wait for me. That was the deal.

Dad's terrified gaze lands on me. The absolute pain and anguish on his face silences all of my own fears, all of my own needs. I've got to fix this.

"Andy," I whisper softly as I slowly kneel in front of her.

Andy sniffles loudly, then turns her stormy blue eyes towards me. Crimson splotches dot her freckled cheeks, her dark curls soaked with fallen tears. Taking her hands in my own, I squeeze them tight, and aim the most affectionate smile I can muster towards her.

"Pops made his choice. We gotta respect it, darlin'." My voice comes out even, despite the waves of grief crashing against the shore inside me. Andy and Mom need my strength right now. They need a strong Beau, protector Beau, there's no room for me to fall apart too.

"It's just not fair." Andy's bottom lip trembles. Another tear slowly slides down her cheek.

"Who told you life was fair?" I repeat the family motto with a gentle wink.

The phrase startles a wet laugh out of her, and she angrily wipes her tears away with the backs of her hands. Thankfully, the tension dials down just a little, but Andy still clings tightly to Dad's shirt. His fingers lovingly sift through her long brown curls, untangling the knots that have gathered from her day. A few moments later, Mom wanders in with a tray of cookies and glasses of lemonade. None of us are hungry or thirsty, but we put on the show, acting like our world isn't falling apart.

Once Andy and Mom flee to the back porch, I turn my gaze back to Dad. Exhaustion flows from him in huge waves. He's more tired than I've ever seen him. Months of cancer treatment have turned the strongest man I know inside out. The colon cancer diagnosis had been out of the blue. We'd thought for sure that with radiation and chemotherapy he'd be just fine but... when one makes plans, God laughs.

"After the wedding... we'll get with hospice," Dad tells me, eyes distant and empty.

"You're sure?" I ask, voice a hushed whisper.

Dad nods once, swallowing slowly. "It's how I want to go. I want to go gently, quietly, with all of you around me. I'm so tired, Beau."

"I know, Pops. I know."

"You'll have to step up, Andy and your mama are going to need you now more than ever."

I nod quickly. "I know. They can always count on me."

Dad's gaze softens, his fingers linking with mine over his thin thigh. "You've always been the strong one. The good one. We never had to worry about you. I know you're going to do right by them and the farm, but you've got to promise me you'll think of yourself sometimes too. Life is so beautiful when you let love in, Beau. So precious. And it goes by so, so fast. Do you understand?"

"I understand, Pops. It's alright."

Standing slowly, I sit on the couch beside him, tossing my arm over his shoulder to hold him close. Pops has always been the only person closest to my height and width, but now he seems so small, so fragile in my hold. My heart does another dangerous dip and dive, stomach knotted with nerves, but I push it down where it can't hurt me.

I hold him for many long quiet moments, just listening to him breathe. Thinking about how one day I'll forget about the sound of his soft breaths, the smell of his cologne at the end of the day, the hearty chuckle when he finds something particularly funny.

One day he'll just be a memory, and I'll be lonelier than ever.

"You got a date for Andy's wedding?" Mama asks me as I stand in the doorway of her office at the farm.

I wince at the question. "Not yet."

"It's in a month," she reminds me, a sour look on her face.

I know she's thinking about how time is slipping through our grip. Andy's wedding, then however many months we have with Dad afterwards. Time is moving so fast, only to slow to a crawl afterwards.

"I've been talkin' to someone online. I'll invite him." The lie just slips out. I'm not sure what really possessed me. Maybe it's the idea of Pops worrying about me, Mama being stressed. I don't know. But the lie doesn't feel quite as wrong as I expected.

"Really?" Mama asks, eyes lighting up with curiosity.

"Just for a little bit. It's long distance."

"Long distance?" Mama repeats skeptically.

"Yeah, mostly over the phone. That sort of thing."

Mama hums and eyes me shrewdly, all the weight of a stare only a mother can truly give. "Beau, you've been my son for thirty-six years, and you've never been one for many words. How do you date someone mostly over the phone?"

The little dig isn't unusual, by now I'm not sure people think it's a dig when they talk about my lack of talking. Most of the time I don't have much to say. A man of action instead of words, most of my teachers in school used to write on my report card. Even my football coach liked that about me, especially when I came out. Easier to ignore the elephant in the room if the elephant isn't blabbering about it. It probably helped that I was bigger than most of our linebackers even back then.

"I can talk enough when I need to, Mama. Anyway, you got those orders for the new sprinkler hoses in lot thirteen? We talked about it a few weeks ago. I'm afraid the blueberry bushes will die if we don't get it fixed."

"On back order," she murmurs distractedly, face turned towards the computer screen. "I'll try another vendor. I meant to tell you... it just slipped my mind."

Now's the time to mention the other thing I know she

6

won't like. "Have you thought about taking the next few months off? Anna can cover the front office in the meantime." After all, the girl has been shadowing my mother since high school.

Letting out a weary sigh, she throws herself back into her office chair. Her normally vibrant red hair is a messy nest on top of her head. I'm not sure she's even brushed it recently. Dark circles rest under her eyes. For the first time in my life, I can't fix something for the people I love most. And that in itself is enough to bring me to my knees.

Leaving Mama to it, I head back to the front office. Everyone greets me with friendly faces, but there's still that annoying element of pity in their eyes. What am I going to do? Mama will be expecting me to have a date for the wedding now. Probably much to her relief after spending years harping on me to date, to get out there, to find someone.

It's not like I don't like dating. I just don't trust most people. The times I have tried to date haven't exactly gone well. People take one look at me and expect one thing. But my heart aches for something else. I ache for someone to hold me like they cherish me. For someone to take on the world with me when life is just a little too hard to bear. But most days I'm not sure that person exists. So maybe, I should fake happiness. Like I fake everything else.

With my mind made up, the farm disappears behind me in a cloud of dust. The setting sun dips below the trees along the road, casting orange and pink hues along the earth that I know better than the back of my hand.

An empty house greets me. Like always. Sometimes my most fervent, slightly frightening dream is to come home to a house with someone waiting on me. A smile, a kiss to my cheek, and arms that can hold me when vulnerability hits me. That's a landslide of a dream though, one that I'll keep dreaming, until the loneliness consumes me.

After a few chilled beers on my back porch, my fingers have a mind of their own. Googling about fake boyfriends is about as easy as one would imagine. Only books appear when I search, which is frustrating. I'm not much of a reader. Some of them do look entertaining though.

Sidetracked.

An hour of searching later, a social media website for a company called *The Boyfriend Experience* comes across my phone. Interesting. It seems mostly legitimate. A service that provides fake boyfriends for weddings, work events, and even just for companionship. The young woman that owns the place seems friendly enough. She's got tight blonde curls and a sweet smile that eases a lot of my discomfort at the idea of doing something so far-fetched.

What if everyone figures out that I've hired someone? The only person that might see through me would be Colby, but he's been so caught up in his own grief over the loss of his husband that maybe it'll slide right by him. Maybe I can convince everyone I'm happy, that someone loves me. If I can give my dad just an ounce of peace before he passes, wouldn't it all be worth it?

I'm not much of an impulsive person but I fill out the survey, type up an email, and send it off without a second thought. The silence of my house has never been so loud. So deafening. Even the cicadas outside seem quieter, hushed after my quick decision. But I know it's the right one. If only to get me through the wedding, so no one wonders for a minute how I'm doing.

Not that they would wonder. After all, I'm strong, steady Beau. The one that never falls apart.

CHAPTER TWO

TREVOR

The scent of whiskey and expensive cologne lingers on me like a bad kiss. Trudging out of the downtown Atlanta skyrise, I try to ignore the disapproving stares from the staff. Everything feels a little too raw after a weekend playing pretend. Worn a little too thin from acting. But that's also the best part. Being someone else, being desired, being wanted because they can't have me. No one can.

Warm, muggy air slaps me in my face, a stark difference from the frozen air-conditioning of the fancy building I just exited. Pulling my weekend bag a little higher up on my shoulder, I walk a few blocks until I'm sure I'm alone. Never know with fake boyfriends. Sometimes they want to keep me so badly that their brains go decidedly wonky and decide to follow me.

It's happened a few times. Enough to put me on edge. Forever.

The Boyfriend Experience saved me in a lot of ways. When I hate myself a little too much, I spend a few days pretending to be someone else. Fake boyfriend Trevor is perfect and lovely. Fake boyfriend Trevor has no *issues*. Trevor is the perfect clean slate of a human just ready to be what anyone dreams for the right price. Escort Trevor can be too. Trevor will be anything if the dollars stack up enough.

Which is exactly why my job works so well for me. Most of the time. Playing pretend makes it easier for me to shut off the parts of my brain that sometimes yell too loud. The meanest parts of my brain.

The ride to the clubhouse is quick despite the congested downtown Atlanta traffic. The driver is thankfully silent, because I don't think I could take idle chitchat after the past few days at the stuffy penthouse. Giving the driver a hefty tip, I hop out of the car to stride into the high-rise with a little pep in my step. Everything is about appearances. If I sell it well enough, no one will ever question *what* I'm selling.

"Hey, Scott." I shoot the sweet older security guard a wicked grin, and inch my way towards the elevator.

Scott eyes me carefully. "Trevor. Coming from a job?"

I salute him with a teasing wink. "Three days. Heading up to see Claire now. Are the other boys upstairs?"

Scott nods, then lets his gaze return to the front entrance. "'See you on the way out."

Sending a wave over my shoulder, I swipe my badge to enter the elevator. I lean against the wall with a relieved sigh, pinching the bridge of my nose to hopefully avoid a migraine. Fifteen floors are all I've got to get my shit together. Shaking my arms out, I paste a grin on my face, just in time for the doors to slide open to *The Boyfriend Experience* headquarters. Aptly nicknamed the clubhouse. Basically, the place is an entire office floor dedicated to the four of us and Claire, along with her assistant, Davis.

White marble floors, white walls, colorful art pop accents, and the sound of my best friends laughing is enough to calm my frayed nerves. A very particular giggle has my lips twitching up in a smile. Bypassing the main room echoing with laughter, I head back towards Claire's office.

"Boss lady!" I shout, putting on my most panty-melting, charming smile.

Claire aims a death glare my way. "What did you do?"

I blink slowly at her, hoping to project total innocence. "Nothing?"

She huffs while tapping her perfectly manicured nails against her pristine desk. "When you call me 'boss lady,' usually you've fucked up."

"That's a Pavlovian response you've got there."

A laugh escapes her, despite her clearly wanting to be annoyed with me. I pop my hip and lean against her desk, grinning sweetly down at her. Claire saved my ass years ago. I'd left home with nothing to my name. We'd grown up together in the rich upper crust of Manhattan, but she'd fled out of state for college. Family life hadn't been good for her either. When I needed a place to land, there wasn't any other option but Claire.

New life, new Trevor, new everything. Thanks to Claire.

Another loud laugh makes me look over my shoulder, but Claire's office impedes my view.

"I've got another job for you," Claire says while carefully handing me her tablet.

Sweet. The email is already pulled up on the screen for my review.

Name: Beau Callahan
Age: 36 years old

Kinks: Uhm... I don't really have any. I've been told I'm a romantic at heart.

Sex included in boyfriend experience: I don't think so

Length of time: three days in July for my sister's wedding

Lodging: My house in Florida

Comments: *Hi... I'm not too good with words. But I'm reaching out to hire a fake boyfriend for my sister's wedding. My dad is sick, and this is my sister's big day. Everyone's on me about bringing a date. I don't want to detract attention from her day. I want to hire a fake boyfriend to be on my arm, support me, and make the day as good as he can. Bonus points if he likes the silent type.*

Seems pretty to the point. Weddings are actually some of my favorite experiences. Most people are happy when they attend a wedding. Happy people at weddings have less chances of people being awful little shits. And I *hate* awful little shits. But the guy seems a little boring. Usually, I get the kinkier johns. The ones that want to call me a slut or enact some weird fantasy that could probably land them on *Dateline* if they aren't careful.

"Seems boring," I point out with a deep frown.

"Maybe it's time for a change of pace. I can't always send you to the ones that ask to bite, choke, and call you a filthy slut."

I wink dramatically at her. "I am a filthy slut though."

"Trevor," Claire admonishes me with a steely look.

"Fine. Trip isn't far. Weddings are easy. There's not even any sex though. Are you sure you don't want to send Benji? He's so... sunshine."

Claire playfully smacks my thigh. "You know he hates when you call him that."

"It's his legal name!"

"Still." Claire carefully takes the tablet from me. She keeps her eyes on the tablet, finger restlessly tapping at the screen. "I'm sending you on this experience. You need a break. The boyfriends will agree."

My cell phone picks the perfect time to start vibrating. We stare at each other for a few stilted moments, before Claire throws her hands up in frustration. The phone silences, but the weight of the call is enough to reiterate that she's probably right. A break to Florida for a few days could probably do my brain some good. I'd rather die than admit she's right though.

"Whatever." I push off the desk, flicking her pen off just to rile her up.

Her loud guffaw follows me out of the room. Following the sound of laughter, I drop my duffle bag off by the communal shower entrance before heading towards the main room.

Benji lies on the large sectional, dressed in only low-slung sweatpants, while letting Eli carefully paint his nails light blue. For a moment I stand there, taking in the sight of my best friends. Sometimes it still blows my mind that they decide over and over that I'm worth keeping. Worth spending time with. Worth anything at all for that matter.

"Trevor?" Jackson whispers from beside me.

I jolt and aim a glare his way. "You scared me."

His dark brown eyes turn shrewd. "Rough weekend?"

Punching his shoulder, I make my way past him toward the kitchen. "Exactly the kind of rough I like."

"Trevor."

"My God, why is everyone obsessed with saying my name like a swear word. What have I done to incur such wrath?"

Jackson follows me into the kitchen, radiating the brotherly energy he can never help but exude. He's not even the oldest. But he's big brother Jackson, our protector. The one I call when a john gets a little too rough and I'm too scared to call Claire. He's probably just feeling a little protective after what happened a few weekends ago. At least, that's how I explain away his behavior away as he follows me around the kitchen like an overly keen puppy dog.

"Back off," I whisper, annoyed.

Jackson huffs, grips my chin between his forefinger and thumb, tilting my face for close inspection. Against my better instincts, I allow him.

"No bruises."

I tear away from his grip with a scowl. "It was a normal experience this time. I promise."

Jackson hums, then crosses his giant arms against his broad chest. Shaved head, dark brown eyes, caramel skin, and the body of a professional athlete, Jackson is the agency's favorite top. I can see why. I get it. The man exudes daddy energy despite being only twenty-something. But he should know by now that I don't require that type of care. I can take care of myself.

"The energy in this room is stifling." Benji pops the fridge open to grab an energy drink. He looks from Jackson to me, gaze calculating. "Nice few days, Trevor?"

"Uh-huh." No longer hungry, I head back out to the living room. Plopping down on the couch, I tap my feet against Eli's. "Are we going out tonight?"

"No can do. I'm playing sugar baby again to that older guy. I'll be home late."

"Sex?"

Eli vigorously shakes his head. "Just a pretty thing on his

arm. He's sooooo nice. I'll be sad when he finds the real thing."

That's the worst part of the job. Forming a manufactured connection with someone, only to lose it when they find something real. Rarely happens for me, at least on my end. Sometimes I act too well, and the johns fall in love with me. Those are the times I'm glad we all live in the same high-rise, with tight security down below. Telling someone that's paid for you, *I'm not in love with you too*, is inherently dangerous.

"How was your three-day extravaganza?"

"Good," I answer with a lazy shrug.

Eli arches one eyebrow. "Just good?"

"Made bank. So yeah, good."

Eli presses his foot hard against mine, before tickling the bottom of my foot with his toes. I kick him until we devolve into a small play fight on the couch. Benji jumps over the back of the sofa, effectively stopping our wrestling.

A few moments later, Jackson strolls back into the living room, dressed in an impeccable black suit. He flicks a goodbye wave toward us.

"Heading out. I'll be back late."

"Jeez, I come home and everyone leaves," I tease.

"I'm not going out," Benji replies with a small frown.

Jackson playfully flicks Benji's ear. "Be good, Sunshine."

"I'll put a snake in your bed."

Jackson scoffs. "I'd like to see you do it."

Benji angrily narrows his eyes at Jackson. A couple of seconds pass before Jackson crumbles under the stare, dipping down to sweetly kiss the apple of Benji's cheek.

"Just kidding, love you, Benji."

Benji's face transforms into pure sunshine, dimples on display, light blue eyes twinkling. Scary how fast the man can go from terrifying to downright angelic. We all watch Jackson leave, turning at the same time to look at one another once the door closes shut behind him.

"So?" Benji asks.

Eli jumps up from the couch in a hurry. "I've got to go get ready."

Benji and I look at each other, then quietly agree with no discussion that we'll go our separate ways for the rest of the evening. Good for me.

I spend an hour or so in the gym, take a shower, then return to my mostly empty apartment a few floors below the clubhouse. I snuggle down onto the blankets of my bed with my phone to do what I always do when I take a job. Social media stalking my future fake boyfriend.

Beau Callahan has no online presence at all. Nothing. What the hell? What kind of man has absolutely no social media?

All I can find is a business in Northeast Florida for a family farm that hosts seasonal events and lets people pick their own fruit throughout the year. One of those sorts of places. They even have a pumpkin patch in the fall. I absolutely do not get absorbed in looking at all the photos of families picking pumpkins.

But that's when I hit pay dirt.

Finally, a picture of Beau Callahan. I only know it's Beau because it's from the sister I assume whose wedding I'll be attending. Andy Callahan posted a picture and tagged Clay Road Farms. Beau leans against a fence, a ball cap obscuring a good portion of his face, and he's petting a night-sky-black horse. But I can see the smile on his lips even from the bad angle of the photograph. Scruff covers his chin, and he's dressed in worn-to-hell work jeans, boots, and a faded work shirt that has Clay Road Farms blazoned across the back.

The back of his shirt is stretched taut against the solid line of his back. He's a big guy, almost level with the horse. My stomach does a few flips just at the sight of him. Oh yeah, playing fake boyfriend to Beau Callahan won't be a pain at all.

The flight from Atlanta to Orlando is splendidly short. Is it a little silly to take a flight for what would've been a seven-hour drive? Yes. But also, there's zero chance of road rage from me if I'm sitting in business class with an Arnold Palmer.

Humidity smacks me in the face the moment I step through the airport sliding doors. The sticky summer heat almost makes me gag, the thick air stuck in my throat. With a heavy sigh, I tie my hair up in a messy bun to prevent it from sticking to my neck.

Families eager to get to the theme parks in Orlando bustle around me. A young girl bumps into my side, and apologizes with a smile, so I just smile gently back at her letting her know it's alright. I watch her disappear with her family, long blonde curls dancing as she skips while holding her mother's hand tightly. Happy families. Must be nice.

"Trevor?" a deep voice calls out to me.

My brain takes a few moments to reboot when my gaze finally lands on Beau. My God. It's like looking directly at the sun. The photo I found of him online holds no comparison at all to the beauty of a man that stands before me. Beau is wildly tall, towering over everyone else at arrivals. Leaning against his truck, his forearm presses against the roof, dark green ball cap on his head. But it's the warm smile that makes him feel a little less large and a lot more sweet.

A whistle rents through the air from the tired parking cop, which I take as a sign to quickly hustle towards the truck. Beau comes around the truck, opens my door, and gestures for me to climb inside. I hop in with my most charming smile. Beau takes it in stride, smiling sweetly right back at me, then slams his own door shut.

"Beau Callahan," Beau says with just the hint of a shy smile. He holds his hand out for me, and I take it, giving him a firm good shake. Beau grins.

"Trevor Thomas."

"Good flight?" Beau asks conversationally as we make our way out of the airport arrivals area.

"It was fine," I admit, because it was exactly that. "Glad to be back on solid ground though."

"Don't like flyin'?"

His southern accent isn't too deep, but I like the way it softens some of his words. Makes him sweet in a way that makes him seem even more approachable.

"I am impartial to flying. It's always nice to get off the plane at the end."

Beau hums his agreement, then carefully guides the truck towards a toll road heading away from the airport. Silence envelops us for a little while, enough that I can make out the soft country music flowing from the truck speakers. Despite the family farm branding on the outside clearly making it a work vehicle, the truck is nice inside and cleaner than you'd expect.

Every now and then Beau hums along to the music, relaxing me even further in his presence. There's something gentle about him, something calming. Some clients raise my hackles immediately, usually for the best. Sometimes I need to be able to protect myself in very vulnerable moments. It happens very far and few between because Claire does painstaking background checks on johns. Doesn't mean it never happens. Usually, we just don't tell her the details, instead opting to tell her *never book this john again*.

I get the vibe Beau Callahan isn't going to be a problem.

"So, your sister's getting married?" I ask in hopes of striking conversation so that we don't sit in silence the entire way to his house.

"Yes, sir."

And then that's it. Beau doesn't elaborate further. So, I'm going to have to do most of the heavy lifting to get him to talk. No problem, he mentioned that in his application.

"How old is Andy?"

"Almost ten years younger than me. She was a happy surprise. She does the advertising and marketing for the farm."

"That's fun!" I say excitedly, but his lips just quirk up a little.

"Definitely more fun than my job."

"What do you do at the farm?"

He puts the blinker on to shift lanes, looking to his right, so I can finally get a good, up-close look at his face. Good God, the man is unfairly handsome. Square jaw, the right amount of beard, full lips, dark brown hair, and dark blue eyes, the color of the sky after a summer storm. I bite my lip as I appraise him, and his eyes flit to my mouth, before slowly meeting my gaze. A gorgeous flush rises on his cheeks as he looks back out at the road.

"I maintain the crops," Beau explains. "I'm also the boss of all the workers on the farm. It can be hard if we have a low crop year, but I know it's not really my fault. The land will only yield what it wants depending on the weather and other things out of my control."

"Sounds like hard work," I admit honestly.

He taps his fingers restlessly against the wheel again. "Not if I'm paying attention."

"To what?"

His lips quirk up under his beard. "The earth, my intuition."

What a nauseatingly endearing answer. We ride the rest of the way in silence, but I don't feel the need to fill it. Which is unusual for me. Just over an hour later we pull up to a gate that blocks off the entrance to a gravel road. Beau presses a button on a remote attached to the visor above him, and the gate swings open. Dirt kicks up behind us even though Beau's driving insanely slow. Must be because of the truck.

A house appears at the end of the driveway when we break through a copse of oak trees. The house is stunningly beautiful, although not cookie-cutter, or perfect by any stretch of the imagination. White sidings cover the outside and there's a wraparound porch. It's not big, just a modest size, but it looks absolutely lovely. Real farmhouse chic.

"Welcome home," Beau tells me with a shy smile.

Grabbing my duffle from the back seat, he easily slings it over his beefy shoulder. Wind blows through the trees, cutting shadows across the front yard. Flowers in a kaleido-scope of colors line the edge of the house. Bees flit around the flowers but pay us no attention as we make our way into the house.

Light wood floors, warm honey walls, and family photos hung in a haphazard fashion. Beau's house screams cozy. It's less HGTV and more well-loved home. Everything about it works in an odd sort of way. Something painful starts to bloom in my chest, but I push it down, far away where it can't hurt me.

Beau leads me down a short hallway and gestures at a door on the right. Peeking my head in, I find a small guest room, with a bed covered in a homemade quilt.

"Cozy," I tell him.

Beau shines with pride. "You hungry? I can cook us something here. Your flight got in a little early and no festivities start until tomorrow. I figure I'll wait until tomorrow to toss you to the lion's den."

"That bad?"

"Ah." Beau takes off his ball cap and anxiously runs his hand through his hair. "Not bad, they're just a lot. Especially to outsiders."

"Well, I'll have to make them think I'm not an outsider."

Beau eyes me for a few moments, gaze slightly narrowed. "How old are you? The agency said you're of age."

I send a lazy smirk his way. "I'm plenty old enough, Beau. I'm twenty-two."

Beau whistles, eyes going wide at my admission. "You're a kid," Beau whispers in disbelief.

"I'm a forty-year-old at heart, don't worry about it. You'll see."

He thoughtfully rubs a hand over the stubble on his chin, but doesn't argue, just gives me a tight nod. Awkward energy radiates off of him. I oddly feel the need to fix it.

"How about you show me around town?" I ask, hoping to ease the awkwardness between us. Everyone needs to believe we're boyfriends by tomorrow for the rehearsal dinner. "You need to pick up your suit?"

Beau heads towards the kitchen. I follow behind him like a scorned puppy.

"Yeah, sure. I do need to pick up my suit actually."

"Well, we can cross that off our list as you show me my boyfriend's hometown. Give me the works."

Beau sends a complicated look my way. But I just smile at him. My mission these next few days will be to keep him comfortable, make us believable, and earn my pay. I've endured worse.

CHAPTER THREE

BEAU

Trevor is so damn young. He's also unfairly gorgeous. All tan skin and golden hair that falls in soft waves, just barely brushing his shoulders. And the way he looks at me screams trouble. Even when he thinks I'm not paying attention, I can feel the heat of his assessing gaze. Raking over me with all the weight of a physical touch.

I definitely made the right decision in ushering him out of the house.

Instead of the work truck, I get us into my antique Chevy that I use to run errands around town. My classic girl doesn't have air-conditioning, so we roll the windows down, letting the whip of the wind cool us against the damp heat outside. Trevor is a great sport and doesn't complain. He just sits patiently in the passenger seat with his elbow out the window, eyes keenly absorbing the farm landscape we pass on the short way into town.

We strike gold when one of the diagonal parking spots in front of the suit shop along Main Street is empty. I park us carefully, leaving a wide berth beside the cars next to us to avoid getting dings to my truck. Trevor wordlessly follows me out of the car and into the sweltering heat. His head slowly turns both ways to take in the long expanse of Main Street. I try to see it from his viewpoint but it's impossible after living in Clay Springs all my life.

Brick-covered roads, with a long sidewalk down the middle of Main Street with blooming flowers in the middle. The wind blows the sweet scent of jasmine toward us from where it climbs and covers a gazebo. Inside are swings that, during the spring and winter, are frequently occupied by young couples entwined. A gentle, genuine smile covers Trevor's face as he absorbs downtown Clay Springs.

"It's like something out of a movie," Trevor says in awe. "You seriously get to live here?"

I grunt an affirmative answer. He follows me without a word into the suit shop. Mrs. Carmichael waves at me from the register, her hair still buzzed short after her numerous rounds of chemotherapy last year. I give her a hug over the counter, and she pats my cheek when I pull away.

"Beau Callahan. You get prettier every time I see you."

Heat slowly creeps up my neck and cheeks. "Thanks, ma'am."

"I've known you since you were born, and you still refuse to call me Cathy."

"Sorry, ma'am."

She scoffs at me with a teasing smile. "Your suit is all done. Want to try it on before you leave just to make sure?"

I nod and follow her to the back, almost forgetting that Trevor is with me. I only remember when Mrs. Carmichael brings out the suit and her gaze dips to the side.

"Who's this, Beau?"

When I turn around, I find Trevor leaning against the

partition separating the dressing rooms from the store. Trevor's smile is wide, his hands tucked into his pockets. I feel myself get hot all over again just at the sight of him.

"This is my boyfriend, Trevor."

Trevor practically glows. "Hi, ma'am."

Mrs. Carmichael rolls her eyes. "Not another one of you. The ma'am stuff makes me feel so old." She shushes me when I go to interrupt her. "I know, I know. Hard to break a habit." She does air quotes with a roll of her eyes and says, "My mama raised a southern gentleman."

"Well," Trevor says, with a conspiratorial smirk, "my mama didn't raise a gentleman at all. Tell me what to call you."

And Mrs. Carmichael has the gall to look flustered as she clumsily hands me the garment bag containing my suit. Almost slipping through my grasp, I catch it just in time. She gives me a rough shove into the dressing room. I enter with a shake of my head. It takes me a bit of time, but I get the suit on. Andy wanted us all in light gray suits with pale pink shirts. I can't deny my sister anything in this life, despite feeling decidedly funny in the get-up. Suits are not remotely my thing.

Trevor and Mrs. Carmichael's hushed whispers filter into the dressing room as I put the finishing touch of tying the tie Mrs. Carmichael presented to me with the suit.

"Well?" I ask as I exit the dressing room, running a nervous hand over my head.

All whispering ceases.

"Oh, you look so handsome, Beau." Mrs. Carmichael's eyes water a bit at the sight of me, so I look at Trevor instead. But he's almost as bad. His blue eyes are narrowed in on my shoulders, dipping down to my chest, then slowly flickering back up to my face.

"Handsome, indeed," Trevor says gruffly.

"Lucky you, dear."

Mrs. Carmichael manhandles me until I face the mirror, running her hands down the fabric to smooth any wrinkles in the suit. Once she's satisfied with it, she pulls away with a curt nod, and winks at me in the mirror. After I change back and pay, we leave the suit shop with Mrs. Carmichael promising to catch up with Trevor at the wedding.

I hang the suit up in the little sliver of space between the seat and the window in the cab of the truck. Leaning one arm atop the truck roof, I aim a smile at Trevor.

"Wanna see more of downtown? Or do you want to see the real Clay Springs."

Trevor's eyes turn mischievous. "Show me your Clay Springs."

"You got it." I tap the roof just once, then climb back into the truck.

We make our way back out of town, through the suburbs of Clay Springs, and back out to the rural country that I have always preferred. Sun breaking through the trees casts shadows along the old pavement road. I know these roads by heart. Like the lines on the palms of my work-roughened hands.

Country music crackles from the radio as we make the slow drive along my favorite back roads. A few times Trevor hums along like he knows the songs, but I don't think he does. His soft hums comfort me in the small space of the truck's cab. Out of the corner of my eye I watch enraptured as he takes his hair down from the messy bun, so the breeze gently blows through it. The wind tangles and knots it, but that seems to only make Trevor's smile widen.

The road turns from old, cracked concrete to compacted clay dirt. Trevor aims a confused look my way, but I just smile reassuringly at him.

My family's farm looms in the distance, until finally we pass by. The large sign announcing Clay Road Farms is teal with oranges, sunflowers, and blueberries in the logo. It's been the sign as long as I can remember, a little weathered, faded with age. But it's still the beacon that reminds me I'm close to home.

"That's my family's farm. Andy's wedding on Saturday will be hosted there."

"It's huge," Trevor comments softly. His gaze follows the farm until the truck is too far past it for him to keep looking. "How many acres do you own?"

"Well, the farm has about three hundred acres here in Clay Springs. It's been in the family for about five generations now. We export some of the citrus and other fruit, but most of our earnings now come from weddings to seasonal and weekend events."

"I can't wait to see it." Trevor shoots me a soft smile, lighting me up inside. He's got a great smile. A plush top lip, slightly bigger than the bottom, and his teeth are perfectly straight, unnaturally so. But everything about Trevor is beautiful, even sweet.

I restlessly tap my fingers against the wheel during the final fifteen minutes of the drive to our location. The truck comes to a slow stop in front of an old chain-link fence with a padlock. I jump out, unlock the fence, then drive us through, only hopping back out to lock it behind us.

"You bring me here to kill me?" Trevor teases.

"Nah, too many people have seen you in town now."

Trevor laughs, warm and deep, with his head tossed back. His voice is sweet and deep, just a bare hint of an accent that I can't recognize. Almost as if he's worked really hard to erase it. I pull up at the edge of the river and park by the bushes. Heat bugs rattle my senses as I open the truck door wide. They're too loud in the summer, overwhelming and piercing like a train passing right by me.

"God, are those crickets?" Trevor asks, sweeping his hair back into a messy half bun.

"Cicadas," I correct him.

He nods without looking at me, clearly distracted. I rest a hand on the small of his back to guide him to my intended location. A slightly overgrown trail cuts through the bushes, leading to my own personal oasis.

I don't frequent as much as I did when I was a kid now that I'm an adult. But my younger cousins and distant relatives keep the path well-worn.

The trees get just a little thicker right before giving way to a startling turquoise spring. A gasp from Trevor tears through the sound of the cicadas. He pauses beside me, disbelieving eyes on the placid water in front of us.

"You've got your own spring?"

"You wanna swim?" I gesture awkwardly toward the water. "I keep a couple of changes of clothes in my truck in case I get messy at work."

Trevor laughs derisively, aiming a blinding grin my way. "Of course I want to swim!"

Scrambling out of his clothes, Trevor stands in just a pair of tight black boxer briefs that leave nothing to the imagination. A quarter could bounce off his ass. Round and gorgeous, just like the rest of him. Smooth, golden skin, a little bit of light blond hair, and firm muscles that ripple each time he shifts even a little. Jesus, my fake boyfriend might as well be a supermodel.

"Well?" Trevor lifts one knowing eyebrow at me.

Heat slowly creeps up my neck. "Oops."

Not wanting to make a fool of myself in front of him, I undress slowly. But by the time I'm done, he's not even watching me anymore, his toes are already dipping into the spring. When I come up beside him, he looks coyly up at me through his eyelashes.

"It's been a while since I swam in a spring. The key is to jump right in, right? No second-guessing?"

I nod at him and tangle our fingers. "Together?"

He takes a fortifying breath. "Together."

And then we jump.

A gasp tears from me as I break through the surface of the water. The trick is to let my body acclimate to the perpetually seventy-two-degree water, but it always feels a little bit like dying. Silt at the bottom of the spring stirs under my feet, but the water remains a crystal light blue.

Trevor breaks through the surface with a laugh and a violent shiver that cracks his teeth. Sunlight slits through the trees, highlighting all the golden strands of his hair. Like honey, or the center of a daisy. Yellow's always been a happy color to me. Trevor reminds me of the color yellow. Sweet as honey, happy as a sunflower inching towards the sun.

"God, I'd forgotten," Trevor complains, his teeth chattering loudly.

I chuckle softly. "It's a good jolt to the body."

Trevor reaches up to expertly remove his hair from the tie, letting the soft strands cascade to his bare shoulders. I watch enraptured as he dips his head back, wetting the golden locks in the turquoise water. He comes back up with his hair slicked back, longer now than it was when it was dry. Dipping down, he treads water instead of reaching on his tiptoes to touch the bottom.

Sun slashes through the trees, catching on the mostly still water of the spring. Trevor uses his hand to block out the sun and look behind me at the river beyond.

"How many gators come in here?"

"They stay away from the spring mostly," I reassure him with my best comforting smile. "They prefer the river. It can happen though. Don't swim fast and they won't eat you. Swamp puppies are just as scared of you as you are of them."

"So comforting," Trevor murmurs in obvious disagreement.

His baby blues shift back to me, sending a terrifying thought through my head. *Kiss him.* A moment of tension passes over us before Trevor breaks it by playfully splashing me. And then it's on. We wrestle in the water like children, splashing, and laughing under the bright sun. Both of us let out soft pants when we finally pull away, grinning like loons. God, Trevor makes me feel like a kid again. Some kind of magic.

"How'd you become a fake boyfriend?" I ask because I am so curious about the mystery of Trevor.

Trevor hums thoughtfully as he lies back to float along the surface of the water. Every firm muscle along his body is on display from this angle. We might be in a spring, but my blood heats to boiling, especially when he reaches out to tightly circle his fingers around my wrist. To not float away, as if I'm his anchor.

"Matter of circumstance. Helps me pay the bills and I'm good at it. Plus, I like helping people." Makes sense. Trevor

34

kicks his feet, so he spins around on the surface of the water, a little smirk playing at his lips. "What about you, handsome? Why'd you need a fake boyfriend?"

I blow an exasperated raspberry. "I don't have much time to date with the farm and my family."

He gently squeezes my wrist once, then releases me to sit up in the water. Bobbing in the water in front of me, he tilts his head this way and that, considering me with a thoughtful look.

"Are you a virgin?"

Jesus. Heat creeps up my neck and down my chest, no doubt painting me with shyness. "No."

Trevor hums again, narrowing his eyes suspiciously at me, then disappears under the water. He pushes the hair from his eyes when he resurfaces. The water moves out of the way between us until he's standing right before me, on his tiptoes, almost close enough to touch.

"You're a sweetheart, Beau Callahan." Then he kisses the apple of my cheek. His lips linger against my skin for just a moment, soft and warm. I strangely feel like I've lost something when he pulls away.

We swim for a little while longer before climbing out. The sun's just starting to hit the edge of the tree line, telling me sunset is only a few hours away. Trevor yawns, stifling it against his forearm. Time to get him home. My home. Back to my house. Jesus.

Hidden from each other on either side of the truck, we shuck out of our wet underwear, tugging our clothes back on.

Once back at the house, I head straight to the kitchen to cook dinner. I'm definitely one of those guys that's better at the grill than anything with the stove. So, I pull out the chicken breasts I marinated the other day and head out to the back porch. Trevor disappears into his room, so I let him be.

The back porch of my house is heaven. It's built up to the level with the house and the wood is stained dark. I've got a grill, a couple of cozy chairs, a hammock, and a great view of the forest line behind the house. Birds sing loudly in the spring and summer. Deer even sometimes visit my yard. The porch is my little oasis. I don't bring many people here, but I oddly don't mind Trevor being in my space.

He's a quiet, gentle guy.

A few moments later, the soft padding of Trevor's feet reaches my ears.

"What's for dinner, handsome?"

"Grilled chicken with rice and vegetables."

The chicken hits the grill with a sizzle, along with the skewered vegetables. My gaze lands on Trevor leaning against the railing at the end of the porch, looking out at the forest. He's changed into an old T-shirt and sweatpants, the comfy sort of clothes that only people that know him really well probably see him in. My chest puffs out a little bit at that thought.

His cell phone vibrates in his pocket, and his face visibly hardens. With a grimace, he pads barefoot out into the yard, to stand under a large live oak. As the food cooks, I watch him carry on a conversation that has the lines of his body poised for attack. He doesn't speak much, mostly listening intently. By the end of the conversation the man looks borderline sick.

"All good?" I snap the tongs before flipping the chicken.

Trevor waves his hand dismissively. "Nothing important."

I highly doubt that's true, but I don't know him well enough to argue. Not that I'd argue anyway. He leans heavily on the railing, staring so hard out at the yard that I'm mildly worried he'll catch my grass on fire. But the tension slowly leaves him as I finish cooking. His head tilts up towards the sky and he closes his eyes with a gentle, uninhibited smile.

Sometimes words leave me. Almost like I used up my quota of them for the day. Trevor doesn't press me for more than I can give him. We eat dinner in companionable silence, just Trevor making happy noises when he takes small bites of the chicken. I bite back a smile. Silent through the entire meal, it's as if he hasn't had a home-cooked meal in years. Maybe he hasn't.

After dinner, we stand quietly at the sink, passing dishes back and forth until every dish is sparkling. Trevor sends a soft, contented smile my way before letting out a jaw-cracking yawn.

"Night, Beau." He lifts up on his toes to softly kiss my cheek. "See you in the morning."

"Night," I say quietly.

He disappears into the guest room, leaving me with what can only be described as a stampede of buffalo running wild in my chest. Only once I'm alone do I press my fingers to where his plush lips grazed my cheek, wishing to carry the feel of his lips into my dreams with me.

CHAPTER FOUR
TREVOR

Too-bright afternoon sunlight accosts me when I finally blink awake. Shit. I definitely slept in. Hurriedly grabbing my phone off the nightstand, I ignore the texts in the boyfriends' group chat. It's almost noon. Double shit. The rehearsal dinner is tonight. I can't believe I slept for over twelve hours.

The phone call from my mother last night had been enough to send my brain into insomnia territory. But then Beau had been so endearing with dinner, so sweet, that her intended manipulation had turned into more of a sizzling frustration than a worrying demand. Usually, a call from one of my parents can cause my anxiety to spike, sending me into a few days of sleepless nights, but not this time.

Last night I lay in bed, just listening to the sound of the cicadas beyond the window. Only the random hoot of an owl broke through the sound of the loud insects. The scent of cedar lingers on the sheets, like they'd been tucked away waiting for use. Somehow it had all culminated to lull me into a peaceful sleep. Finally, I'd conked out at midnight, but I'd assumed I'd wake up in the morning aching for a workout.

Obviously not.

Rushing through my morning, well, my *afternoon* routine, I decide to let my hair air dry around my shoulders. Quiet fills the house. I softly pad through the house, peering into rooms, but don't find Beau.

The loud clunk of machinery in the garage has me heading that way.

Soft rock music greets me along with the sight of Beau bent over a truck even older than the one we rode in yesterday. Sweat dots his shirt, making it cling to him in the most delicious way. He twists some tool in the engine and grunts when nothing happens. I need to stop ogling him.

"Morning."

"Afternoon more like it," Beau points out without looking at me.

"Sorry," I reply sheepishly. Embarrassment floods through me but disappears when Beau looks at me over his shoulder, a soft smile spreading over his lips.

His gaze rakes over me, before meeting my eyes again. "We got nowhere to go until this evening, sweetheart. Don't worry. You sleep good?"

Sweetheart. Jesus, I'm almost a puddle at his feet. The word just rolls off his tongue, sweet as honey.

"The best I've slept in ages," I tell him truthfully.

He winks and returns to tinkering with the engine. "The power of a decade-old quilt sewed with love and washed a million times."

He's probably not far off. "Can I sit and watch you?"

Beau chuckles, rotating his wrist to do something deep

inside the engine. "Sure. 'Bout entertaining as watching paint dry though."

He really has no idea. A metal barstool sits nearby, so I park my ass on it to watch him work. Pulling out my phone, I take a few stealthy shots of him, sending one to the boyfriends' group chat.

> Look at my fake boyfriend for the weekend

JACKSON
> I think he's taller than me

> 6'5"ish I think

JACKSON
> I have an inch on him

> Every inch matters wink

BENJI
> No flirting in the group chat

> We are literally just talking

ELI
> Stop flirting!

JACKSON
> We could just be sitting in the same room and you'd accuse us of flirting because y'all think you're funny

BENJI
> I know I'm funny

> ANYWAY! THIS IS ABOUT ME!

JACKSON
> Oh he's yelling

BENJI

Everyone be quiet and let Trevor talk

Beau is delightful. I hope I can survive this wedding weekend with him.

JACKSON

Sex?

Not paid for

ELI

Yeah, Trevor isn't returning home without fucking that. Look at his BACK. That is SERIOUS back.

Thank you.

BENJI

You're going to give it away for free?

Maybe

JACKSON

Good luck, babe. I gotta go. Duty calls.

BENJI

Bye babes.

ELI

😌

"Who's got you smiling like that?" Beau asks, coming to a stop right in front of me. A greasy red rag drags over his fingers, wiping the oil from his perfectly large hands. The man really is unfairly hot without even realizing it. The absolute best kind of men.

"My best friends," I say, wiggling my phone at him.

"Good friends if they make you smile like that."

I shrug. "They're okay."

Beau laughs deeply and walks by to lay the tools down on his workbench. He smells like sweat, hot summer days, and hard work. A shiver threatens to roll through me just from his dizzying proximity. And then he does the hottest thing a man can do. At least in my opinion. He pulls off his shirt, wipes his face, then pops one hip against his workbench.

Christ. I tried to not stare at him too much in the spring yesterday. He's got a broad firm chest with lots of dark hair sprinkled across it. Beau has the kind of muscle born from hard work, not time in the gym. My muscles are made for pretty, but Beau's are for long days working under the sun.

"Trevor?"

"Sorry." I shake my head violently to rid myself of fake boyfriend musings. "Did you say something?"

"I said we need to leave here around five to get to the farm in time. It's pretty casual but I'm planning to wear nice clothes."

"Right," I say, hoping my voice sounds even.

"You sure you're alright?"

"Great!" I go to hop off the stool, to flee, but Beau rests a gentle hand on my forearm. All my brain cells narrow in on his touch, the slight grease on his fingers.

"Do you want to help me?"

I blink slowly at him, confused. "Help you?"

A smirk tugs at his lips under his beard. "With the truck."

My gaze pings over to the truck, raised up, hood up too. I've never even touched an engine before. I'll probably break something. Ruin it. Like everything I touch. My thoughts must show on my face because Beau pulls his hand away, finishes wiping it with the rag, then tips his head towards the beat-up truck.

"It's old. Easy to fix a mistake." He heads towards the truck, and I follow, unsure of why my body won't listen to my brain. *Flee.* I should be running. Beau leans against the hood, pointing down at the engine. "I'm rebuilding the engine. It had half a million miles on it. These Fords have great shells, but the engines conk out at a certain point. You see, people use trucks hard, put them away wet. So, the engines go fast."

My mouth goes dry as I watch him point out different parts of the engine, still shirtless, his sweaty shirt now wrapped around his shoulders. Belatedly, I realize his gaze is back on me. I swallow slowly, nodding as if I'm following along. A small chuckle breaks free from his lips, and he shakes his head ruefully.

"Anyone ever taught you how to change oil?" Beau asks, curious, not judgmental.

I shake my head. "Definitely not."

He quirks his fingers in request for me to come closer, and I do, because I'm an idiot. The smell of grease and engine wafts over me, mixed with the sweet smell of Beau's skin and sweat. Taking my hand in his, he guides it to where I need to go, and helps me tug out a stick that's covered in oil.

"This tells you the health of your oil," Beau explains, voice low, soft, sending a shiver down my spine despite the heat in the garage. "I just changed it, so it looks pretty good now, but when it's bad you can easily tell. When it's low too."

I nod, pretending like I understand an ounce of what he's saying. He proceeds to show me how to change the oil, and how to change a battery too. If I ever need to do anything to my car, I'll know now. The man is exceedingly patient, tender even as he painstakingly teaches me about the intricacies of a truck engine. When we're done, I'm astounded to realize a few hours have passed by, making it time for us to get ready for the rehearsal.

Beau eyes me up and down, still shirtless, hair slightly messy from running his hand over it. We silently part ways in the hallway, as he heads to shower. I keep the water cold for my own shower, trying to wash away the want that's boiling up in my veins.

———

Beau's version of nice clothes is hilarious. Dressed in dark jeans that probably haven't been worn to the farm yet, hence making them nice. Boots peek out from under the denim, and he's sporting a light blue polo shirt that has definitely seen better days. But I can't say he looks bad. He just looks like Beau.

He flushes at the sight of me when I meet him in the foyer of his house. I bite back a smile. Tight black dress pants, dress shoes, a striped shirt that plays up the color of my eyes. The nail in the coffin for Beau seems to be me rolling my sleeves to my forearms. His eyes linger on my left forearm just a little too long, as a deep blush fills his cheeks.

It seems Beau appreciates my efforts. He clears his throat awkwardly, then jerkily nods towards the front door. "Ready to go?"

"Yeah, handsome."

Beau laughs in frustration. "Stop with the nicknames. I'm not that kind of guy."

"But you can call me sweetheart?"

"Yeah," Beau says as he opens the front door for me. "'Cause you're a sweetheart."

"And you're not handsome?"

Beau just shakes his head in exasperation as we climb into the truck. I'm beginning to seriously think Beau has no idea just how handsome he is. Not even just handsome. But he's beautiful too. From the top of his head all the way to the tip of his toes. Everything about Beau Callahan checks a box for me. Even those damn ball caps that he usually wears.

Foregoing the classic Chevy, we load into Beau's work truck. Finally, I get to see Clay Road Farms in all its glory. The road kicks up orange dust until it turns into the gravel road that leads deep into the farm. A small parking lot is dotted with cars that I assume belong to Beau's family and friends.

Summer means the sun stays out a little longer, but it's low enough in the sky now that the heat is gentler when we carefully climb out of the truck. A large wooden open-air barn looms on the other side of the property, with glowing fairy lights hanging from the trees surrounding it.

"That's the event building. It used to be a barn, but we converted it about a decade ago," Beau informs me.

I twist my fingers around his as we make the slow journey towards the barn. His hand squeezes mine in reassurance, either for me or for himself. Beau worries at his bottom lip a few times, then squares his shoulders the closer we get to the barn. I've noticed how Beau seems to always be getting ready for a confrontation since I've been here. Beau seems to steel himself against every interaction he has with others.

"Beau!" a young woman yells out.

She's clearly Andy, his sister, as the resemblance is uncanny. Andy is about my height, with long brown hair curling all the way down her back. Sweet sun freckles pepper her face. Brown eyes meet mine as she takes in our joined hands.

"Oh, Beau." Andy lifts up on her toes to sweetly kiss his cheek, then aims a gap-toothed smile my way. Only beautiful people in Clay Springs, I swear. "I'm so happy you could make it! I know it means a lot to Beau."

"I'm happy to be here." Impulsively, I lean forward and kiss her cheek.

Andy flushes bright red, then looks back over her shoulder. "Come meet everyone. You're the gossip of the town."

"Shit," Beau mumbles under his breath as Andy drags me further inside.

An overwhelming amount of people fill the space. But it appears most are family, so Beau stays mostly relaxed at my side. His hand envelops mine again even as Andy shows me around, introducing me to various people.

"Look! Beau's boyfriend exists!" Andy says, voice teasing to lessen the sting of her words.

A man with black curls, stubbled cheeks, and dark brown eyes stands beside another man with light brown hair and a full beard. Both stare at me for a moment, confusion on their faces, before their gazes ping to Beau.

"Since when?" the brown-haired friend asks, eyes sharp on Beau.

Beau shifts on his feet. "Didn't want to steal any of Andy's shine."

"I'm Joey, this is Lee," Joey says, the one with the dark curls. He nudges Lee with his elbow.

"Lee." Lee sends me a hesitant wave.

"Nice to meet you both."

"We grew up together," Beau explains quietly, for only me to hear.

"Ah, the best friends. Are you going to grill me?" I shoot a smirk at both of them, satisfied when Lee flushes a vivid crimson.

Joey's eyes narrow. "Do we need to grill you?"

I shrug lazily. "Not if you trust Beau."

Lee opens his mouth to argue but Andy silences him with a fierce stare, eyes wide. "Let's introduce you to my parents. These losers have had enough of your time."

"Hey!" Joey shouts behind us, voice full of laughter.

"Sorry about that. They're not always idiots. They're just really protective of Beau," Andy whispers against my ear.

"To be expected."

Andy aims a warm smile at me as she guides me towards a group of elders standing at the other side of the barn. Beau plods behind us, rubbing at his arms, clearly uncomfortable in his clothing.

His father is the spitting image of him, but thirty years older. The man looks tired though, in a sickly sort of way. His mother is slighter, with fair skin and dark red hair. I gently shake his mother's hand but take his father's in a firm shake that has him grinning in a soft, pleased sort of way. One thing I know is to always firmly shake another man's hand. That wisdom was ingrained in me early on.

"Trevor," I tell them as I step back.

Beau moves his hand to rest on my shoulder, his grip a comfort against my oddly sudden nerves. It's easy to take a step closer to him, resting against his side where I somehow perfectly fit.

"Nice to meet you, Trevor. You've got the most beautiful eyes I've ever seen." Mrs. Callahan sends me a wink. Mr. Callahan laughs at her and aims a tender, heartbreaking look her way.

"Thanks, ma'am."

"Call me Cindy."

"You can call me Mr. Callahan or sir," his father says, earning him a soft elbow to the ribs. "Just kidding. David will do just fine."

A warm smile, soft eyes, everything a good fake boyfriend gives. But oddly, I'm not having to fake it as much as I usually do. Beau's hand is a constant weight against my shoulder, settling the weird anxiety bubbling up inside me. As they make conversation, I let my gaze trail over the barn, taking in the scenery.

Two long tables fill the barn, decorated with baby's breath and other farmhouse-chic decorations. Andy's warm laugh pulls my attention towards her and her fiancé. Close to her age, with a military-style crew cut. The way he looks at her radiates love, and I get it. There's something inherently sweet about the Callahan siblings. Whoever gets to keep Beau for real will be extremely lucky.

"So, what do you do, Trevor?" Cindy asks me as Beau and David finish discussing the farm.

"I'm still in college."

Cindy's eyes sharpen. "How old are you?"

"Twenty-two, ma'am."

Her eyes slide over to her son, unease radiating off of her, then back to me. "Did you meet on one of those apps," she whispers conspiratorially.

I can't help but let out a loud laugh. If she only knew. "Sort of. But we've been dating a few months and you'd be surprised how little age matters when you have the important things in common."

"And what are the important things?"

I let my gaze go back to Beau, lingering on him for just a

moment. I meet her eyes again with a tender, lovestruck smile.

"Love and family."

Cindy makes heart eyes at me for a moment. She pats my cheek in a loving way only a mother can do.

"Alright, everyone. We're going to practice the wedding, then we can eat!" a tall blond man shouts from the edge of the barn.

We file outside, and Beau returns that possessive hand to the small of my back. I kiss his cheek as we walk, and he stumbles just a little, making me bite back a laugh. He's so easy and I love it.

"That's a serious weapon you've got there," Beau whispers to me.

"What?"

He curls his hand tightly around my hip as we walk. "Those sweet lips."

"You're a real smooth talker, Beau."

"Not usually."

He helps me get to my seat in the front row. I kiss his cheek again, putting on a bit of a show, and he distractedly presses fingers to his cheek as he walks to the back to join his family. The rehearsal goes on under the large oak trees to the left of the barn.

"Hey," someone whisper-shouts from behind me.

I rip my gaze from Beau and turn around to find a guy close to my age leaning against the chair next to me. The guy has gorgeous auburn hair past his shoulders, pale skin, and a deep scar that lines the left side of his face. Ouch. He's sort of androgynous in a way that I know would send a large amount of people clamoring for his attention.

"Yes?" I whisper, not wanting to interrupt the rehearsal.

"You're Beau's boyfriend?"

"Yes."

"You're kind of hot."

"Thank you?"

"You got any friends you can hook me up with?"

I shoot a curious look back at Beau to find his gaze already firmly on us. I send him a thumbs up and he frowns, deeply. Oh boy.

"Girls or guys?" I ask, whisper hushed so no one around us can hear.

"Guys."

Ah, okay. "What are you looking for?"

"Anyone will do."

"Uh," I say, wracking my brain. "What's your name?"

"Harper."

"Okay, Harper, here's the deal." Turning around in the seat, I face him fully, leveling him with the sternest gaze I can muster. "There are apps that can get you what you want. I can show you. But a sweet boy like you, you want the real thing. Trust me."

Harper wrinkles his nose in displeasure. "You don't know me."

"Trust me," I repeat.

Harper huffs and throws himself back in the seat. "Whatever."

"Who are you related to here?"

"I'm Colby's dad's sister's nephew."

I literally cannot keep up with that. "Are you related to Beau at all?"

Harper actually looks affronted. "You aren't from the South, are you?"

I shake my head. "Not really."

"Okay, well, let me teach you a lesson." Harper leans forward again, elbows on his knees, and levels me with a shrewd, assessing sort of look. "Everyone here is related in some way or another. Blood doesn't matter. One time Beau saved me when I fell from a treehouse in the woods and broke my leg. He carried me all the way back to my house, kept my mom from losing her shit. He's as much a cousin as anyone else."

Loud claps interrupt us as the rehearsal finishes with Andy and her fiancé giving a kiss that's presentable for the surrounding family. People mill about chatting, but Beau beelines right for me and Harper, frown still marring his gorgeous face.

"Harper," Beau says gruffly, a hint of reprimand in his voice.

"Beau." Harper grins up at Beau. His smile is beautiful and wide. I bet he gets away with just about anything.

"Are you up to no good?"

Harper bats his eyes. This guy is too much even for me. But I can't help but smile at his antics, which I guess is the point when Harper winks at me.

"I'm up to exactly the right amount of good. You're looking nice tonight."

Beau lets out a little "uh-huh," then wraps his fingers around mine, using them to tug me out of my seat. My stomach goes warm and fuzzy at how easily he handles me.

"Dinnertime, sweetheart."

"Sweetheart?" Harper mutters sourly under his breath just before pretending to gag.

"Bye, Harper," Beau says loudly, attempting to end the conversation. Only once standing do I notice the sweet golden retriever wearing a service vest sitting sweetly by

Harper's feet. My eyes flick back to Harper, and our gazes meet hard. A deep frown covers his face when he realizes I've noticed the dog, his irritated gaze swinging toward the barn.

Beau guides me away with a warm hand on the small of my back. And I let him. The sun sets behind the trees as the lights dangling from their branches glow brightly. Warmth floods through me, both from the company and the sight of a family full of love for one another. Beau leads me to the middle of the table to sit by his parents. He keeps a loving hand on my thigh under the table all through the meal.

CHAPTER FIVE

BEAU

Rain on a wedding day is supposed to be good luck. A loud crack of angry thunder rushes through the house just as we finish getting dressed for the wedding. Summer in Florida can guarantee about two things —rain in the afternoon and oppressive heat with humidity that resembles a dip in a swimming pool. Either way you're getting wet.

"That doesn't sound good." Trevor comes out of his bedroom, dressed in a beautiful navy-blue suit, hair loose and just barely brushing his shoulders. His beauty stills me, just for a moment, until I force myself back into action.

"It's good luck, isn't it?"

Trevor smirks, eyes crinkling at the corners. "I'm not sure that's actually true."

My phone vibrates in my pocket, and I let out a frustrated huff. Andy's harsh cries filter through the phone speakers, causing emotions to ricochet through me. Trevor winces and comes to stand beside me in the kitchen. His presence calms my already alert nerves.

"Beau." Andy sniffles a few times. "It's ruined!"

"It's not, Andy. The wedding is in two hours, it'll be over by then."

"But the chairs will be all wet!"

"Trevor and I will come wipe them down. Don't you worry about it. Stop crying, Mom will be so upset if your makeup looks bad."

"I don't have any makeup on yet." Andy cries harder into the phone.

My sister crying has always torn me to pieces. I look helplessly out the window at the angry storm clouds in the sky. If only I had the power to make them disappear. Brothers should have that power.

"Andy, I promise. We'll figure it out. Trevor and I will leave now, and make sure everyone's got a plan B. You don't worry about it at all."

Andy's sniffles soften, until she's just barely hiccuping. "Okay."

"I'll see you soon. Stop worrying."

I hang up with a sigh, pinching the bridge of my nose hard. Jesus.

Trevor slings his suit jacket on a hanger, then wrangles me out of my own to hang it up as well. He aims one of his comforting, sweet smiles at me.

"Let's go save the day."

And that's what we do. The rain ends just as we arrive at the farm. The day is hazy, a mist hanging overhead, but the rain clouds look like they're gone as we get to work. An hour passes us by as we wipe down every single chair until they're mostly dry for the guests.

The trees drip moisture as they sway in the wind but I'm placing my bets on us finishing our task before the wedding starts in an hour. Thirty minutes until people start arriving to take their seats. It'll work out. It has to work out.

Trevor and I hustle back to the truck to slide on our suit jackets. He carefully helps me into mine, fingers lingering along my broad shoulders as he brushes his hands over my chest to straighten it out. Next, he fixes my tie so that it's lying flat. His baby blues flit up to my gaze. With a nod, he clucks his tongue approvingly. Something in his eyes makes my knees go just a little weak.

"You look perfect," Trevor tells me, voice warm and low.

I swallow, my mouth suddenly dry. "You too, sweetheart."

Trevor chuckles softly before pulling away, his gaze far away despite being right in front of me. "Let's do this."

After helping Trevor to his seat, I leave him in the capable hands of Harper. To the back, the little barn has two sides, one for a bride and one for a groom, so I make my way into the bride's suite. I shield my eyes as I enter so I can't see the ladies half-dressed.

"Can I look? Everyone dressed?"

A round of laughs echo around the room.

"You can look, Beau," Mama says from the other side of the room.

With a bashful smile I remove my hand from my eyes to survey the room. A few of my female cousins and Andy's friends wave at me from where they stand in their blush-pink bridesmaids dresses.

But my gaze lasers in on my beautiful little sister. Her hair falls down her back in soft waves over the ivory lace body-hugging bridal gown. I remember when she gripped my hand tight before jumping into the springs, when she had no front teeth, and when she was impossible to find while playing hide-and-seek. She's all grown up now. Lost to me.

"You look beautiful, Andy."

Andy's smile is watery. "Don't make me cry, Beau."

"I won't." Kissing her warm cheek, I steel myself against the tears wanting so badly to fall. "Everything's all ready for you. Are you ready?"

The bridesmaids around the room sigh dreamily for Andy. We all help her get outside, avoiding the wettest spots around the farm. I squint to make sure that Ethan is already waiting with his groomsmen, and when I see he's there, I hold on to Andy's hand and wait for her bridesmaids to walk ahead of us.

Dad stands from the chair in the back row we'd saved for him. His breaths are a little short and pained as he takes Andy's hand. I kiss his cheek but let him take over for Andy. I run up the outside of the row to join Trevor at the front.

"She's all good?" Trevor whispers against my cheek as he kisses me.

"Perfect."

I take his hand in my own, twining our fingers as the wedding march floats through the trees. Everyone stands to watch my beautiful sister walk down the aisle. I do my best to hold back tears, but I've never been really good at keeping them from falling. My face is a mess by the end of the ceremony. Thank God I had the forethought to bring a handkerchief. I roughly wipe at my face as Andy and Ethan kiss.

"Top ten best weddings I've ever been to," Trevor says, voice a little raw.

"Really?"

"Oh yeah. So much love here." Trevor places a hand over his heart, eyes misty. "I can feel it. You guys are a real family."

"What about your family?" I ask because I'm curious to know about him.

His face shutters closed. "My family is nothing like this."

"I'm sorry."

Trevor's face transforms to hide every ounce of sadness. I can't explain why but that sends a pang of my own sadness through me. To know he's hiding from me, pretending. He might just be my fake boyfriend, but all I know how to do is care for people. The urge to pry him apart, know his tells, know what could ever make him sad, is so great that it almost threatens to boil over.

"Now we party," I tell him.

Another earth-shattering grin is aimed my way. My heart does a little skip in my chest. I try to ignore it, but it's hard to do that when Trevor is so perfect. But I do my best to remind myself he's being paid to be perfect.

I love my family, but they're loud and obnoxious. Even more so at events like a wedding where there's an excuse for loudness. Probably why I've spent much of my life on the outskirts, always being the helper, because after a few hours with them, my head pounds. It does now too, but everything's a little better with Trevor by my side. In an unexpected turn of events, Harper and Trevor might actually be becoming friends.

Which is dangerous if Harper finds out what Trevor does for a living. Because Harper cannot keep a secret. That boy has looser lips than a bullfrog on a lily pad.

Trevor's deep laugh breaks me from my reverie. He'd wandered to the bar to get us both a beer, but he was stopped by Colby. I use his distraction as a chance to take Trevor in when he's not keen to my assessing gaze. Suit jacket off, on the seat beside me, so his strong shoulders are on display. Trevor's not short, probably average height for a guy. He's muscled too, the kind from the gym. And his smile is wide and sure in a way that says it doesn't take much to fake being a nice guy.

Sensing my stare, his warm gaze slides over the crowd to meet mine. My heart does another one of those traitorous rolls and bursts in my chest. His eyes soften, and he bites his lip, then hurriedly ends his conversation with Colby. All to come back to me. To take a seat beside me with a tired release of breath.

"Weddings are so much work," Trevor informs me, sliding me a still-cold beer despite him being waylaid by Colby.

Leaning back in my chair, I take a slow sip. People are eating and mingling, but I know the dancing will start soon. My sister is a family girl to the roots, so she used our distant cousins' bluegrass band for the reception. Notes from the guitars and banjos waft over us, easing my discomfort from all the people around me.

"How are you doing?" Trevor asks softly.

His fingers come up to play with the hairs at the nape of my neck, sending jolts of lightning throughout every one of my extremities. Touch has always been a double-edged sword for me. At times I crave it, but at other times it makes me uncomfortable. Probably why I've never been a one-night-stand type of guy. A stranger's touch usually makes me feel like I've lost something. But Trevor's touch is a steadying pressure, dancing along all the good nerve endings in my brain.

"I'm alright," I whisper back.

Trevor tips his beer back to take a taste, showing off the arch of his elegant throat. He carefully surveys the crowd, then zeros in on the dance floor. "What are the odds of getting you on the dance floor with me later?"

"Pretty good after one or two more beers."

"Good to know."

"So, you're in school. What do you want to do?"

"I'm getting a psychology degree."

"That's a lot," I admit honestly.

Trevor kicks me softly under the table, lips tilting up in a smile. "Sometimes. And you? You'll run the farm until you retire?"

I nod as I take a sip of my beer. "That's all I've ever wanted. It's what I know."

"Nothing bad about that."

Humming softly in agreement, I push my beer away from me. Angling my head towards him, faces only inches apart, I easily hold his gaze. From this close, I can clearly hear the sharp intake of breath from Trevor, like my proximity can still shock him. A stray lock of his hair tickles my chin. The golden strand twists easily around my finger, so soft, like the silky petal of a sunflower. I tug gently, then move it away, tucking the strand back in with the rest of his hair. Softly, and slow enough so he can track my movements, I skim my fingers down the length of his arm, coming to rest at the curve of his elbow.

"Trevor," I say softly, an edge of need in my voice.

"Oh boy." A shiver rolls through him, and he squeezes his eyes tightly shut. "You said no sex."

"We can do a lot of things that bring pleasure without having sex."

Trevor's pupils blow wide at my words, swallowing up his

gorgeous baby blues. Deft fingers twitch in my hair, grip tight, then tug me close enough that our lips are only a whisper apart.

"Beau," Trevor murmurs, lips softly grazing mine. An almost kiss. A blink-and-you-miss-it kind of kiss. An *I need more,* just the hint of a kiss.

"Hiya," a voice says loudly from behind us.

I don't pull away from Trevor. Instead, I just turn my head to take in Harper. The man doesn't look remotely guilty for interrupting us. Actually, he looks pleased-as-punch. The brat.

"They're going to cut the cake soon," Harper announces with a knowing grin.

"Okay," I tell him, hoping he'll disappear.

Harper wiggles his fingers at me in the imitation of a wave. "Just thought you'd want to know."

I stare daggers at Harper's back as he disappears towards his edge of the table. Trevor's wearing a teasing smile as his gaze follows Harper through the crowd.

"You look so familiar."

I turn my gaze to the other side of the table to find one of Ethan's family members standing, gaze calculating where it falls on Trevor.

Trevor swallows, but his smile is pasted on. "I have one of those faces."

The man cocks his head. "No, I've definitely seen you before. What's your line of work?"

"I don't work. I'm in college," Trevor says, voice cold and distant. I've never heard his voice like that before, not sure I ever want to hear it again.

"Wait... aren't you—"

"I think that's enough," Trevor interrupts, eyes full of fire.

The man's gaze pings between me and Trevor again, taking in Trevor's fingers in my hair, the proximity of our bodies. A mean smirk curls the man's lips to the side, but I stare at him with every ounce of *fuck off* my body can muster. He holds up his hands in defeat and backs away towards the table at the other side of the barn.

When I turn back to Trevor, his eyes are closed tight. His fingers drop slowly from my hair. An ache the size of a canyon opens inside of me just at the loss of his sweet touch. He firmly cups the bottle of beer in both palms and returns his calculating gaze to the wedding guests.

"Trevor," I plead, needing to have his attention back on me.

He shoots me a half smile. "It's okay, Beau."

The problem is that I can already somehow see through his carefully constructed defenses. A little hitch to his voice tells me that for a second, he was vulnerable, and he didn't really enjoy the feeling. A little furrow forms between his brows, his mouth twitches at one corner as he attempts to fake a painted-on smile. But I know and maybe that's enough for now.

Time ticks by slowly. I mingle with my annoying family since I'm the epitome of a good southern boy. Trevor gives everyone his most award-winning smile while plastered to my side. But something changed after the interaction with that man earlier. I wish I could go back to before Harper interrupted us. I wish I could go back. The band switches to a drowsy love song, once everyone is winding down for the night. I take that as my chance.

I find Trevor happily chatting with Harper at the edge of the barn. Holding out my hand, I patiently wait for him to slip his hand into mine. His eyes flit from my hand and up to my eyes in question. One of those sweet smiles tilts the edges of his lips up, and his eyes sparkle just enough to make me smile in return. When he slips his hand into mine, I feel like I could spin the earth backwards like Superman.

We bump into a few dancing couples as I guide us through the swaying bodies on the dance floor, until we're at the very center. I tug him into the cage of my arms so that he's flush against my body. No place we don't touch, but it's still not enough.

His hair is a little sweaty from the heat inside the barn, curling up slightly where it brushes his shoulders. Suit jacket abandoned long ago; his shirt sleeves are rolled up to show his forearms. He's achingly beautiful, perfect for me.

Swaying off beat to the calming wedding music, I tug him closer with a tight grip on his slim hips. His skin is warm even under his dress shirt, burning against the warmth of my palms. He fits so easily against me, like he was made for me. Such a dangerous thought.

"Beau," Trevor says my name like a dreamy sigh. He loosely loops his arms around my shoulders, fingers tangling together against the nape of my neck.

I've always been a big guy, in size, and in nature. People count on me. They know that I'm going to take care of them and get things done. *Call Beau* is the motto I've heard most of my life. And I wish for just a moment that Trevor felt he could call on me. That he could count on me. I bet every guy that gets him for even a moment feels the same way.

Song after song, we stay silent, just basking in the moment together. So wrapped up in Trevor, in his soft gaze, I don't even realize the barn is slowly emptying.

"Andy and Ethan are leaving," Colby whispers, seemingly

ashamed for interrupting us. I shoot him a shaky smile to let him know the interruption is fine.

Keeping Trevor's hand tight inside my own, I lead us outside to watch my sister drive off with her new husband. Andy gives me a sweaty, and too-tight hug. Kissing her cheek, I give her the same wink that used to make her giggle as a toddler. But she doesn't giggle, she just shakes her head at me before disappearing into the badly decorated car. The headlights disappear down the dirt road and a weird pang of loss reverberates through me.

"Take me home?" Trevor asks quietly, fingers still gently holding on to mine.

"Anything you want, sweetheart."

The drive back to the house is silent. I keep Trevor's hand in mine the entire way, resting our joined hands against my thigh. Every now and then I swipe my thumb against his knuckles, and Trevor lets out a soft sigh at the sweeping touch. I wonder how often he's touched just for the sake of being touched. Do people make him feel pleasure because his pleasure means more to them than their own? I doubt it.

In some unspoken agreement, Trevor quietly follows me to my room once we're back home. Tenderly cupping his face in my palms, I press a lingering kiss on his forehead as he grabs my wrists so tight that ripples of pain course through me. I trail kisses down his face, finally nudging his chin with my nose so he tips his head back, giving me better access to the beautiful expanse of his throat.

And that's the way it goes. Finding and kissing every inch of skin I can will be my night's mission. Slowly, I unbutton his dress shirt, and watch as it falls to the floor in a puddle of expensive fabric. Trevor's chest heaves once he's down to just his boxers. Bare to me, every glorious inch of perfect skin for me.

"Take a shower with me?"

Trevor blinks syrupy slow at me, caught in the haze of desire. "Is sex on the table now?"

I shake my head. "Nope. Follow my lead."

"Alright," Trevor whispers, a little unsure, with a hint of color on his cheeks.

When I go to take my clothes off, Trevor pauses me with a hand on my stomach. His stormy eyes freeze me. My heart does somersaults in my chest as I watch him carefully undress me, cautiously, like he's afraid to cross some unknown line. Once I'm down to my underwear, his eyes take me in, before trailing slowly back up to meet my gaze. The moment is fraught with tension, sizzling with heat that I need to dial down to survive the night I have planned so carefully in my head.

I guide him into the bathroom with a hand on his naked back, his skin burning hot against my own. Steam fills the room quickly, ratcheting up the heat rolling from us both in waves.

"Naked or with underwear on?" I ask him softly, trying to give him the upper hand.

Trevor aims a wry smile my way, but it doesn't quite reach his baby blues. "We can be naked without jumping one another, right?"

"I think so."

Slipping out of our underwear, we keep our eyes firmly above shoulder level like we're in the locker room. The shower is perfunctory. We take turns under the water, washing our hair, then finally our bodies. Afterwards, I wrap a towel around his shoulders with another kiss to his forehead. His wet hair hangs around his shoulders, with a few knots, so I gently run my fingers through the fine golden strands. His eyes fall closed at my touch, lips tilting up slightly at my devoted attention.

My feet follow Trevor to the bedroom of their own accord. He drops the towel, leaving him naked for my viewing. He's beautiful, just miles of flawless skin, and an absolutely wicked smirk that leaves me all sorts of breathless. With a grin so wide my cheeks ache, I lift him up, and toss him onto the bed. A breathless little laugh leaves him as I tuck us under the pile of quilts. I pull him to me, bare skin against bare skin, then sweetly tangle my fingers in his damp hair.

"Can I kiss you?"

"*Please* kiss me," Trevor begs, every word filled with intent.

Begging is always my greatest undoing. I press my lips to his gently at first, learning the weight of his lips, the softness of his mouth. His fingers bite into my back as he inches just a bit closer to me, close enough I can feel his hard cock against my thigh. Fucking him would be amazing, but it's not my mission for the night. I want to show him what I want, what I need, and that's simply just to kiss him, to hold him through the night. I'm a simple man.

Trevor whimpers into my mouth as I trail my fingers over his overheated skin. A deep shiver wracks his body when I softly dance my fingers right back up the slight curve of his spine. I keep up the swirling dance of my fingers during the slow slide of our lips. Softly flicking my tongue against his lips, he easily opens up for me. I reach up to pinch his chin, angling his head to deepen the kiss so I can taste all of him. He tastes like wedding cake and beer and something else that's entirely Trevor. Something spicy, but sweet at the same time.

I soften the kiss again, until our lips are just barely grazing each other. A gentle press of my mouth to his own. Trevor's an amazing kisser. Just the right amount of tongue, right amount of tease, the right amount of everything. Time loses all meaning during our endless kiss. The kiss continues even as he rolls on top of me, strong thighs bracketing my waist, his hands gripping the headboard so tight that his knuckles turn white.

He pulls away from my mouth with trembling thighs and I grip them tight, letting my thumb dip into the curve of his abdominal muscles. His skin is perfectly soft under my hands. Resting his forehead against mine he releases a slightly panicked laugh.

"You're gonna kill me," Trevor whispers.

His words carry an odd sense of relief.

I lean up to kiss him again. "Nah. Want to stop and go to bed? Kiss some more? Whatever you want, it's yours."

Trevor doesn't answer with words, instead he just presses his sweet mouth back to mine. Chest to chest, his heartbeat wild against my own. Our hard cocks slide together, the friction delicious and almost unbearable. Shocks of pleasure race down my spine, urging me to seek relief.

But we both ignore our desire because that's not the focus of our kisses. The focus is the sweet molasses-slow intensity of kissing someone just to kiss them. No rush, no urgency, just lips sliding against lips. Only the tender onslaught of want and need and the decadent knowledge that, even if only for a moment, our mouths belong to one another.

His kiss grows softer as he rests heavier against me, half asleep from our lazy kissing. Pulling away, I tenderly rain kisses over his cheeks, his forehead, his closed eyes. Rolling him over, I pull him against my side until his head is safely tucked into the crook of my neck, his thigh thrown haphazardly over my hip.

Warm gusts of his breath tickle my neck as he seemingly breathes me in, his fingers play with the hair just below my belly button, causing sparks of pleasure to dance along my skin. All tangled together is how we fall asleep, slowly and then all at once. And I try to pretend that my heart isn't galloping away at the idea of letting him walk away in the morning.

CHAPTER SIX
TREVOR

Dreams are dangerous things. The dreams that come at night with their inky darkness making it hard to breathe, and the dreams that inspire hope. I've found it's best to attempt to have neither of them. But life rarely goes my way.

I'm having the most delicious dream of my life. I'm in Beau's house and bright sunlight shines through the windows, slashing in streams against the walls. Laughter fills the air, the kind of joyful laughter from a decidedly happy toddler. When I look around, I find pictures of a family filling the walls. A family that includes me.

A warm hand wraps around my neck that startles me even in my dream. I look over to find Beau, older, but still as handsome, and he's grinning at me, corners of his eyes wrinkled. It's the gentle smile that tells me he's thinking sickeningly sweet thoughts about me.

I blink and we're outside with two children playing in a treehouse in the backyard. He takes my hand in his own and kisses my knuckles, showing off a wedding band on my finger.

A cold, sticky sweat covers my skin when I gasp awake. Looking around nervously, I remember that I'm in Beau's home. That's why I dreamt such a vivid dream. Just my brain going berserk because I'm not home in my own bed. That's all it is. Early light of dawn filters in through the windows facing the backyard. The gentle chirp of birds that signal morning has come filters in through the gauzy curtains covering Beau's bedroom windows.

Time to go home.

Beau grunts beside me and reaches his arm out for me in his sleep. A few more hours remain on the fake boyfriend clock. I let him tug me back down into his strong arm. I snuggle deeply against him, stupidly taking comfort in his arms. His heart pounds beneath my ear, strong and steady. Just like him. I run my fingers along the veins of his forearm as he slowly joins me in the land of the living.

"Mornin'," Beau says, voice still sleep gruff and low.

I tenderly kiss the hollow of his throat, feeling his pulse jump against my lips. A grin breaks loose from me, and I press my lips harder against his sleep-warmed skin to hide it. "Morning."

"Mmm," Beau hums sleepily, tangling his fingers in my messy hair.

And then we just lie there. We freaking lie there as his fingers slowly comb through my hair, picking out the knots from sleep. I've never had a john do that before. Just treat me like a real boyfriend, like they enjoy my presence, like they enjoy *me*. I press my forehead against his chest, taking a steadying breath to calm my wild heart.

"So, what do you do when you leave here?"

"Probably another client or two this summer. Back to school in the fall."

His fingers stutter a little in my hair, but otherwise he doesn't speak. I trail my fingers down his side, along the dip of his ribs, and nuzzle my cheek against his chest hair. I've never been a big fan of body hair, but Beau has just the right amount to catch on my fingers as I rub my hand over his chest. Strangely, it's comforting.

"Your flight is in a few hours," Beau whispers dejectedly.

I press tighter against him, needing to burrow into his warmth. A clock chimes in the distance and my heart cracks in half. "Just a few more minutes."

"Whatever you want, sweetheart."

The words are so sweet, I almost believe them.

Beau drives me back to the airport with the attitude of a man seeing his lover off to war. Keeping my gaze off him and his unfairly perfect forearms is my only mission. Away from his perfect, horribly beautiful face. A man like Beau could never want a man like me, I remind myself, repeatedly, until my brain is forced to accept it.

Just keep my eyes trained on the rolling landscape out the window. When he finally pulls up at the airport, getting out of the car feels like an impossible act. After three days. What the fuck is wrong with me?

"Well, Claire will send you a survey asking about your experience." I play with the edge of my shirt, twirling my finger around a stray string. I should cut it. "You've already paid for it."

"Trevor."

I swallow hard, keeping my gaze aimed out the window. "Thank you. This weekend was actually pretty great."

"Trevor, will you look at me?"

Shaking my head violently, I'm unable to bear even the idea of looking at him. A parking cop blows his whistle and angrily points at us with wrath in his eyes. Time to flee. I pull the handle and push the door, but Beau tugs me back, and his mouth slams into mine with all the force of a car crash. He kisses me like he's going to miss me. Like he can memorize the weight of my lips. And God, I kiss him the same way back. Which is absolutely bonkers. I've clearly lost it.

A pathetic whimper escapes me when he pulls away. His breath fans across my cheek, sending a ripple of want through me. I wish I could turn back time. The safety of his arms, of his bed, of his home, is incomparable, stealing all the relief I usually feel when returning home.

"If you ever need me, you know how to find me." He swipes his thumb across my bottom lip with a rueful smile. "Goodbye, Trevor."

Words no longer exist in my lizard brain, stealing my ability to reply without sounding like a bumbling idiot. I hurriedly grab my bag, quickly fleeing into the safety of the busy airport. Check-in is a blur, so is getting on the plane, so is the entire flight home. I don't have any memory of the day until I'm standing in front of the all-too-familiar high-rise in downtown Atlanta.

None of the boys are at the clubhouse when I walk in. Even Claire is gone. The startling reality of being alone makes me feel sick enough to vomit. Dizzying nausea hits me with all the force of a Mack truck. Jesus. I can't be alone now. Not if I want to stay sane.

Anyone up for margaritas?

JACKSON

I'm in. Wacky Sunday?

BENJI

I'm on a job

ELI

I'm in!

BENJI

Wait there should be a rule against this

ELI

We will drink one in your honor

BENJI

Whatever you bitches

JACKSON

Excuse me?

BENJI

Sorry sir

ELI

barf

The Cantina in an hour?

JACKSON

Didn't you just get back from the airport?

Yes

Eli: Damn that bad?

No, it was that good.

JACKSON

We will be there in an hour!

Jackson always has my back. I wash quickly in the communal showers, brush a comb through my hair, and toss on a new set of clothes.

Nothing smells like Beau anymore. That realization hurts more than it ever should. I close my eyes for a brief moment to try to recall the scent of him. Blue skies, fresh-cut grass, cedar lingering on sheets, and hard work. Going the rest of my life without that smell seems truly unfair. Life isn't fair though. It's cruel and then you die.

Downtown Atlanta is fine, but it's never felt like home. Despite me living here since I turned eighteen.

The Cantina is a newer Tex-Mex restaurant that we've been meeting up at lately. It has the biggest margaritas I've ever seen, and it doesn't cost an arm and a leg. I easily spot my best friends because Jackson is a towering behemoth of a man. He really missed out by not playing basketball professionally. I know the pain of that for him though, so I feel like shit for even thinking it.

"Spill," Eli demands the moment I take a seat at the table. His big doe eyes blink at me in fear and worry, which I hate, but I also oddly appreciate. Sometimes it's nice to be cared about. The operative word is sometimes.

"I had a job this weekend." I take a large gulp of the margarita Jackson slides across the table. "I think I accidentally started to make it more real than I should."

"Ah, kid." Jackson shakes his head, leaning on his elbows.

I grimace as I play with a coaster. "I know."

"And what if it was real?"

Eli is always like this. He sees the best in everyone. A hopeless romantic at heart where I'm more of a realist. The odds of a john falling in love with me, or my friends is zip to none. *Pretty Woman* is just a lovely fairy tale, an urban legend, not a true story.

"Eli," I scoff with a roll of my eyes.

"It's not impossible!" Eli argues testily.

Jackson taps the table between us like a good referee. "We're here to listen to Trevor. If he thinks it can't happen, then it can't happen. What do you need from us?"

I pinch my nose to fight angry tears from falling. "I've got too much baggage for this."

"Trevor." Eli reaches across the table to take my hand in his with a kind smile. Nausea sends my stomach swirling at his perfect, sweet kindness. "Falling in love isn't a bad thing, even if it's just for the weekend, even if they don't love you back. Sometimes it's nice just to love, to know you're capable of it."

"Ugh." I angrily yank my hand away to roughly press my heel to my forehead.

"In other news, the bartender is eye-fucking the shit out of Eli." Jackson stealthily nods towards the bar. We all sneak glances that way.

Eli smirks, sending the bartender a coy wave. I try not to laugh when the classically handsome bartender waves back, smiling like a lovestruck dope. Eli is so easy to love. My best friend. He's a couple years older than me but I don't think age really matters when you connect with someone. Eli is proof of that.

"Think I should go for it?" Eli asks while biting his lip.

I kick him under the table. "One thousand percent."

Eli kicks me back softly, then climbs from the table with a dreamy sigh. "You're okay?"

"I'm fine," I promise him, and I mean it. I'm always fine.

Eli sweetly pats my head and happily skips off towards the bar. Jackson and I watch on for a few minutes as Eli leans against the bar, butt wiggling a little as he sways on his feet to flirt with the bartender. The man sure has game, without even trying. Must be so nice.

"You know that not everyone hires us because they have some ulterior motive."

"Ugh, Jackson," I groan with a bitter laugh. "Seriously. I get it."

Jackson skewers me with an assessing look, one dark eyebrow raised. He's not the eldest of us fake boyfriends, but his energy has always been of the boyfriend wrangler. Even our protector. But he's also wickedly smart and plays the stock market in a way that feels borderline illegal. I'm not sure he even needs to be a fake boyfriend. I think he honestly just likes it.

"You know we love you, right? You're not just a boyfriend, but our best friend."

Ugh, damn Jackson and his ability to see right through me. To see right to all my deepest issues. I'm not sure I'll ever accept that Jackson, Eli, and Benji actually love me. To my core. Sometimes I feel so rotten, so unlovable. Doesn't everyone though? At least, that's how I reassure myself that I'm just deeply normal.

"I do know, I swear." I reach across the table and pat his stubbled cheek, earning me a pretend bite to my hand. "Be nice to me!"

"We love you."

"Yeah, yeah. I love you too."

Elijah's raucous laugh has us turning back towards the bar. His face is an inch from the bartender's and they're whispering amongst themselves.

"Wanna see a movie?" Jackson asks as he throws a couple of bills down on the table.

"Sure."

"New Ryan Reynolds?"

I sigh dreamily. "You really know the way to my heart."

Jackson wraps a comforting arm around my shoulders, keeping it there through the entire walk to the theater. Because Jackson knows me so well, he orders us a large Coke and a giant-ass popcorn to share. The cinema is honestly one of my favorite places in the entire world. The air-conditioning is always on blast, it's quiet when the movie is on, and the snacks are ace. What else could I ask for?

Jackson even springs for the fancy recliner seats so we kick back and attack the popcorn as the ads start. We fight over the popcorn for a while, idly chatting during the previews. He catches me up on his boyfriend shenanigans, and I listen, comforted by the soft tenor of his voice.

"You sure you're okay, kid?" Jackson asks, just as the lights are dimming.

Worry rushes through me, just for a moment, that maybe he can really see me. See through Trevor to the core of me. But when I glance over at him, his gaze isn't knowing, only concern radiates from him. Concern is an easier emotion for me to handle from him.

"I'm sure," I say, the lie as easy as breathing.

CHAPTER SEVEN

BEAU

Octobers at the farm are usually full of joy. All the pumpkins, the kids in costumes, the families making wonderful memories. Even though all that is still happening, it's tinged by the bittersweet last few days my dad is going to be alive. Everything would be worse if we had no idea what hospice was or how the last few days would look.

Colby is an invaluable resource to us. The loss of Marcus, although terrible, has imparted him with knowledge that has made everything about my father's illness just a little easier. Colby's been there every step of the way, someone I can lean on. Which isn't the usual for me.

My dad has been a strong, steady foundation in my life. He joined a big family, the Smiths, without a blink and worked his way into the community. His love for my mother is something that I grew up admiring and being simultaneously envious of because I want to love someone like that. With every ounce of my soul.

"How are you doing?" Colby asks as he joins me on my parents' back porch.

I tiredly seesaw my hand back and forth. "At least we've known this is coming for a long time."

"That's the best and worst part about cancer. You know it's coming, but it still feels like it's happening so fast."

I take a deep, steadying breath, attempting to calm the noxious worry eating away at me. "Mom... this is going to be so difficult for her."

Colby shoots me one of his soft, reassuring smiles. "It'll be hard at first. Especially since they've been together almost forty years, but she's strong. She'll be okay."

"Is this hard for you? Reliving it all in a way?"

Colby thoughtfully runs a hand over his short stubble. "Not really. Yeah, it still sucks because that's my uncle, but it's different when it's your spouse."

"I hope I never find out," I admit honestly, then immediately feel like shit. "That was insensitive."

"Beau," Colby says firmly, but nicely, a sad look on his face. "You are allowed to be insensitive right now. You're allowed to feel pain. I won't hold anything against you. Is your boyfriend going to visit soon? That might help."

My eyes close tightly against the lie, against the pain of thinking about Trevor. It had seemed like such a brilliant idea to hire a fake boyfriend right up until the moment he left. Because everyone asks about him all the time now. I don't even know where he is or how to find him. Even though I want to find him, would love to find him.

"I really need to get back to the farm."

"Beau." Colby makes a pained sound before clapping my shoulder, effectively stopping me from fleeing. "The farm is fine. It'll be fine until you can get back. I promise. If you feel idle, there are other things we can do."

I squeeze my eyes shut against the pain. "Like what?"

"Wanna break an engine down and put it back together like we did with Grandpa?"

A weak laugh escapes me. We haven't worked on an engine together in ages. Probably not since we were kids. When Colby was a teen and I was a pre-teen, rebuilding engines with Grandpa was what kept us out of trouble. The man sure knew how to keep his grandkids distracted. Even Andy helped out with the cars when she was little.

"It couldn't hurt."

Colby playfully nudges me with his elbow, aiming that bright, sweet grin my way. I can't help but smile back at him. A couple of half-working vehicles just waiting to be fixed fill my parents' garage. That's the nice thing about being in a family of men like us, there's always a car around that you can fuck around with.

A few hours tick by as we work in the garage, tinkering around with one of the cars. Just the comfort of silence between us. Something about the smell of grease, of engines, comforts me to the marrow of my bones. The smell reminds me of hard work, days spent with the comforting presence of family. My mind drifts away as we work, so I'm no longer worried about the farm, about the future, about my mom or Andy. Until all I am is a man with my hands on an engine in the crisp Florida autumn air.

Until Andy comes running out of the house frantically looking for us.

Until her terrified eyes and tear-streaked face tell me everything.

When I look back on that day, that run from the garage to

the house felt like a million years. Like a million miles. But it only took me seconds. Just like it only took seconds for my dad to draw his final breath. The final goodbye.

One day is all I allow myself to be miserable. One day to wallow in my sadness. Then I pick myself back up and plan the memorial service. Thankfully, Colby's there to help me with that too.

Impulsively, I even sent an email to *The Boyfriend Experience* asking if Trevor is available for two days.

Hi, Beau,

Sorry to be the bearer of bad news but Trevor is not available. If there's another boyfriend that could fit the bill, please let me know and we can schedule him for three days from now.

Wishing you all the best,
Claire

Despite my grief and how hard the past few months have been with my father's declining health... my mind still frequently drifted to Trevor. I wondered if he'd ever take me up on my offer to come back here. If he'd ever need me.

Three days with him were enough to know something special flowed between us. Something rare. No one is a good enough actor to fake chemistry like we had. But I can't focus on Trevor now, even though he's been my favorite thing to focus on. A little piece of joy that I tuck away to pull out when I need it most.

Clay dirt kicks up behind me as the truck rolls towards the farm. It's Wednesday and it's closed to the public. We use that day to harvest crops, plant, or prepare for events. Today we're preparing for my father's memorial service on Friday.

After trying to help, most everyone shoos me off. Maybe for the first time in my life no one wants my help. So, I do the only thing I can think of to do. A few hours out with the sunflowers will cure me. Sometimes a man just needs to stand among the sunflowers, look up at the cloudless sky, and think big, scary thoughts. I've been doing that a lot lately. Just thinking. Most of my thoughts are about how I'm closer to forty than I am to thirty without much to show for it.

I've got the farm and my family but nothing else.

Andy's starting a new family of her own with Ethan.

What do I have?

I leave the farm feeling better than I did when I arrived. The land has always had a way of calming me, rooting me on earth when I feel like all the suppressed emotions inside me could float me away. Instead of going straight home, I head to my parents' place to check on my mom. Uncle Patrick's truck is in the driveway when I pull in with a soft sigh.

The soft sound of crying greets me as I push through the front door. I call out to my mom with a wince because I hate making her feel embarrassed for being sad. But I know she'll feel that way around me.

"Mom?"

"Hey, Beau," Uncle Patrick says to me as I enter the living room.

Mom wipes at her face and aims a watery smile at me. "How's the farm?"

"Mom, don't worry about the farm right now. Uncle Patrick and I have it covered."

Mom nods at me before standing on shaky legs. I envelop her in a tight hug, cradling her against my chest, and pretend not to hear her soft cries. Uncle Patrick lets out an anguished sigh and heads to the kitchen to make a cup of coffee. I hold Mom until her tears taper off. She gingerly pushes away at the scent of coffee floating in the air. That's one thing that'll always get her relaxed, a nice mug of coffee. She can drink it before bed. That's always been my mama's way.

Sitting at the kitchen island, we quietly share our coffee together.

"I brought some food over and put it in the fridge," Uncle Patrick says. "People keep dropping stuff off at our house, or at the farm. Lots of people love you, sissy."

Uncle Patrick kisses my mom's cheek, gives me a hard slap on the back, then disappears out the front door. The house is quiet for a few minutes as Mom sips at her coffee, hiding behind her hair a bit.

"I've got the service all planned. It'll be a hard day, but I think we'll all feel better once that's done. Once we can kind of officially say goodbye."

She angrily wipes at her eyes. "I know you're right."

I send her a soft smile, trying to ease her pain just a little. "I usually am."

"That too."

"Want to have dinner with me tonight?"

Mom shakes her head, swallowing roughly. "I want to be alone for a bit. Between you, Pat, and Andy... I'm not getting much of a chance to be alone. But I think I need to be alone in this house, feel it for a bit."

"If you're sure."

Mom sweetly pats my cheek with another watery smile. "I'm sure, baby. Go on home to your place and try to get some rest."

With one final kiss to her cheek, I leave her alone to grieve in her own way. I want to be with her, to make her feel better, but I can't police what she needs right now. Colby warned me of that. So, I head back home to my empty house, in my empty truck. Maybe I should get a dog. Whiskey isn't too rambunctious anymore. She seemed to be a great comfort for Colby after Marcus died.

Lots of maybes fill my life right now.

Too many maybes.

CHAPTER EIGHT

TREVOR

Keeping track of Beau for the past few months has been my newest, most painful hobby. I stalk the Clay Road Farms social media account way more than is healthy. But it's worth it when every now and then I get a glimpse of Beau in the background of a photo. Visiting Andy's account is fruitless because I'm honestly too scared about what I might find.

Worry for Beau is constant. About the family that I only spent three days with but felt more welcoming than my own ever had. Most of my days are spent at the gym, working out so long that everything hurts. Eating is perfunctory. Something I do to keep my muscles bulging just how the boyfriends that hire me like them. The nights with fake boyfriends are endless, mind numbing, painful in a way that's impossible to put to words. Like small cuts slicing away at my soul, which is what I always needed before, but now it doesn't feel nearly as good as before Beau.

And then one day in October, Claire calls me.

"Hey!" I shout into the phone as I pause the stair climber. "Is there an event going on at the clubhouse this weekend?"

"No," Claire says firmly which immediately has me on edge.

"Uh."

"Do you remember Beau Callahan?"

My heart skips approximately ten beats. Maybe this is how I die. By cardiac arrest just from the sound of Beau's name.

"Yes," I say, voice an octave too high to be normal.

"He reached out wanting to hire you for his father's funeral. I had the feeling you might want to know despite being booked for the weekend."

Oh, God. I dip to my knees on the stair climber, then press my forehead to my knee. Sweat dots my chest and arms, my back too. The ache of a good workout is long gone, only to be replaced with absolute heartache for Beau.

"What'd you tell him?"

"That you're unavailable."

"Shit." I stumble off the machine, then stagger towards the locker room. The phone is slippery in my hand from sweat. I almost forget that I'm even on a call, so distracted with thoughts of Beau.

"Was that a mistake?" Claire asks softly, even a little warmly.

"Can you..." I trail off, then take a deep, clarifying breath. "Tell him I'm available?"

"I can, yes. What am I doing about your booking with Nolan? He's been consistent about booking you."

"Benji."

Claire breathes deeply into the phone. "Benji?"

"Yeah, he'll do it. He can deal with it."

A few moments of stilted silence filter through the phone line. I never bail and I never rock the boat. But the idea of passing over just one more day with Beau to spend it with someone else who has an affinity for pain play, well, my heart won't allow it. Which is entirely new for me. The guys that make it hurt are usually my favorite, not the gentle giants that treat me like I'm as fragile as glass.

"Do you want me to reach out to Beau to let him know?"

"No," I tell her firmly. "I'll head there now. Also, only charge him your cut. Don't take a cut for me."

"Trevor," Claire says, voice a frightened murmur. "I hope you know what you're doing, honey."

"Everything is fine."

Except when I hang up with her, I know not everything is fine. And I know that for sure when I get home, hastily pack a bag, grab my keys to my shitty Toyota Corolla, and point my car towards Clay Springs. The seven-hour drive takes me just under five. Probably less to do with speeding and more to do with my total dissociation and need to just... get there.

My heart beats wildly as I slowly pull up to the gate in front of Beau's property. I didn't think this through at all. Thankfully, a large truck pulls up on the main road behind me, coming to a stop to investigate.

"Trevor?" a familiar voice calls out.

I lean my head out the window to find Colby standing just outside his truck. When he notices it's me, his smile widens. He jogs towards my car, coming to a stop by the driver side window.

"Oh wow, he could really use you right now. Are you surprising him?"

I swallow hard against every rotten emotion swelling to the surface. "Yeah, it's a surprise."

Colby winks at me, before typing a code into the gate pad. "Be sweet with him. The past few days have been rough."

I watch him with detached fascination as Colby runs back towards his truck, then disappears across the road to his own property. The gate beeps when it's fully open, so I take that as my cue to pull on through. The road is more winding than I recall in my dreams. My car comes to a squeaking stop in front of the still all-too-familiar house. I really need to get my brakes checked.

A ragged Beau steps through the front door with a confused look my way. But at the sight of me, he softens like the weight of the world is falling off his broad shoulders. I make a mad dash to him without even grabbing my scant belongings. Beau gratefully slumps against me like he trusts me to hold him up. I pull him tight to my body. Beau might be taller, broader, and physically stronger than me, but I can still easily bear his weight.

"Lets go inside," I whisper as I gingerly guide him back into the house.

Gently, I push him down onto the couch, and take a seat next to him, pulling him against the curve of my body. His head rests against my chest with all the pain of someone that's lost the dearest thing to them. I know that pain, know that hurt. Everything inside me demands that I try to heal it, to take away that hurt. All I can do is be here for him when he needs me most.

I play with the dark brown hairs at the nape of his neck. His hair is longer than a few months ago, curling more at the edges. The house is exactly the same though, which I find comforting for some odd reason I can't explain. Like Beau is too big of a force to change too much. Too steady to be rocked.

Beau doesn't cry, but I think it's an almost-thing. I hum some song I don't know the words to as I comfort him with my touch, gliding my fingers through his hair, tenderly massaging the base of his neck.

My heart cracks wide open for him. The fierce need to make this better, make it easier on him, is stronger than anything I've ever felt. I watched him make everything easy for his family for Andy's wedding. Watched him bend backwards for them. And I know he's doing that now too. So, I'm going to be his shoulder through the funeral. Then I'll go back to the clubhouse. Back to my life.

"The agency said you weren't available," Beau says softly.

The urge to tell him all my secrets, all my truths, bubbles up inside me. Threatening to boil over like a steam engine barreling towards the end of the tracks. But I can't, not now, not with him just barely hanging on. Maybe one day, when we find one another again outside of this messiness, but not now. All he needs from me now is my weight to bear the heaviness of his grief. I'm going to be for him what I needed so many years ago.

"It was a misunderstanding. I'm here now."

Beau rolls his head to look up at me. I push him down until his back is on the couch, so I can tenderly cup his face. His beard's a little longer than I remember too. More wiry, more wild. I oddly like it. I run my finger under his lip and smile down at him.

"There you are."

"My dad died."

"I know."

Beau shakily covers his eyes with his forearm. "My dad's gone," Beau says, voice trembling.

And then Beau's crying, big, wracking sobs that break my

already fractured-to-pieces heart. I carefully wiggle so that I can lie down over his body, pressing my weight down on him. His arms wrap around me, holding me tighter against him as if I can sink into him.

I can't say how long we lie there as Beau cries, tears thick, chest heaving with barely restrained sobs.

"Can I take care of *you*, Beau? Tell me how I can do that."

Beau presses his fingers into the small of my back, tugging me somehow even closer. "Just be here with me until it's over."

Brushing my lips across his forehead, I bite my cheek to keep myself from crying. Only the orange hue of light shining through the windows tells me the time. I leave Beau asleep on the sofa, and rummage through his fridge for food. The shelves are almost empty. What's he been eating? From the state of things, it looks like he's probably not been eating well for the past few weeks.

A flier on the fridge door for a local pizza place catches my eye. That'll be it. I place an order for delivery and give them the gate code I watched Colby enter earlier. Hopefully, Beau won't mind. And then I get to work cleaning the kitchen. The place isn't messy, but I don't think it's up to Beau's usual standards. At least not from what I recall from my last visit.

The pizza arrives just after I finish cleaning. I give the delivery kid two twenty-dollar bills and close the door quietly behind me. Maybe it's the sound, or maybe it's the sweet smell of the pizza, but Beau rouses from his short nap with the heel of his hand pressed hard against his forehead.

He blinks at me a few times, then his tired gaze flicks between me and the pizza.

"I thought I dreamt you," he says, voice dripping with exhaustion.

And that breaks my heart too. "Nope. I'm here. At least until after the funeral."

Relief washes over him and the tension bleeds from his shoulders.

"Come eat?" I ask gently.

Beau quietly follows me into the kitchen. We don't even sit down. We just stand around eating pizza slices out of the box. Tiredness radiates off Beau in a way I've never felt it radiate off of someone before. All my protector urges rise to the surface seeing Beau half-broken the way he is now.

After he's eaten a few pieces of pizza, I manhandle him into the bathroom.

"Take a nice hot shower, then we'll get you into bed to sleep."

Beau doesn't even try to argue. I shut the door firmly behind him so that he has privacy. The sheets have seen better days, so I change them after spending an odd amount of time trying to find new ones without violating his privacy. Clean sheets always make me fall asleep just a little bit faster and easier.

Steam floats through the door when Beau pushes it open. He's in just boxer briefs, gracing me with the sight of his big barrel chest. Still just as beautiful as this past summer.

Gingerly tucking him into the bed, I rush through a shower for myself. The steamy air still smells like him, like blue skies, the outdoors, and everything beside the word strong in the dictionary. Digging around under his sink, I don't know why I'm surprised to not find a blow-dryer. This is Beau Callahan. So, I forgo the blow-dry and instead haphazardly run Beau's comb through my hair.

Beau is halfway asleep when I crawl into the bed beside him. He blinks those sleepy dark blue eyes at me and smiles just enough to make my world rotate on its entire axis. I'd do anything to keep him smiling like that. As if just my presence beside him soothes him, he promptly falls asleep.

Sleep eludes me as I watch him. Too wired from the absolutely wild day I've had, plus the long drive from Atlanta. My fingers have a mind of their own and trace his broad, expressive eyebrows. Then I scratch at his beard a little, just soft enough to leave him sleeping.

My eyes drift closed as I tenderly run my fingers through his still slightly damp hair. I snuggle up against him, smiling like a loon when he wraps an arm around my waist to tug me closer. With the weight of Beau's arm around me, I fall into the deepest sleep I've had in years.

Gentle fingers combing through my hair wake me. When I blink my eyes open, I find Beau leaning over me, a soft, pleased smile tilting up his plush lips. Without thinking, I lean up to slide my lips against his in a tender kiss. Morning breath be damned.

"Morning," I say, my voice still sleep husky.

"Morning," Beau echoes.

"How are you doing?"

A sweet, shy smile tilts his lips up at the corners. His eyes are just shiny enough to worry me. "Better now."

I can't let this be about me. Everything needs to be about him. So, I build my walls up higher, so high that I know not even I can climb over them. I wrestle Beau out of bed. Breakfast will be the pizza and eggs that I scrounge out of the fridge. Tried-and-true breakfast of warriors.

We eat in silence on the back porch. Instead of the sweltering high heat and humidity of summer, the air is warm, less sticky. A light breeze washes over us, gentling the warmth of the day. Once Beau finishes his food, I carry it back inside to start on the dishes. Beau stares out into the forest with a contemplative look as I work.

Returning outside, his heavy gaze swings to me. Emotion visibly overwhelms him as he swallows thickly, throat working to hold back his tears. His fingers grip the chair tightly, knuckles white from his strength.

"It's gonna be alright," I tell him.

He nods tightly once, then slowly unfurls from the deck chair. My heart does a little skip in my chest as he makes his way over to me. Looping my arms around his strong shoulders, I let my hands hang loose at the nape of his neck. His eyes close in what I like to imagine is relief.

This is caring for someone without wanting anything in return.

And Beau is the only person that could elicit this from me.

I pepper kisses across his face until he relaxes against me, his hands a warm, steady weight on my hips. The warmth of him bleeds through my clothes, until it feels like he's warming me from the outside in. Frozen glass around my carefully protected heart could melt under Beau's gentle care. Dangerous. This man could never want me if he knew, no one ever wants me. Love is conditional, earned only by being good, by being perfect.

I shake myself from my morose thoughts. "What do you need from me?"

Beau sweetly nuzzles the side of my face. "Can you just stay here at least through the funeral?"

"I'm already doing that, love." I skim my nose up his cheek, smiling at his soft sigh. "What do you need me to do? You want me to check on your mom? On Andy? Go to the farm?"

Beau sighs loudly, resting his weary head on top of mine. Exhaustion bleeds from him, and I ache to take it all away. "Just be with me."

I pull him tighter against me, as if I can pull him into myself. "That I can do."

Being by Beau's side, comforting him, isn't a hard task. Even in his deep sadness, the man is extraordinarily gentle. His family welcomes me back into their arms like I was never gone. Like I've always been here, at the farm, a part of their family.

His mother hugs me a little too tight, but I let her. While Beau busies himself in her kitchen, I sit quietly with her on the back porch. Just keeping her company.

"You have an outfit picked out?" I ask her, trying to be as sensitive as possible.

Cindy's lips lift into a bittersweet smile. "He picked the dress out before he died. It's light pink with green and pink flowers. He loved it. It made him smile to see me in it."

"That's beautiful."

Emotions choke me. The grief and profound love are so palpable. It's hard to believe some families are full of this much love for one another. That some people can love their spouse this much, enough to be brave for them in their last days. The very idea overwhelms me. My family was nothing like this close-knit one. Maybe before everything went to shit there were glimpses, but most of the time my family was neglectful at best.

"How's college?"

I clench and unclench my fingers to derail my thoughts. "Good. Just one more semester."

"What's your degree again?" Cindy asks in only the way a mother can. Gentle, but curious.

"Psychology. My goal is to be a licensed clinical social worker. A therapist."

She sizes me up for a few moments. "My son has always been the strong one, it's the lot in life he inherited. My pregnancy with Andy wasn't easy, and he was older by the time she came along. Then she was born with lung issues, so she was sickly." Her eyes go distant for a few moments, before falling back on me. "I've been hard on him, more than I should. Especially through all of this. Made him grow up too fast. You'll be good to him?"

"Yes." The promise isn't a lie either. Despite the fake nature of our relationship, I will be beyond good to Beau. I'll take care of him for as long as he'll allow. "He's a good man."

Her eyes quickly flick behind us, then back to me. "He's a great man. Speaks highly of you, you know. Beau's never settled with anyone before. Never wanted for much. Wanting you means you're top shelf in my book."

Warmth suffuses through me at her approval. Unable to bask in her sweetness for another second, I leave her alone outside, and join Beau in the kitchen. I find Beau at the window above the sink, staring forlornly out at his mom. For a moment I wonder if he was listening, but it's too far away for that. The look on his face is one I haven't seen yet, not able to parse the thoughts flowing through his head.

"She likes you," Beau murmurs softly, sounding unusually distracted.

I don't know how to respond to his statement. But I don't have to because Beau turns around, grabs my cheeks with his still soapy hands, and kisses me firmly on the mouth. I'm so shocked by the kiss that I barely have a chance to reciprocate before he pulls away. His eyes are closed tight, a deep frown mars his beautiful face. But he stays quiet, as usual. Too many thoughts filling his head to put them into words.

After finishing up dishes, we head back to his house. Beau wants to check on the farm, but I won't allow him. Employees and other family members can handle that task. I am sure that they'll be able to set the service up for tomorrow without him hovering over them.

"What am I supposed to do now?" Beau asks, confusion lacing his voice, as we walk back into his house.

"Most common advice is to sit with it."

He huffs in exasperation. "I don't want to do that," Beau says, voice cracking on the words.

I nod, despite not understanding myself. "But that's how you move forward. You've got to feel it, Beau. Let yourself feel it."

He slowly covers his face with his hands and lets out a rib-breaking, anguished cry. The sort of cry that comes from the very pit of his grieving soul. His heartbroken sobs reverberate through me, to the marrow of my bones, to the pit of my hardened soul. The cry of a man that's lost something he knows he'll never have again. To know you'll never hold that loved one again, never smell their sweet smell, never see the glimmer of love in their eyes when they catch sight of you. It is a pain you can't know until you live it. I wish Beau wasn't living it, I'd do anything to spare him his pain. Anything.

Before Beau can crumble to his knees, I carefully catch him, lowering us softly to the ground as I bear his weight. Painful, gut-wrenching sobs tremble and shake through his burly frame. All I can do is hold him. Tears well in my own eyes and a few even dare to fall. But I ignore them. Because this isn't about me, it can't be about me, it's about him. I gently sway Beau in my arms, rocking him back and forth until his sobs slowly quiet to hiccuping cries.

I can't say how long we sat there in the middle of his living room. Could be minutes, could be hours. All I know is that by the time I've got him showered, back in bed, and I'm curled around his sleeping body... I know I'm in deep, deep trouble when it comes to Beau Callahan.

CHAPTER NINE

BEAU

The memorial service takes place on an unfairly beautiful October day. Not one cloud smudges the large expanse of blue sky. A gentle breeze blows over the farm, carrying the fresh scent of the citrus groves from deeper on the property. My father would've loved the day. He would've smiled, tipped his head to the sky, and said *no rain today, son.*

Sometimes I miss him so deeply my heart aches with it. I'll never hug him again. Never feel his large palm slapping my back after a job well done. I'll never pick blueberries off the bush and eat them from the palm of his hand like I did as a child. So many memories now only in my mind. My memories of him are now just a perfect time capsule.

Easily five hundred people dot the property. Just for the memorial alone.

To say I'm overwhelmed would be a gross understatement.

I grip Trevor's hand tightly as we join my family at the front. Rows and rows of chairs are full, and at least two hundred people stand at the back. Workers with their hats off, held to their chest in respect. It's easy to forget how loved my family is, how ingrained in the community we are. But moments like this when everyone rallies around us, the reminder is bittersweet.

Colby joins us in the front row, along with his parents, and on the other side of me, my mother grips Uncle Patrick's hand like a lifeline.

I keep a firm hold on Trevor's hand, afraid if I let go, I'll fall apart. His hand is a steadying weight as he tries to carry some of the emotional baggage of the day. Trevor's smile is tremulous as he aims it at me, but I'm grateful for it all the same. Thankful for him. Just his presence beside me brings me stark relief.

The service doesn't last long thankfully because I'm not sure I could withstand too much. A local pastor speaks fondly about my father's life, and I fight back tears the entire time. When it's my turn to get up, to stay a few words, I can't. I'm frozen to the spot. Andy looks at me in confusion, but I can't physically move. For the first time in my life, my body won't let me stand.

Colby squeezes my shoulder hard as he stands, then heads towards the makeshift stage. He says a few words of thanks that filter in and out of my brain without absorbing them. The service is over in what feels like the matter of minutes.

Trevor attaches himself to me, holding me up when my knees feel too weak to bear my weight. A good old southern meal follows the service, under the open barn reserved for special events. Andy's wedding had just been here months ago. Now the place is sullied by the loss of my father.

I don't remember eating, but I assume I do because

Trevor takes a plate from me with a tender smile. His hand is warm in mine, keeping me rooted to the earth when I so badly want to float away. To disappear. Just see my dad one more fucking time.

The hundreds of people slowly trickle out until just close family is left. Unable to not stay busy, to not do something, I start to clean up, but Trevor's hand comes down hard on my arm.

Trevor's eyes are sharp as he squeezes my forearm. "Don't."

I squeeze my eyes tightly shut to blot out the day, to just forget everything.

Colby joins us with an understanding look. "Why don't you both go home, it's been a long day."

The walk to the car is silent. Tension radiates off me in painful waves, tightening my jaw, pulsing in my veins. Once we're alone it eases, as if Trevor's presence alone is enough to calm the terribleness of the day. Maybe it is.

Closure doesn't feel as good as I expected. On the way back home, our fingers stay interlocked, the heat of Trevor's skin blending into me. Every now and then he rubs his thumb across my knuckles, sending little sparks dancing along my skin. His touch is a comfort like a warm blanket, fresh out of the dryer. An inexplicably simple thing but it carries such taut relief. Sadness a tidal wave over me, grief the ugly destruction in its wake, but having Trevor eases the ache, making it somehow easier to withstand.

This man made one of the worst days of my life bearable.

Everything with him is real.

Nothing about Trevor feels remotely fake. Not anymore.

"Trevor," I whisper into the pitch black when we park in front of the house.

"Yeah?"

"I want you."

His smile is blinding, although it doesn't reach his eyes. "You've got me."

"No, you don't get it. I *want* you."

Disappointment floods Trevor's face. "Oh."

"But not just for sex," I hurry to explain, needing him to understand. "I want to hold you, kiss you, and hold you tight while you dream. I want it all. I want everything."

Trevor's fingers bite hard into the skin of my forearm, almost hard enough to break skin. His breath audibly caught in his chest, sounding painful to my ears. The breath releases with a whiny, angry whistle. For a moment I wonder if I've misstepped, only until he closes his eyes tight on a shaky inhale.

"It's real for me," Trevor admits, fear coloring his voice.

"Can I have you?"

A hush falls over the cab of the truck for a moment. Trevor's gaze pings back to mine. Something in his dark gaze fills me with unease. "I can't promise you anything beyond tonight. Will you be happy with just tonight?"

"I'll be happy with just one millisecond holding you."

Trevor laughs softly, but it's fake. It's easy for me to tell now, the difference between real Trevor and fake boyfriend Trevor. He blinks open his eyes to aim those gorgeous baby blues at me, freezing me to the spot. "And that's why this feels so fucking real. For today, I really am your boyfriend. Okay? For today."

"Okay." I tug him until his warm weight presses into me, until he's carefully straddling me in the tight quarters of the truck. The weight of him against me settles something in my uneasy soul. Solid and firm. Trevor's not a small man at all, but he's small when he's in my arms. "Kiss me, Trevor."

Trevor's eyebrow arches, lips tilted up in a sexy smirk. "Is that how this is gonna go?"

"Yeah." I tug him down until he's only a breath away. "Now kiss me."

The kiss is soft, a gentle glide of lips. Slowly the kiss deepens, until I feel like I'm falling into him. Everything spins around me, so I grab him tight, my fingers pressing into his hips, surely hard enough to bruise. The weightless feeling inside my cavernous chest urges me to hold on tighter, to keep us both grounded to the earth.

Trevor pulls away from me panting, hair a messy halo around his face. "Take me inside?"

Problem is I don't know if I can quit kissing him long enough to leave the truck. I figure I can do both things. Trevor laughs into my mouth as I back him up towards the door, devouring his mouth the entire way. God, the taste of him makes me crazy, makes me reckless, makes me *need*.

His mouth is the best thing I've ever tasted. He tastes like the end of a long time waiting, like all wishes fulfilled, but he mostly tastes like *mine*. The thought might be dangerous, but it's so very real. At least for tonight.

A tortured whine drops from his wet lips when I pull away slightly to kick the door closed behind us. His hands run up my back to tightly grip my shoulders. A wicked smile spreads across his mouth and his eyes dance with mischief. My God, he's beautiful.

"Take me to bed, Beau."

I love the way he says my name. The word floats from his lips easily, with a deeper meaning I can't decipher. Sliding my hands down his back, my hands cup his ass for a moment. A relieved sound escapes him when I slip my hands down to his thighs and lift so that he's forced to wrap his legs around my waist. And he goes, just like that. His long legs wind around me like they were made to be there. Maybe they were.

Trevor trails his lips down my neck, grazing his teeth along my overheated skin. When he bites gently on the tendons of my neck, I almost lose my grip on him. Once we reach my bedroom, I haphazardly toss him onto the bed. A small, delighted huff escapes him as he bounces on the bed. He leans up on his elbows to aim a coy look at me through his blond eyelashes. Perfect teeth press down on his bottom lip, and that just won't do. If anyone's going to bite one of his lips, it's going to be me.

My suit jacket falls in a flurry after I toss it to the floor without a care in the world. I start to undo my dress shirt, but Trevor shakes his head, and scoots to the edge of the bed. He wiggles his fingers for me to come closer, so I do. Nimble hands run up my chest. Slowly, making my heart flutter dangerously, he undoes the buttons of my shirt, one by fucking one. Trevor gazes up at me the entire time, so much heat in his eyes that I'm afraid the house might burn down. Those baby blues will be my undoing. Being undone by Trevor is as close to heaven as I'm probably ever going to get.

He pushes my shirt off, fingers trailing softly along my skin, and pulls my undershirt over my head, so I'm left shirtless in just my dress slacks. A couple of beats pass by as he just stares at my chest, as if he hasn't seen me naked before. But this is in a different context, so maybe it means more now. I can't be sure. All I know is I'll die if my lips aren't on his while he's got that look on his face.

Placing my knee on the bed, I lean forward until he's forced to fall back. Blond hair fans out beside his head, a little mussed from the day, but he's still so effortlessly gorgeous. He's perfect, and for tonight, for this small sliver of time, he's all mine. One hand lifts up to gently cup my face, and his eyes shift between mine, searching me for an answer to some unknown question.

"You gonna make me yours, Beau?"

I nod against his hand, placing a dry kiss to his palm. "I'm gonna show you."

He arches one single eyebrow. "Show me what?"

"What it's like to be loved, sweetheart."

Trevor gasps sharply, closing his eyes so tight it looks borderline painful. He takes a few deep, calming breaths, then opens his eyes to aim those startling baby blues at me.

"Call me Levi," he whispers, eyes once again searching mine. "That's my real name."

Oh. The tension in his body, flush on his cheeks, alerts me to the fact that he doesn't tell many people that truth. It's an honor for me to know his real name, know the real him. Behind Trevor's fake boyfriend persona is a man that so desperately needs to be loved.

I kiss him in thanks for trusting me with his secret. Running my hand up and down his arm to calm him as best I can, he shivers underneath me despite still being fully clothed. I undress him without taking my lips from his, which is a particular skill I never knew I had. Maybe it's a skill just for him, just for this grand moment.

I devour him as I kick out of my own clothing. Licking into his mouth, I attempt to memorize the flavor of him, the flavor that's all mine. When I press down on him to line up our hard cocks, he bucks against me, letting out a pained cry that I eagerly swallow down.

"Shhhh," I whisper into his mouth, desperately trying to soothe him.

He gives me a jerky nod, eyes firmly shut. I rain loving kisses over his cheeks, his closed eyes, his forehead, while running my fingers through his silk-soft hair. I kiss him and kiss him, ignoring how hard both of us are. Finally, it's too much for him. Need vibrates from his body and his hips restlessly buck up into mine, seeking friction, seeking pleasure. Time to give in.

Reaching into the nightstand, I clumsily fumble around until I return with a condom and lube. Levi lets out a relieved sigh at the sight of the supplies.

"Next time, I'll eat your ass until you're begging for it, but tonight I'll just use my fingers, get you nice and wet, then slip inside you like you were made for me. Alright, sweetheart?"

Levi squeezes his eyes tightly shut for a moment, before nodding, blinking those gorgeous eyes back open to take me in. He watches, gaze heavy, eyes lidded, as I gently press a lubed finger inside him. A gasp rattles out of him as he bears down, welcoming me like I was made to be there. I go slow, gently gliding my finger in and out, getting him used to the feeling of having me inside him. But I must go too slow, despite the hazy glow of the evening, because he tangles his fingers in my hair and tugs my gaze to meet his.

"You better get inside me or I'm going to lose my shit," Levi demands, voice throaty and full of warning.

I shake his hand from my hair and teasingly bite his thumb. He hisses as I let go. Shifting onto my knees, I roll the condom on, and lube myself up. Levi's eyes are hot on me the entire time, watching, and waiting for my next move.

I lean over him, one forearm braced beside his head. "Like this?"

Levi nods and firmly presses his lips to mine. I hook his leg over my arm, lifting so that I can notch my cock against his entrance. He welcomes me easily, like he was made for me, like I was made for him. I kiss him through the slow glide home, until my hips are pressed flush against his ass. He whimpers softly into my mouth.

I rock into him, gently, more of a grind than a thrust. He pants against my mouth, eyes wide, fingers making half-moon indents into my shoulders. Curling a hand into his hair, I hold on tight, and kiss him through the slow pace I set. I could go like this all night, just making love to him, eating his whimpers and moans and every breathy exhale that tells me Levi is actually enjoying himself.

"Beau," Levi whimpers against my cheek when I turn my head to pant against his shoulder. "Beau, please."

The "please" is what does me in. That single word is what makes me a fool. I turn back to him and tangle both hands in his hair this time, forcing him to keep his gaze on me as I increase the pace of my thrusts. Every couple of thrusts I swivel my hips, stretching him, rubbing against the spot inside him that makes him see stars. His thighs tighten on me each time until finally they're trembling against my sweat-slick ribs.

His heels kick against my thighs as I stop going slow, stop taking my time, and thrust inside him all the way, only to pull out slowly, and keep the pace up until he looks almost delirious. Gorgeous splotches of crimson bloom across his cheeks, so I kiss them, because I have to taste his flushed skin.

Fingers bite into my skin so hard that I think I might bleed. He lets out a loud gasp, more shock than pleasure, before stilling underneath me with wide, almost frightened eyes. I'm afraid for a moment before I feel his warm release splashing between us. He came untouched. Levi goes absolutely boneless underneath me. I start to pull out but a firm hand on my neck holds me in place.

"Where are you going?" Levi mumbles, all sex drowsy and sweet.

"Pulling out, you came."

Levi shakes his head tiredly. "Finish inside me. I want it."

Jesus Christ. My hips flex before my brain can even catch up. I grind into him, conscious of his oversensitivity, and only a few thrusts later my orgasm crashes through me. My orgasm is borderline violent in its intensity. I know it's because of Levi. He lets out a satisfied sound, a smile tugging at his lips. I nuzzle into his neck and breathe the clean, summer scent of him in. My Levi.

I pull out of him as gently as I can, careful the condom doesn't slip off. On shaky feet, I walk to the bathroom, turn the shower on, and take care of the condom. I lean back on my heels to check on Levi and find him still spread out in an exhausted heap on the bed.

I head back into the bedroom and lean over him on the bed. Blue eyes blink up at me, still a little glazed. A chuckle escapes me at the sight of him. I tenderly push his messy hair from his face.

"Wanna join me in the shower, sweetheart? Let's get all clean before bed."

"I cannot go again," Levi mumbles in disappointment, eyebrows furrowed. I wonder how often he's allowed to say no, how often things are demanded of him that he doesn't want to give.

"Not a sexy shower, just a get-clean shower."

He easily lets me manhandle him out of bed and into the bathroom, every ounce of fight bled out of him by the orgasm. The bathroom is thick with steam. Sliding the glass door open, I push him through, then quickly follow him inside. I carefully push him under the water, tilting his head back for him so that I can wash his hair. He stares at me the entire time, through shampooing, conditioning, and finally rinsing. I rush through washing my own hair, then return my attention to him.

My fingers skim over his body behind the loofah, memorizing every dip, every muscle, every sun freckle that I can find. His stomach contracts at my touch, all the muscles dancing under my curious fingers.

"Beau," Levi murmurs sleepily.

I can only smile at him and position us so we're under the spray of the shower at the same time. The water rinses us clean, but we stay there for a little while longer, until I'm afraid the water might turn cold. I run the towel over his miles of skin until he's dry, then he takes the towel from me to dry me off next. Once dry, he stands in front of the mirror for a moment, inspecting his reflection with a shrewd intention. As if he's lived here all his life, he rattles through my drawers until he returns with a brush that I haven't used in years. Haven't needed really.

After his hair is thoroughly brushed, he tiredly stumbles towards the bed, and faceplants on the sheets with a heavy groan. Chuckling, I pull the duvet over him and join him under the sheets. Levi quickly turns over to wiggle himself into my arms, pressing his body tight against mine. A smile creeps across my face without me even realizing.

"Night, Levi."

His breath puffs against my chest, fingers pressed tight to my back. "Night, Beau."

"BEAU."

My whispered name wakes me up in the middle of the night. When I open my eyes, I'm greeted by the sight of Levi leaning over me. His hair is a mess but he's so beautiful my heart hurts with the force of it.

Levi straddles me under the sheets, his warm, naked body sliding against my own. His hard cock brushes against me, forcing a hiss of pleasure from my lips. He leans down close to my face in the dark. Lips brush against my own softly with both of our eyes wide open.

"Will you make love to me?" Levi asks, voice hush quiet.

My hands tighten painfully on his hips. "That's what you want?"

He nods softly, hair brushing my face. "Show me."

Levi scoots back a little to grab a condom and lube off the nightstand. When he settles back down on me, he wastes no time wrapping the condom around me, then slathering me with lube. He reaches back to prep himself, and I cup his ass in my hands, spreading his cheeks to make it easier for him. A moan of pleasure rattles through him at my rough touch.

A frustrated sound escapes him just before he kneels over me. I wrap my hand around his neck, my other on his hip to support him as he takes me into his warm body. This feels different than earlier. There's an edge of urgency to Levi's movements.

I sit up so that he's nestled in my lap, so I can see his face more clearly. Tears swim in his eyes. I want to take his pain away, ease his sadness. I tangle my fingers in his hair and tug him close as he grinds down onto me. Small sounds of pleasure escape him each time he grinds down onto my cock. His fingers dig into my biceps, holding on as he takes me so deeply inside him that I wonder if he'll feel me for days afterward. He feels so good, pleasure rapidly builds at the base of my spine, demanding insistently that I come, but I push my pleasure away to focus on him.

"Tell me."

Haunted eyes flit quickly between mine. "I wish this was real."

"It is real." His cock is burning hot against my skin when I tightly squeeze at the base, tearing a gasp from him at my almost too rough touch. "Doesn't it feel real to you?"

Levi nods, then immediately shakes his head, indecision floating off of him in thick waves. I don't know how to fix this, how to reassure him that what I feel for him is real, despite the reality of our fake boyfriend situation. Nothing about this is fake anymore. It hasn't been since he returned and held me as I wept with awful grief.

"Do you want me? Really want me?" Levi asks as I flip us over, voice small and thready. His hair fans on the pillow around his head, making him the picture of an angel. Fallen from heaven just for me to love.

"Sweetheart, I don't know what you're asking of me."

Levi raises his hand to cup my cheek, imploring me to hear him. "Do you think you could actually really want me?"

Even though I don't know what he's asking for, I give him the answer that my heart says is right. The answer that feels right in the very depths of my sorrowful soul.

I press a kiss to the skin over where his pulse pounds,

finally lightly kissing the very hollow of his throat. "I want you so much it hurts. I want you for keeps."

An anguished cry leaves his lips when I pull out, only to slam back in, hitting that spot that makes him see stars. I kiss him, eating at his mouth, needing to taste his pleasure as I pummel into him over and over. Tomorrow, he needs to feel this, have the reminder of me deep inside his body. Keeping one hand in his hair, I use the other to drag his thigh up higher against my side, deepening the angle until we both moan at the feel. God, he feels like heaven.

"Beau," Levi begs, voice broken. "Make me come."

"Not yet," I whisper, voice firm.

He claws helplessly at my back. "Please."

I'm not ready for it to be over. Not by a long shot. That goes for everything with Levi beyond this moment too. Levi's eyes are glassy as he stares up at me, lip caught between his teeth. God, the way he looks at me could end me. Suddenly, my orgasm means nothing, only his pleasure matters.

"You want to come?"

Levi nods rapidly, a deep flush across his chest and neck. "Please."

Grabbing his still lube-covered hand, I lower it to his cock, helping him wrap his trembling fingers around himself. "Make yourself come, then."

I rise to my knees and tug him higher up into my lap, changing the angle in a way that has a delicious moan falling from his kiss-bitten lips. I slowly grind my cock into him, his eyes flutter closed at the ecstasy of it. His hand tugs furiously at his cock with each of my thrusts, perfectly timed with me. The tendons in his throat pull taut as pleasure races to overtake him. An absolutely mad urge to see him come, see him fall apart overtakes me.

Even in the dark of the bedroom, everything about Levi is achingly gorgeous. I wish I could take him into my mouth, edge him for hours, feel his trembling thighs around my shoulders as I take him to the very brink. Next time, because there will be a next time. His head arches back to reveal the gorgeous line of his throat just in time for him to come with a silent cry. The fierce pleasure etched across his face almost undoes me.

My teeth grind together when he tightens around me like a vise, his cum painting his fingers and chest. The sight of his head tipped back in blissful pleasure sends me hurtling towards my own borderline violent release. I've never had sex like this before, felt such an easy connection with someone. This is true intimacy. And he's going to leave. I'm going to lose him too.

I tilt onto my hands with a soft grunt, cock still gently thrusting in and out of him as my orgasm slowly wanes. Levi lies there, still as a marble statue, while I delicately clean us up so we can fall back asleep.

His lips move softly against my own, my favorite kind of kiss. Sometimes a kiss says more than a million words. His kiss hushes the runaway thoughts threatening to send me careening off the cliff. His kiss grounds me, the taste of him something I know I won't forget for years to come. Mouth familiar and soft to mine, his lips quiet my brain, quiet my terrifying worry about the impending doom of morning.

Levi blinks slowly when I pull away to tug him into the safe cage of my arms. "You said for keeps."

My heart pounds as I run a comforting hand up and down the damp skin of his back. "Sweetheart."

"It's real for me," Levi murmurs, shivering hard.

Those are the last words Levi says to me. Because when I

wake up, the sheets are cold, and every trace of him is gone. The odd sense of losing two people overwhelms me, momentarily breaking down the walls I so carefully built up over the years.

First my father.

Now Levi.

Will anyone ever stay?

CHAPTER TEN

TREVOR

I thought by leaving New York City that maybe I'd finally escape my parents' manipulative clutches. My parents are in prison. There are over one hundred federal prisons in the country, so surely the likelihood of either parent being incarcerated near me was small.

False. God laughs when you make plans.

Especially when it's me.

Months of manipulative phone calls from both parents begging me to deposit money into their prison trust accounts has me finally giving in to agree to visit my mother. Who else is going to visit? The rest of our family hates them. I'm an only child. The guilt to at least go see her a few times a year weighs so heavily on me that usually I end up giving in. Despite how seeing her kills me afterwards.

The clubhouse is quiet when I wander in on a Tuesday afternoon. Soft voices filter from Claire's office. Davis, Claire's assistant, sits at his desk, clearly on the phone with a prospective client. He sends a small wave my way, so I wave back with a pasted-on smile. Doubtful he'll notice.

Claire does though. As always. Her eyes narrow dangerously as I stride into her office, carefully gathering intel on what could possibly be going on with me. The door of her office closes gently, and I lean heavily against it, feeling weighed down just at the idea of the conversation ahead of me.

"Which one?" Claire asks, leaning back just as heavily in her chair.

"Mother."

"You want me to come with you again?" Claire's voice is gentle, nurturing, as it usually is when the topic of my parents comes up.

I nod, unable to say the words. With a heartbroken sound, she stands, tugs her skirt down like the proper lady she is, then comes towards me to wrap me up in her slender arms. No tears come, despite the anguish rising inside me just at the idea of having to see my mother again. Everything about seeing her is so draining. The sight of the prison, the sounds of the place, and the smells. Dreadful experience every time.

"Let's get it over with," Claire announces with false cheer when she pulls away. "Have you given them money again?"

"Yes," I admit, defeated.

"I wish you'd stop." Claire cuts a look at me, not cruel, just slightly judgey. That's just Claire's way. Growing up together, she knows my parents, and all their manipulation tactics. Her parents weren't too dissimilar from my own.

"Hard to say no."

Claire hums as she grabs her purse. She leaves her office, heels clacking on the floor. I follow along behind her like a lost puppy.

"I'm gone for the rest of the day," Claire tells Davis. "I'll be back tomorrow. Let the other boys know I'm reachable by phone. Also, don't schedule Trevor for anything for two weeks."

My heart races. Two weeks? I can't go without pay for two weeks. "Claire—"

"Pay him the standard boyfriend rate," Claire interrupts, eyes on her phone as she types.

"Yes, ma'am." Davis nods, staring up at her, waiting for her to look, but she pointedly ignores him. His besotted gaze follows us until the elevator doors close.

Claire presses the button for the first floor, still typing away at her phone.

"Are you and Davis...?" I trail off, waiting for her to look up at me.

The only sign she heard me is the little tic in her eye that I know means she doesn't want to talk about it. "Pointless."

"Why?"

"You know I don't date. Being asexual and all. Also, look at what we do. There's no way he'd... anyway it doesn't matter."

Now my gaze turns hard. "Claire."

She waves her hand dismissively at me as she steps off the elevator. "Doesn't matter, Trevor."

It does matter but neither of us are very emotional people, so I don't know how to goad her into talking about it with me. Usually I just wait people out, instead of pushing them to talk. Maybe on the drive to the prison Claire will open up.

We quietly climb into her fancy sports car, and she peels out of the garage into the bright spring sunlight. Once we're out of the city, we roll the windows down for a blast of crisp air.

The few hours' drive passes dully, especially since Claire

stays buttoned up, her eyes firmly on the road. Her fingers are so tight on the wheel that I'm worried she might permanently lose blood flow. I go to speak, say anything, just fucking words, but she turns the radio up to preempt me from putting my foot in my mouth. Thank you, Claire.

With every mile we get closer, the harder my heart pounds against my ribs, until I feel almost dizzy with the force of my racing heart. Claire parks the car in the lot after we check in at the security gate.

Since she's not on my mother's visitor list, she can't join me, and for some reason that causes me even more anxiety. Seeing my mother alone is like going up against an army.

Anxiously stepping out of the car, I brush off my crisp black suit, doing my best to get out the wrinkles that formed during the drive. My reflection in the window of the car shows my blond hair messy, windswept. That won't do at all. Mother will hate it.

I walk around to Claire's side of the car and dip down, patiently waiting until she rolls down her window. She aims eyes full of the brimstone of Hell as I wiggle my fingers at her with the small, anxious smirk I've perfected over the years.

"Bobby pins?"

Claire sighs in abject irritation, but still fumbles around in her purse for a few bobby pins anyway. I move over to the back window, then do my best to get my hair into the semblance of a short cut style. It's hard, considering my hair's current length, but once it's good enough, I head towards the prison without a backward glance. Head up, back straight, take no shit.

The sterile prison and fluorescent lights greet me like a slap when I step through the noisy automatic doors. Once through the metal detector, I head straight for the check-in desk.

"Here for?" the older female guard asks. She radiates annoyance and yeah, me too, lady.

I awkwardly clear my throat. "Lyla Shaw."

The guard rolls her eyes. "Of course you're here to see Ms. Priss. Look at you."

Discomfort rolls through me, but I bite my tongue to keep from giving a sarcastic reply. She returns my driver's license, the one with my *real* name, then another guard leads me back to the room where inmates take visitors.

Since it's a low-security prison, inmates are allowed to meet at tables, instead of behind glass. I almost wish I had the separation though. It would add a layer of protection that my heart so desperately needs.

Unease settles in the pit of my stomach as the guard leads me to the table already occupied by my mother. Her fake smile beams at the guard, but the guard leaves without acknowledging her pretend sweetness. The smile predictably drops the moment we're alone.

"You could visit more often," she says snidely.

"I have my own life."

She scoffs and rolls her eyes, clearly already over me. "Doing what? I know you're working with that Claire girl. Just because I'm in prison doesn't mean I don't get informed of your... ways."

I stare at her, hiding my expression so she doesn't know she's gotten to me. "Do you mean being gay? Or being an escort?"

Her expression tightens at my words. Leaning forward, her eyes glare daggers at me. "Don't get sassy. Did you deposit more money in my account?"

I deflate under her stare, already exhausted from our brief interaction. "Yes."

A winning grin spreads over her face. "Good. For your father too?"

"Yes," I repeat dully.

"Good, good." Her fingers tap on the table as she glances quickly around the room. "Your hair looks awful, by the way. I don't know why you insist on keeping it long. It's so proletarian of you. You should get a gentleman's cut."

"I like it long," I murmur, but she either ignores me, or purposefully doesn't hear me.

"Is that suit off the rack?"

The line of questioning needs to be stopped before I lose my shit in the middle of federal prison. By losing my shit, I mean by walking out without another word.

"It's Tom Ford."

She huffs, clearly finding my answer acceptable despite wishing she didn't. Her hair is a little more gray than it used to be, but otherwise the color still closely matches my own. I inherited my light blond hair from her. My father's hair is black, probably more salt and pepper now after the past few years. But I'm surprised she's not maintaining her perfect shade of blonde. Lyla Shaw always maintains appearances.

"Well, this visit was nice and all. But you know why we have these. Looks good for my record when my son visits."

"I graduate in a few months."

Her eyes cut back to me, a hard glimmer in them. "Finance?"

I want to melt into the earth. "No."

With a roll of her eyes, she stands from the table. The guard returns and escorts her to the exit, leaving me alone. The prison fades from my view as I walk out towards Claire and the waiting car. My head stays down, counting the taps of my shoes against the hot black asphalt. When I lift my head, the sight that greets me is Claire sitting against the hood of her car, cigarette dangling from her fingers. Fuck if that isn't a good view.

I gingerly take the cigarette from her extended fingers. I inhale the smoke, letting it burn my lungs until my eyes water at the sting. Sitting between her legs, I lean back so that she can pull the bobby bins from my hair. The strands fall to my shoulders, blowing with the soft breeze that passes over us.

"So?" Claire asks, voice gentle.

"She's still a raging bitch." I take a pull from the cigarette, letting the acrid smoke blow into the breeze. The only time I ever smoke is after drama with my parents or a particularly bad boyfriend experience. Claire doesn't know about the second though. I'll keep it that way.

Her fingers comb gently through my hair, forcing my eyes to fall closed at her tender care. "You need to stand up to them. Cut them off."

I flick the ash off the cigarette, frowning deeply. "They'd have no one."

She hums softly. "They don't have you either, baby."

A laugh bubbles out of me, but it's a laughter full of sadness, full of pain. It's such a beautiful day outside. Makes me think of Beau. Where he is, what he's doing? Does he ever think of me? It's a nice wish. Even if he does think of me, it's just about the persona, about Trevor. The perfect fake boyfriend is all I'll ever be. Not worth much more than that.

But sometimes just the *idea* of him, the memory of Beau, can calm the violent ocean of pain inside me. The pain that says I'm only worth what I can be bought for. His gentle smiles, the warmth of his touch against my overheated skin, the looming promise of what his love could do to me if I deserved it... it could destroy me.

Once we're back in Georgia, the sun has almost set, and Davis is gone from the clubhouse for the day. Claire settles at the desk, eyes still keenly aimed at me.

"I know this is a really weird question to ask, and it's crossing a million fucking lines, but would you happen to have Beau Callahan's number?"

Claire's gaze doesn't tear from me. Her eyes sharpen, but her mouth quirks up just a little, as if fighting a smile. My stomach curdles with nausea as she stares at me, only easing once she taps at her keyboard, then writes a number down on a sticky note, pushing it across her desk for me to hastily grab.

She taps her perfectly manicured finger on the sticky note just once. "Be good, Trevor."

A smirk tilts my lips up as I reach for the sticky note. "I'm always good."

Claire grabs my fingers, gives them a hard squeeze, before letting go. "I love you."

I hold the note up and nod in thanks. The note burns a hole in my suit pocket the few moments it takes me to go down a couple of floors. My cold, mostly empty apartment below the clubhouse has never felt less like a home to me. Gaze sweeping the room, I realize that there's nothing here, nothing has ever been here for me. Going through the motions is all I'll ever do. All I'm capable of.

I carefully place the sticky note on my kitchen counter with shaky hands. Unable to be in the same room as temptation, I head into my room to shower away the awful day. Even the shower, soft sweatpants, and a cold beer from the fridge can't calm my racing thoughts.

Two empty bottles later, I stand at the kitchen counter, eyes staring without blinking at the hot-pink sticky note. The numbers that'll get me to Beau. Maybe it's the alcohol, maybe it's everything with my damn mother, maybe it's just the need to know he remembers my name, remembers me at all, but I don't know what to blame my impulsiveness on when I dial his number with trembling fingers.

One ring.

Two rings.

And then...

"Hello?" Beau's soft, sweet southern voice filters through the phone.

My breath stutters in my chest, words stuck like rocks in my throat. Pressing the heel of my palm to my forehead, I just listen to Beau breathe for a moment, listen to him move around wherever he is, probably in the living room. It's so easy to imagine. I can even smell the sweet, cedar smell of his sheets without even trying. A phantom smell. A phantom loss.

"Levi?" Beau asks, voice trembling.

A cry gets caught in my throat. I cover my mouth with my hand, desperately doing anything I can to hold in the sobs that want to wrench loose.

Once I've gathered myself, I ask, voice hushed, "For keeps?"

Silence, unending silence, and then a softly whispered, "For keeps always, sweetheart."

A smile breaks through the tears slowly inching their way down my cheeks. The taste of the tears invades my senses, enough to overpower the taste of Beau that my brain summons from the deepest well of my imagination. The line is quiet for a few beats, just us on the phone together, and I think maybe that's enough. Just to know someone, some-where, could want me enough to play for keeps.

We sit on the phone for a while, resting in gentle silence, until the moment becomes too much for me to bear. After hanging up, I sit alone in my empty apartment. Without even saying a word, Beau made me feel less alone than I ever have.

Tears swim in my eyes as I save his number in my phone under My Beau. Because even though he's not mine, can never be mine, the idea of him will always be enough.

CHAPTER ELEVEN

BEAU

Life goes on. Swimming through grief for my dad while simultaneously missing Levi is a double-edged sword of seemingly unending pain. Plus, Colby is still going through it over Marcus, so I'm back to the standard of being everyone's rock. While absolutely no one is there for me.

I think about Levi far more than is healthy. I wonder where he is, if he's happy, if he thinks of me. The stark loss of him rattles around my now oddly empty rib cage. Does he feel the loss of me too? Wherever he is, does he feel the pull that I feel when I reverently whisper his name right before falling asleep? Months ago he called me, just once, and hearing his voice felt like a lightning strike straight to my heart. But words aren't enough to tell him to come back to me. For real.

Despite the workday being over, there's always more to do. The past few weeks I've been working on a secret project. A lush garden is slowly coming to life in my backyard. The wooden pallets have been built, the dirt put in, and now I get to do the rewarding part. Planting.

Ten gardenia bushes fill the back of my truck. Special order from across the country in California. Some new breed that's supposed to have double the blooms. My mama has always loved gardenias. She says they're the southern flower of love, the southern rose. Filling my garden with gardenias is all I can do in hopes that they'll bring love back to me.

The sun bears down on me, breaking sweat out across my neck, under my shirt, any place sweat can reach. Swiping my ball cap off, I run my forearm over my forehead to catch some of the sweat threatening to drip down my flushed face. Birds sing in the forest behind my house, happy with the humid air and bright sunshine.

A sudden whistle startles me so badly that I almost scream. When I slowly turn around, a smirking Andy strolls toward me with her hands on her hips. Dark curls up in a bun, torn denim shorts, and a faded T-shirt, she looks just like she does in all my childhood memories. Just a little older now, more of a woman than a rambunctious child following me around the farm.

"What's going on here?" she asks, eyes carefully surveying my garden.

"Ain't you ever seen a garden before?"

Andy rolls her eyes dramatically. "Duh, loser."

I take a swipe at her with my dirty hands, but she dips out of reach, laughing loudly at my brotherly antics. "No, but seriously, what's with three plots of gardenias? Mama said you special ordered them through the farm account, then brought them back here. What's up?"

Needing to tell her the truth bubbles painfully inside me. A few weeks ago, I'd told Colby, and something inside me had snapped a little. Freedom from the shackles of a lie that I don't regret, but that still hurts to bear. Her eyes are shrewd as she stares at me, waiting for me to give up the truth.

"I planted them for Trevor," I tell her, the truth as easy as breathing.

Confusion clouds her expression for just a moment before her lips form a perfect *oh*. "I never asked after the funeral... you're not much of a talker. I assumed when we didn't see him again that something happened."

"I hired him."

A myriad of expressions flick over her face before settling on confusion once again. "You hired him?"

I nod slowly, putting my hat back on to prevent the sun from beating so hard down on me. "A fake boyfriend."

"Fake boyfriend," Andy repeats slowly, clearly trying to understand. "Like from one of my books?"

"Basically."

"Huh." She takes a step closer, then gently pats my bicep. "You tell Mama?"

"No," I say loudly.

"Alright, alright." Her eyes sweep across the burgeoning garden, gaze a little misty. "You need help? I've got some time."

The offer is sweet, but I need to do this alone. Only a handful of days with him rooted him inside my chest, like one of these plants.

"No help. I need to do this on my own."

"Fair." Andy nods at the bushes lined up along the raised beds. With a soft smile, she wanders over to steal a gardenia bloom off the plant. Lifting it to her nose, she takes a deep inhale, smile growing as she lowers it back down. "Reminds of being a kid." She spins the bloom in her fingers, then raises her distant gaze to mine. "Pops always grabbed them off the bush out back, putting them in a glass bowl so that the entire kitchen smelled like them. The smile on Mama's face was always so blinding when he did that."

A rock forms in my throat at the mention of Pops. The loss of him still feels so visceral, like not much time has passed at all. If it feels that way for me, I can only imagine how it feels for Andy and Mama.

"How's Ethan?"

A frown forms on Andy's face as she keeps spinning the flower between her fingers. "The Mediterranean; that's all I know. The life of a Navy wife."

"And you didn't want to go with him?"

Andy shakes her head firmly. "Wasn't an option since he's out to sea. Plus, I don't know, I kind of wanted to stay here with everything going on."

"I've got it all handled here just fine, sis."

Her eyes lift to mine, assessing in a way I've never felt before. I bristle under her stare just a little, unable to meet her too-knowing gaze.

"You've handled everything for so long, Beau. It's not fair for you to keep doing that."

"I'm used to it."

Andy scoffs. "That's the whole damn point. Maybe it's time for you to stop worrying about taking care of everyone else and steal some of the joy for yourself for once. You hear?"

"My life is pretty joyful."

"Is it?"

Andy skewers me with a hard, borderline angry stare before grabbing another bloom from the bush. Walking back over to me, she lifts onto her tiptoes to place a kiss against my sweat-slick cheek.

"I love you so much, Beau. I hope this garden brings you all your wishes."

Only one wish is my goal. I don't know how to tell her that though. A blaze of dirt sprays behind her truck as she leaves me behind.

The heat of the sun lessens as the day goes by, making it easier to finish planting the gardenia bushes. By the time I'm finished, the smell of their blooms is so heady that a smile creases my lips. For just a brief moment, I imagine showing this to Levi. The smile on his face would rival the eight wonders of the world, I know it. Making him smile was one of the most joyful experiences of my life. God, I hope I get to do it again one day.

"You're extra quiet tonight." Joey pointedly clinks his beer with mine to bring my attention back to him.

The downtown brewery is busy, scattered families and couples loud for Friday night. Once a month I get together with my best friends to catch up on our lives. Seems a little silly considering both of them work at the farm. But it's a tradition we've always had since we were old enough to drink, so it seems pointless to end it now.

"I'm always quiet," I reply seriously.

Joey scrunches his nose up in blatant disagreement, dark curls dancing in the breeze. "I said *extra* quiet."

"Hmm." Taking a sip of my beer, I lean back harder against the metal chair.

"You started without me?" Lee complains with a huff as he takes the seat beside Joey.

Joey slides the beer he ordered for Lee across the table, eyes firmly on our best friend. The tension at the table rockets for just a moment, then dials back down when Lee takes a grateful sip of the beer.

"Thanks, my favorite."

Joey stares at Lee for a brief moment, then drags his gaze from Lee, settling it back on me. "I know."

"Are we all just going to drink and stare at one another?" Lee's gaze flits over the crowd as he sips at his beer.

"We're not staring at one another," I point out.

Lee fake laughs. "Beau, the jokester."

"You know me." I smirk softly, enjoying the gentle ribbing.

"Savi starts first grade in just a few weeks." Joey pulls out his phone to show us a picture of his six-year-old as if we don't see her frequently at the farm. Slim to none passing up seeing a new photo though.

Her grin is just as wide as Joey's, curls just as dark, but her light green eyes belong solely to her mother. A truly awful woman that I could never stand and can stand even less now that she's putting Joey through a hellishly contentious divorce. Joey is an amazing man, one of my very best friends, and he married a pregnant Danica after dating only a few months. The man is a saint.

"First grade." Lee stares down at the photo, throat bobbing, before taking another slow sip of his beer. "Seemed like she was just born the other day."

"Yeah," Joey agrees fondly.

"Divorce final yet?" I ask, trying to be delicate, to not put pressure on what was a gaping wound just a few months ago.

Joey sighs loudly, obviously still frustrated. "Mostly. Just finalizing up the custody split now. I want fifty-fifty but Danica wants sole custody. She makes everything so damn difficult."

"You need anything from us?" Lee angles his body on the metal chair to fully face Joey and puts a gentle hand on Joey's shoulder.

They've always been more touch oriented than me. Even back in high school. Lee and I were some of the only queer kids at our small rural school. Lee's closeted though, was back then too, whereas I had the support of family to come out, Lee most definitely did not. Coming out didn't go as well as it could've considering I was the star quarterback, but it's over now. Life goes on. Lee though, I'm not sure he'll ever have the comfort of coming out. No matter how much support I offer him.

The thing is that Lee's parents aren't as accepting as mine and Colby's. His dad is a real piece of work. Most evenings when we were kids, Lee was at my family's table for dinner, then at my house for sleepovers. I guess that's what happens when your dad is known as the town drunk. An angry drunk at that. I can't blame Lee for living life in the closet, not with the drama his father can so easily bring. All I can do is be his friend.

"I heard about your secret gardening project," Joey teases, eyes full of amusement.

I grunt. "Andy?"

Joey nods rapidly, then taps his beer against mine. "She loves to tattle."

My heart thuds dangerously in my chest. "She say anything else?"

Joey's head cocks to the side, his eyes narrowing at me in question. "No. Should she?"

"Nope." I bottle everything back up and focus on the chilled beer in my hand.

The guys know when I'm done, no more words, so they don't push for more. Quiet overtakes us for a little bit until Lee and Joey get to talking about Savi. The hum of their conversation floats over me, giving me the sense of peace their company usually does. Usually, my loneliness is at an all-time low when I'm with them. The two of them never push, never ask me for more than I can give. True friends.

"All done?" Lee nods towards my now empty beer.

I push the empty beer glass towards him, watching quietly as he heads towards the brewery to return all three of our glasses. Joey watches him go; some emotion that is impossible for me to place etched across his face. For the first time tonight, I notice how tired he looks. Not physically tired, but just sort of done. I know that feeling better than most.

"You okay?" I ask in a hushed whisper.

Joey's gaze slides back to me as he rubs at the shadow of his dark beard thoughtfully. "Me? I'm great. Good. No complaints."

"Sounds a little over the top."

A startled laugh shakes out of him, making my lips tilt up. "I'm alright, Beau. Promise."

I don't quite believe him. "If you say so."

Lee returns with his hands empty, a pleased grin painted on his wide lips. "Ready to go?"

Joey stares up at Lee for one tortured moment. Seemingly shaking himself, he slowly rises from the table. I follow along behind them toward the parking lot. They split off towards their vehicles with waves, and I walk the rest of the way alone.

Stars blink above me in the cloudless night sky. Resting my forearms on the truck roof, I stare hopelessly up at the stars. I wish. Oh, I wish. If the stars do grant wishes, then I deserve one the most. Don't I? Just one wish.

"Levi," I whisper to the sky. The name is a fervent wish on my lips and in my forever lonely heart.

CHAPTER TWELVE
TREVOR

Only the blood angrily pulsing in the bruises scattered around my body remind me that I'm still alive. Another too-rough client that used me to the brink with my permission. "Stop" so close to falling from my lips but ultimately unable to. Because I deserve every ounce of pain rained down on me. Some sick side of me thinks if I let myself be hurt enough, that'll make up for all the years I benefited from the money my parents stole.

The pain makes my brain blissfully shut off. No thoughts of anything but the way my body is a vessel to someone else's pleasure. No pleasure had for myself.

My walk of shame up to the clubhouse is all too familiar. At least this time I have the cover of night to make up for it. I should go back to my own apartment, but I crave the comfort of a friend. Jackson didn't answer my texts but I'm hopeful he's there, ready to patch up my wounds with a steady, quiet hand.

I sniffle quietly to avoid being heard and tiptoe toward the living room. My brain is still rattled from receiving the assignment from Davis for Colby, Beau's cousin. Even the suggestion of it had made me so ill, so dizzy with nausea that I'd done the only thing I could think to do. I passed a client off to Eli. Passing clients off to each other isn't weird or abnormal, we all do it quite often. When one of us isn't in the mood for a certain client, a certain act, we pass them off to one that we think is better fitted for it.

Normally Claire is none the wiser.

But after I'd orchestrated the handoff to Eli last week, I dove headfirst into every client that requested rough sex. Every client that could wash my brain of Beau's gentleness. Of the weight of what being loved by a man like that could do to me.

If I'm running, if I'm faking, then nothing can hurt me.

Carefully stumbling toward the living room, I limp toward the light of the television that hopefully means Jackson is awake, but I'm willing to accept Benji if I absolutely must. Instead, I'm confronted with the sight of Claire sitting on the sectional with a glass of wine in her elegant fingers.

"Oh fuck," I say out loud, irritated to be caught.

Claire's eyes flash with fear even in the low blue light of the television. "Why are you limping?"

Easing my way down onto the sectional, I aim my gaze towards the television. An old episode of a dating show is playing, a show I know for a fact she's seen a million times. So, she's been sitting here just waiting to catch me. I work my jaw a few times, trying to not clench up and close down.

"It was a rough one," I admit, voice devoid of emotion.

"Should I ban him?"

"Definitely with Eli or Benji," I say quickly, urgently needing her to understand my underlying meaning. The client wasn't mean or malicious, but Eli or Benji couldn't withstand what I'm able to nor should they.

She blinks slowly in understanding, then leans forward to set her wine down on the coffee table. A tremble in her fingers makes my mouth dry with worry. I did that. I made her worry.

"Claire—"

"I'm taking you off rotation."

I wince at her words, letting my chin fall to my chest in defeat. Less at the words and more at her tone. Claire has always threatened to put me out of commission but never acted on it. A year ago, I probably would've argued with her, been spitting with anger even. But there's something nice about the choice being taken away from me. If I ever get the courage to return to Beau, I can tell him that I'm done. That I'm a better man than I was the first time around. Maybe then I'll deserve his love, really earn it.

Claire sighs and unfolds her legs to scoot toward me on the plush sofa. I lean heavily in relief against her when she wraps a tender arm around my neck. Curling her fingers into my hair, she scratches my head, and I sigh softly.

"Listen to me," Claire whispers against my cheek, "you've been hurting yourself for years, you need to stop. Please, stop."

"Okay," I murmur helplessly, unable to withstand her tender care.

"You've graduated, the world is your oyster. Stop letting what they've done control your life. You are an amazing person and deserve happiness."

I rub at my eyes and my fingers come away wet. Great. I'm crying. "I don't know how to be happy."

"I think you know exactly how to be happy. Your happiness starts in Clay Springs."

She's right but I don't want to admit it. Just the thought of Beau brings glorious warmth to my chest. Bright warmth suffuses through me like the sun rising after weeks of night, just by remembering his bashful smile. The smile that I earned, that I put there, simply by being real Trevor, not the ghost of Levi.

"He won't really want me... if he knows..."

Claire gently pats my cheek to bring my gaze back to hers. "Let him decide."

She brushes a sweet kiss across my cheek, then disappears out of the clubhouse without a word, leaving me alone with my own anxious thoughts. I clench and unclench my hands a few times, focusing on the feel of my tingling palms. Everything hurts when I stand up, my body rebelling against the last few days.

My bedroom is empty as always, devoid of any ounce of personality. I grit my teeth against the loud chatter in my brain as I painstakingly shower away my last client. When I toss myself into the bed, my heart hammers painfully against my rib cage.

I squeeze my eyes shut to imagine Beau, the springs, and the smell of cedar lingering on sheets made soft with time.

The memory of seeing Colby's name come across the email assignment from Davis still shakes me to my core. I'd done the only thing I could in my anxious state. I passed

Colby off to Eli in hopes that it would give me more time, spare me the idea of confronting Beau. Not just for him to know who I really am but the absolute awful thing I did to him by leaving without a word.

But I handed Eli off to Colby and now they've fallen in love. Thanks to Eli finding forever love with Colby, I'm finally heading back to Clay Springs. Can't even get out of it either because that'll mean more explanation than I'm willing to give. Anxiety like I have never felt before in my life has my hands trembling, mouth dry. I hate this, everything about it.

What if Beau's found someone that he can make a life with? What if I have to see that... see him in love. Cool, great for him, but I think I'd rather die than see him with someone else. But I'll also die if he takes one look at me and decides I'm not worth playing for keeps.

"What the fuck is wrong with you?" Benji hisses while roughly manhandling me into Jackson's G-Wagon.

"I think I'm having a heart attack," I hiss back, completely serious.

Benji pauses, eyes frightened. "Wait... are you serious?"

"No!" I whisper-shout.

Jackson pauses at the driver side door, eyes calculating. "What's going on?"

"I think Trevor is hyperventilating," Benji says gravely.

Oh. Yes. Maybe that's what's happening to me. It feels like no air can get into my lungs despite my frequent intakes of breath. My body feels like it's slowly dissolving into ash. I'm melting. I bang my head a few times against the door, only stopping when Jackson carefully tugs me away.

Jackson's fingers grip my chin, forcing me to meet his sharp gaze. "Tell me."

"Do I really have to go?"

"No." Jackson releases my chin, folds his arms over his chest, and stares down at me with all the irritation he can seemingly muster. "It's either come with us or tell us why you're acting like a rabid raccoon about making the drive down to support Eli."

Benji gasps theatrically, the little shit. "Are you in love with Eli?"

I pinch the bridge of my nose in irritation. "Okay, hard pass on talking about my emotions with you. Also, two, no, I'm not in love with Eli. That's disgusting. Anyway, we're both bottoms."

"You're vers," Benji patiently and irritatingly points out, as if rooting for team Eli and Trevor.

I narrow my eyes. "I'm not in love with Eli. I'm in love with someone else."

Benji gasps again, this time dramatically placing his hand over his heart. "With whom? Jackson?"

Jackson's eyes comically bug out of his head in alarm. "Please say psych."

"I'm not in love with any of you assholes. Jesus. It's fine. Just get me in the damn car, start to drive, and I'll be fine. It'll be fine. Everything is fine."

Everything is *not* fine. My phone vibrates without ceasing for the first few hours of the drive and the contact ID says *PARENTS' LAWYER - DO NOT ANSWER*. Great. Benji takes the annoying phone from me with a frustrated growl. He huffs through updating my settings so that it's totally silent, no vibrations or noise at all. But the screen still stares up at me as we drive, a haunting reminder of why I've stayed away from Beau for so long. Why I left to begin with. Why I don't deserve a second of Beau's time.

The closer we get to Clay Springs, the more unsettled I

feel. Fear courses through me at the idea of being denied by Beau. Just the thought of him not wanting me could bring me to my knees, overpowering every other thought in my pea-sized brain. Scenery slowly changes, signaling the fast approach of our destination.

Benji turns around in his seat as we pass the sign for Clay Springs. There's pity in his eyes and I loathe it.

"You look like you're going to barf," Benji announces, fear coloring his voice.

"Do not puke in my car!" Jackson shrieks on the edge of hysteria. The car even swerves a little.

"I'm not going to puke." Most likely. Probably. I might.

Benji's eyes turn tender, his hand gently settles on my knee. "You can tell us anything."

"I'm fine," I promise him.

He turns around with a disbelieving sigh, just as we take the turn that'll deliver us to Colby's house.

Jackson carefully parks between two beat-up trucks that obviously belong to relatives of Colby. Both of my friends spin around in their seats to pointedly stare at me.

I plaster a smile on my face. "Leave me alone for a bit?"

They turn towards each other, exchanging some tele-pathic conversation that I'm not privy to. Without another word, they climb out and head towards the house. My heart races as I sit alone in the car. Everything is so impossible; everything is too much. Time passes slowly as I sit in the dark of the car, attempting to rein in my warring emotions. Nausea overwhelms me so badly that I'm momentarily afraid I might barf. Jackson will violently murder me if I ruin the interior of his prized matte gray G-Wagon.

I climb out of the car and shake my limbs out. What I need is a good old pep talk. I am going to walk in there, look at Beau, and ask him if he still wants me. I'm going to tell him that I've thought about him every day for the past three hundred and forty-two days. Yeah, I've been keeping count. Once my brain and body connect, my feet carry me up the stairs of Colby's farmhouse.

A sign on the front door says to come on in through the back.

I'd missed this too.

I walk around the house to the backyard and just freeze like a deer in headlights. So many faces I know are scattered around... and I am obviously the last to arrive. Alright. I was aiming for fashionably late and instead got here dead last.

Eli notices me first, not to my surprise.

But then the heat of Beau's gaze lands on me with the force of a meteor slamming into Earth. It sends a shiver rolling through my body. One moment Beau's standing beside Colby on the raised porch, then in the blink of an eye he's running full tilt towards me.

A moment of pure fear rolls through me until I catch sight of his beautiful face. The joy in his eyes, the grin on his lips, everything about him is blinding. My heart skips ten beats just at the sight of him. The absolute unbridled pleasure of laying eyes on me. How did I ever think he couldn't really want me?

Beau crashes into me, forcing a grunt from my lips at the slightly too rough contact. Quarterback my ass. This man had to have been a linebacker.

Falling to the ground in a tangle of limbs, his hand gently rests under my head to soften my fall. Even in his frantic need to get to me, he's gentle to the core. I blink up at him, breath painfully caught between my ribs. He looks exactly the same as I recall so fondly in my dreams. Dark brown hair, with a little grayer than I remember. His beard is trimmed perfectly, and his lips tilt up in a breathtaking smile.

"I've been waiting for you, sweetheart."

I laugh in shock underneath him. "Beau."

"Sweetheart," Beau whispers, voice carrying a million emotions all at once. His eyes take in the sight of me, traveling over my face as if making sure it's really me, before his lips crash into mine.

The crowd of Beau's family and friends disappear to the back of my mind. Just for a moment, I let him kiss me like I've been away at war. The taste of his mouth is like finally going home after years away. Homesickness I didn't realize I'd had ebbs away just from the onslaught of his mouth against mine. His fingers tighten in my hair, biting into my scalp, reassuring me that this isn't a fever dream. It's real, Beau is so real. When he tears away from my lips, I chase after him, unwilling to lose him yet.

He chuckles darkly, eyes full of amusement, gazing down softly at me. "Come back to my house. We gotta talk, sweetheart."

"Alright," I agree with obvious trepidation.

Like my weight is easy for him to bear, he easily helps me to my feet, hand firmly gripping mine. Ignoring everyone, we leave the party without a single word uttered between us. This moment needs to be about me and Beau, not anyone else. The anticipation of our looming conversation sends my heart racing dangerously despite our Hallmark-style reunion.

Beau opens the door of his Chevy, then with a gentle hand at the small of my back, pushes me inside the warm cab of the truck. Leaning inside, he carefully buckles my seat belt, and I close my eyes as the familiar smell of him washes over me. Hard work, grass, and engine grease. The smell of home.

I watch him close the passenger door and walk around the front. He dances his fingers along the hood as he walks around the truck, lips tilted up in a beaming grin. He climbs into the driver's seat, starts the engine, and turns his face to me for a moment as if checking to see if I'm a hallucination. My smile is awkward, a breath I didn't realize I was holding escapes me when he starts to drive.

Watching Beau drive is still one of my favorite pastimes. Hand loose around the wheel, his strong forearms bared for me to see. The muscles in his forearms leap as he tightens his fingers around the wheel when we meet a few bumps along the gravel road. I have to swallow and turn away to prevent myself from doing something ridiculous like leaning over and kissing his stubbled cheek. Or telling him I've thought about him every day for months. Or saying three words that'll no doubt scare him away.

Before things get out of hand, I sent a quick text to the boyfriend group chat, just to let them know I'm fine. I'm sure our exit was dramatic, and I don't want them to worry. Not after everything else.

The sight of Beau's house coming into view sends shock waves of pure relief rattling through me. Four days spent in that house made it feel more like a home than my childhood house ever did. No mansion could ever compare to the white farmhouse with a wraparound porch lined with rocking chairs. Beau has felt like home from the very beginning.

Beau's eerily quiet as we walk into the house, hushed even as he points at the couch in silent demand for me to take a seat. My feet take me to the couch before my brain can even catch up. That's the effect that Beau has on me.

"So." Beau stands like a statue in front of me, arms gently crossed over his barrel chest. "You want to stay?"

A man of few words. "If you'll have me."

Rubbing a thoughtful palm over his beard, his eyes stay firmly on me. "Sweetheart, that door has been open to you since last October. Been waiting on you. But you gotta give me some answers. I'll be damned if you walk in here just to walk out again."

I swallow loudly. "That's fair."

"And if you stay, we're doing it right. I'm going to date you, woo you, make you mine. For keeps now, sweetheart."

"Easy as that?"

"Levi." Beau says my real name like a curse, but there's an undercurrent of love that stops my anxiety from spiking. I don't think I like my real name on his lips. "I'm not a complicated man. You want me? You can have me. But there won't be any going back and forth like last time. I'm not hiring you. This time, you're mine because you want to be, because there's something between us that I've been waiting for you to see."

"I saw it too," I interrupt him, not caring a bit when his eyes flash at me. "I just need to be clear. I felt it last time too. I just... I'm not even twenty-five. I carry so much shit with me and I needed to finish my degree, and it all felt so... much. It felt so much. Don't you understand?"

"Yeah, I know," Beau agrees and takes a seat next to me on the couch. He carefully takes my hand in his own, caressing my knuckles with his thumb. "I wish you had just talked to me last time. Tell me why you couldn't?"

Just rip the bandage off. "My real name is Levi Shaw."

He stares at me in confusion. "You told me that already."

A riot of nerves rolls through me. This is Beau. He waited for me, and I came back here for me. To see if we can have something real. So, I owe him the truth, the full truth, so that he can decide what he wants.

"My parents are Turner and Lyla."

He continues to stare blankly at me. It must be so nice to be so disconnected from national-level news.

"Turner and Lyla Shaw. My parents are serving life in federal prison for swindling thousands of people out of their retirement in a Ponzi scheme. They... took everything from people. Most of the country thinks they're the worst villains in the world. And they're right. My parents did evil things, made awful decisions, but sometimes people think that I'm just like them. I mean, they raised me, so I have to be kind of evil too?"

Out of breath by the time I finish, my chest heaves with the weight of my words. But Beau remains staring at me, fingers playing with my hand, gaze warm and intent.

"Can you say something?" I ask quietly.

"Sweetheart, what makes you think what they did is a reflection on you at all? Weren't you a kid?"

Oh God. Beau makes it sound so simple. Tears well up in my eyes because his words are just so matter of fact. So Beau. Something I've struggled with for so many years is just... narrowed down to the truth of one single statement.

"Yeah," I admit around the rock in my throat. "I was a kid."

"Well then, you didn't help them make their mistakes. I think you're trying to do better, right? You finished school this spring?"

I nod as I take a few steadying breaths. "I did. I also don't do the boyfriend anything anymore, just so we're clear."

"Even if you did, that's not something I'd have an issue with."

It's my turn to aim a confused look at him. "You'd be fine with me fucking someone else?"

He chuckles wryly and shrugs his broad shoulders. "I don't know about fine, but sex work is sex work. Matters more to me that I'm the one you come home to at the end of the night, the one you say three special words to before bed."

"Beau." My lip trembles as I fight back tears. "You're perfect."

"Not really." Beau gives me a sheepish look.

"To me you are."

"So, if you don't do the boyfriend thing anymore, what do you do?"

"I graduated with a psychology degree. I want to go on to get my master's in social work so I can become a therapist."

Beau smiles that gorgeous, sweet smile at me. "That sounds perfect for you."

"But there's online degrees for graduate school... so I can do most of it online. Minus any clinical hours I need. It'll take some time. But I need to apply... it probably won't be until next year."

"And you want to do that here with me?"

My face heats under his scrutiny. I can't believe I'm talking about uprooting my entire life in Georgia. But there's nothing left for me there. It's time to quit the agency, I finished school, and my next step is on the horizon. The next step seems unfairly easy sitting here on Beau's couch, in Beau's house.

"If you'll let me."

Beau chuckles again, sending my heart on a rapid gallop through my chest. Everything about Beau makes me feel free and light, like I could fly if I really put my mind to it. No one could ever give me what Beau does.

"I'm going to date the hell out of you," Beau vows, voice low and sure.

"I don't want to talk about me anymore. I left you at the worst possible time. How are you doing?"

My question seems to momentarily startle Beau. Makes sense to me because I'm sure not many people have checked on him the past few months. My darling, sweet Beau, everyone's rock but no one is there for him. That's going to change now that I'm back. I'm going to carry him, just like he's so willing to carry me.

"I'm... okay." Beau squeezes my hand tightly. He lets out a careful, slow breath. "I've been focusing on the farm. Been working on other projects too."

"Tell me," I beg because I need to know everything I've missed.

His eyes twinkle with unrestrained joy. "I can show you."

His large hand envelops my own as he drags me through the house to the back porch. Just as inviting as I remember, even the smell is the same. Sound is a little different now though. The cicadas aren't oppressively loud, in fact I don't hear any at all. Their absence is actually sad to me. The sound of the bugs had been comforting. A distraction from the constant racing of my heart when I was in Beau's dizzying orbit.

But maybe I don't need the distraction anymore.

Beau leads me out further into the yard, away from the house. Something else is different now. That's when I spot it. A garden rests between two large oak trees, but it's not full of plants, instead full of flowers and small bushes. White flowers bloom from the bushes and the scent is heady, like jasmine but with a sharper edge. The warm scent is inherently comforting, filling my lungs until all I can smell is flowers and Beau.

"It's beautiful, Beau."

He smiles sheepishly at me again, awkwardly clearing his throat. "I built it for you."

My eyes go cartoonishly wide. "For me?"

"Yeah. Gardenias are the southern rose... my mama always said they're the flower of love. So, I planted them here to wait for you. I knew you'd come back to me, so I wanted to have this for you... to show you that I was thinking about you the whole time."

"Jesus Christ." I launch myself into his arms with a delighted laugh.

One of Beau's hands tangles in my hair, the other under my ass to hold me close to him as I wrap my legs tight around his waist. My joyful laugh presses into the warm skin of his neck, full of more happiness than I knew was possible. Four days is all it took to fall for this man, and he waited for me, like a man from a bygone era. Deserving him will be my life's mission.

Hope blooms in my chest as I gaze down at Beau. Love radiates from him, through his eyes, his tender smile, even in the wrinkles at the corner of his mouth hidden under his unruly beard. Abundant amounts of love reside within him, so much reserved solely for me.

"Sweetheart," Beau murmurs softly, fingers gently flexing in my hair. "What do you want me to call you? Trevor? Levi?"

"I don't feel like Levi anymore." I tilt my head, so his thumb slides along my jaw. He smiles, warm and sweet. "I thought maybe I would, that's why I asked you to call me Levi that night... but you make me *feel* like Trevor. I'm the real me when I'm with you."

"Trevor, then? And sweetheart when you make my heart skip a beat?"

I nod rapidly against his firm grip. A wide grin spreads across my lips when he pulls me down for a palpitation-inducing kiss. It's difficult to kiss when both of us are grinning, but we make a solid attempt. His beard scratches against my face, and I oddly missed that too. I expect him to carry me into the house, to the bedroom, and make love to me, but Beau always surprises me.

He gently places me back on my feet and carefully fixes my hair with his work-roughened fingers. Seemingly happy with the state of my hair, he pulls away to pluck a gardenia from a bush. One of those smiles that is only ever for me graces his lips as he carefully places the flower between my thumb and forefinger. Gently gripping the bloom, I raise it to my nose to deeply inhale the gorgeous perfume of the ivory petals. It's silky soft against the pads of my fingers.

"I love it," I admit, tone close to reverent.

"Good," Beau says gruffly.

I pull it away and tuck it behind my ear with a content smile. "You going to make love to me now, Beau?"

"No."

"What?"

Beau just laughs, heading back inside the house without a care in the world. "I said no, sweetheart."

"What does that mean?" I call after him.

He pauses halfway up the porch stairs. A careful, heated look is aimed at me over his shoulder. "You don't know what no means?"

"Beau!" I gasp in shock, laughing at his seriousness.

"We're dating, sweetheart. Call me old fashioned but I don't fuck on the first date. You can wait."

I watch, mouth ajar, as he walks steadily into the house, without another look my way. What does he mean? He doesn't expect...? There's no way... how long does dating go on in this part of the country? Because I don't think I can wait too long to have his hands on me again.

Breathless and panting, I burst through the back door of the house. Calmly standing at the counter, Beau patiently sorts a small pile of mail. He sends a curious look my way, but otherwise doesn't pay me any attention.

"Beau, you can't be serious."

"I'm very serious," Beau says matter-of-factly.

"Beau."

"Trevor."

"Not sweetheart anymore?"

Beau turns and leans against the counter, arms crossed over his broad chest in contemplation. "I told you what I want. You're going to stay here in the guest room, we'll date, and I'll woo you. We can talk about physical intimacy in a bit."

My jaw drops. "You're actually serious? Why? Why does this matter to you?"

"We skipped a lot of the beginning," Beau explains carefully. "I want to do it all over the right way. Date you, know you, love you, and then I'll make love to you. Think you can be patient with me, sweetheart?"

I blow a raspberry in frustration, which only makes Beau's eye twitch, and a smile curl up the edges of his lips. Visibly fighting laughter, Beau winks at me, before returning to his pile of mail. This is going to be a journey that I know will set the tone for our life together.

"Alright."

"Good," Beau says, then comes towards me to pull me into

his arms. He sways us a little in the kitchen, hands firm on my hips. "It's going to be okay. I promise. You trust me?"

I kiss him on the corner of the mouth. "With my life."

"First things first, we'll get the bedroom set up for you. You brought enough stuff to get you by for a few weeks?"

"About that..." I trail off and rub awkwardly at my neck. "I rode with Jackson and Benji... I just have a duffle bag. But there's nothing for me left in Georgia. There's my apartment but it's mostly empty... I don't have much."

Beau just blinks at me for a few agonizing moments. "You don't have much?"

Time to keep confessing, I guess. "I make decent money with the agency but between paying for school and donating half my income... there's not much left over. My apartment is small. All I have really is clothing and that was solely for being a boyfriend."

"What do you mean donating half your income?" Beau asks, eyes scrutinizing in a way that could probably take me apart, piece by piece.

I anxiously fiddle with the bottom of his shirt, unable to hold his gaze. "There's this fund that accepts donations for my parents' victims. I donate half my income which ends up being about a hundred thousand dollars a year. It's not much but it's the most I can do."

"How much have you donated over the years?"

I swallow loudly. "Probably around half a million."

"Christ, Trevor." Beau shakes his head, then aims a miserable look my way. "Do your parents know this?"

"No," I answer with a bitter laugh, shaking my head firmly. The idea of them knowing is beyond anxiety inducing.

Beau ignores that, seemingly sensing my dropping mood. "Your small car?"

I aim an irritated look at him. "My car is normal-sized, thank you. We can't all have giant work trucks, you know? Anyway, it's still in Georgia."

"You'll come to like my trucks," Beau murmurs, a hint of a tease in his husky voice. *Oh.* "Here's the plan. We're going to get you settled into the guest room, and then we're going to go to bed separately. I got work tomorrow. I'm up before dawn, and you can join me later at the farm for lunch. If you want."

"My bag is still in Jackson's car," I whisper, breath hitching as Beau presses a line of openmouthed kisses down my neck.

"It can stay there. You can wear one of my shirts tonight."

"Beau..."

"Shhh." And then Beau kisses me with so much care my heart cracks at his sweet, undivided attention. I can't think of anything else but the hot press of his mouth, his strong arms, a tight band around my body, and how maybe, just maybe, home is a person and not a place.

CHAPTER THIRTEEN
BEAU

For months, every star in the sky was wished on by me. Thousands of wishes. Maybe even millions. Seeing Trevor come around the corner at Colby's house yesterday was the fruition of so many heartfelt, full-of-longing wishes. I've never experienced joy so deep, so profound, as when his eyes met mine again.

And now he's here. Staying with me. Indefinitely.

Never before has the future felt so grand. But we've both got a lot of work ahead of us. Trevor puts on a brave front, but I know how tender he is deep down. When he'd told me about his parents, I'd seen a pain in him that I wish he didn't carry. One I ached to take off his shoulders.

Last night I tucked him into bed, gently kissed his forehead, swept his hair from his angelic face, desperately wishing I could've kept him from the very start.

But I have him now and that's what matters most.

"Beau Callahan," my mama shouts from across the field.

"That's a mama yell if I've ever heard one. You eat the last cookie?" Lee teases as we both warily watch my mom stomp angrily across the blueberry field, hair up in a messy auburn bun and eyes zeroed in on me. I'm definitely about to get it. Crap. But her rage is softened by her messy hair, hole-filled cardigan, and rain boots. Hard to take her seriously when she looks so much like the Mama that lovingly placed Band-Aids on my knees as a kid.

"Yes, ma'am?" I ask sweetly.

"Don't *ma'am* me." Mama accusingly points her finger with narrowed, suspicious eyes. "Trevor showed up at the party last night. Then you sweep him away without so much as a peep. Where is he?"

Lee chuckles, tosses up his hands, and disappears towards the other end of the field. Lucky duck.

"He just got back into town," I hurry to explain to avoid her impending wrath.

"You'll bring him over for dinner soon, you understand me?"

"Yes, ma'am."

Mama's eyes soften. She takes a careful step closer to me. "Now, is he alright? Are you alright?"

I can't help but laugh because for the first time everything finally seems alright. The past few years have been rough, but now that Trevor's back, maybe I can finally get my own bit of happy.

"I'm doing a lot better now," I admit.

She grins at me, then tenderly pats my cheek. "Good. Now I've got to get back to the office because they're all fighting about some television show and it's all very entertaining. I love working with the younger generation."

With a wink tossed at me, she stomps through the field back towards the office. A few moments later, Lee wanders back over with a teasing grin on his lips. I take my hat off to hit him with it, but he ducks out of the way before I can make contact. Doubtful this will be the last time I'll get anything from Lee over this.

"I gotta get me someone to date," Lee says as we kick at the dirt like kids.

"Find someone, then."

Lee rolls his eyes. "Not as easy for all of us."

"One day, buddy."

Lee scoffs, then lets out a long sigh. "Sure. We should get the gang together again to welcome Trevor back to town."

I rub anxiously at my neck. "I'll talk to Trevor about it."

A truck rattles down the dirt road, kicking up dust, signaling the end of our somewhat tense conversation. The upcoming weekend requires us to visit the sunflower fields for the approaching fall season. Not much to do, but I always like to be involved with anything involving the dirt at Clay Road Farms. If it's planted, I want to know, and I want to help it grow. Just a point of pride for me.

Lee and I walk quietly up to the office, but the closer we get, the more I realize that wasn't just any truck. My classic Chevy gleams under the bright Florida sun. The most beautiful sight greets us as we approach the office. Trevor stands by the driver's side door, elbows resting on the open window ledge, sweet smile on his face. He looks achingly perfect in the too-bright Florida summer sun. My heart does a sweet little kick of something I'm afraid to put words to just yet at the sight of him.

"Handsome," Trevor whispers once I'm in earshot.

Heat creeps up my neck, but I ignore it, because something about him calling me handsome makes me all sort of stupid. Checking the coast is clear, I press Trevor against the truck to give him a hello kiss. His lips easily part for mine, letting me in to taste the sweetness of him. I lean my forearm on the roof behind him to cage him in between me and the truck.

Every kiss between us is like the very first one. Trevor never fights me for dominance, never tries to take over, he just lets me lead. Pretty sure it's because he trusts me, and his trust is more precious to me than any jewel.

"Best hello I've ever gotten," Trevor teases as he caresses my bearded cheek.

"You drove my truck."

His cheeks pinken under my heavy stare. "I did."

"I like it. What's mine is yours." I kiss him again, softer this time. I rock our foreheads together once I pull away from his perfect lips. "I wanna see you drive my truck."

"Definitely not as toe curling as watching you drive it."

"Not so sure about that. Hungry?"

Trevor nods while patting my stomach with a smirk. "Starving."

I twine our fingers together as I tug him towards the farm food truck. The truck is one of Andy's best ideas. Pastries and meals cooked with some of our fruit grown on the farm, along with other locally grown ingredients. On the weekends the food truck can be bought out within only a few hours. But on the weekdays, it's just us on the farm, so Joey, the chef, keeps a limited supply for the employees.

"Hey, boss," Joey calls through the open truck window.

I groan at the nickname. Joey leans halfway out the window, all messy dark hair, and a dimpled grin. Trevor's hand tightens on mine for just a second, before trying to tug loose, but I hold his hand tight. Not happening on my watch.

"You know I hate when you call me boss."

Joey winks again. "That's why I do it."

"Two lunch specials."

Rolling his eyes at me refusing to play along, his gaze goes to Trevor, only to return to me. "Sure. Nice to see you again, Trevor."

They shake hands briefly, but I easily clock the wary look on Trevor's face. His tells aren't as hidden as he likes to think. Joey hums to himself as he disappears back into the truck to make our lunch. No time like now to bring some essential items up, I guess.

"You know I'm out, right? You were my wedding date, funeral date, everyone knows."

Trevor blows out an uneasy breath. "I know. I just... I'm trying to fit into your life here. New people make me nervous... I'm always afraid." He trails off and looks around, eyes seemingly searching for threats. "I'm always afraid someone will recognize me. Put two and two together. Not just because my face was plastered in the headlines when I sat at my parents' trial, but also because well... I was an escort. It was fine before I didn't think I'd ever come back but..."

"Now it's real and you don't want your parents' legacy to ruin it."

Trevor laughs bitterly. "Well, yeah."

"Can you listen to me, sweetheart?" I take his hand back in mine, and tenderly kiss his knuckles, then press his palm to my cheek. "If people find out, we'll deal with it. I'm gonna keep you, that's all you need to know. Right?"

Trevor shifts his palm under my hand to sweetly cup the curve of my jaw. His head tilts a little to stare up at me with a look so fond that my heart aches.

"You're going to destroy me for anyone else," Trevor whispers like it's a secret.

"Good, 'cause I'm the last one."

Trevor smiles, that smile that's just for me, and I pull him tightly against me for a fierce hug. He smells like my body wash and shampoo, something that makes the caveman inside me burst with pride. Maybe a little want too.

"Two lunch specials," Joey calls out behind us. I turn around in time to see Joey hanging out the truck window, an absolutely delighted grin on his face. "Felt bad interrupting but don't want it to get cold."

I hastily grab the tray loaded with the food and guide us over to one of the picnic tables at the end of the row. A few years ago, we had an open-air building built for events, it's just a roof with a couple of hefty support beams, but it's worth it on warmer days like today. Under the shade it's not too bad, especially when the breeze blows, and Trevor's hair gets tossed about.

"Ready for some of the best food you've ever had?" I ask with a smirk.

Trevor looks skeptical but squares his shoulders. "Absolutely. Hit me."

"Alright." I push the tray between us and start pointing out the items. "Barbecue pork sliders, fried plantains, glazed wings with our specialty teriyaki-blueberry sauce, and the best pumpkin cheesecake bites you'll ever eat."

"Any particular order, or?" Trevor stares down at the food with wide eyes.

"Pick your poison."

He starts with the sliders, so I start with the wings. I watch him as I eat, eager to see his reactions, to know his thoughts to something that's a part of me. Part of my life. On the very first bite his eyes slide closed in bliss, and he licks his lips clean once he finishes the entire slider.

"That's fucking good," Trevor says.

I point at one of the chicken wings. "Try a wing."

Trevor doesn't need to be told twice. He dives into the food with all the relish of a starved man. My chest puffs out in pride when the food is so good that he can't even carry on a conversation. Feeding people, bringing them happiness, that's really the best part of my job. Yeah, I'm a farmer at heart, because I love the land, but giving people an unforgettable memory through food and nature, that's also my joy.

Just as we're finishing up, a familiar flash of red hair comes into view. My eyes flick over to the truck to find Joey dipping out of my sight, but not before I catch the embarrassed look on his face. He definitely tattled.

"Trevor!" Mama shouts once she's close enough to rattle our bones.

Trevor's panicked gaze meets mine. "She's right behind me?"

"Yep," I whisper.

"No time like now I guess." Trevor wipes his hands on a napkin, then carefully stands from the table just before he's enveloped in my mother's arms.

Trevor stands awkwardly for a moment, then slowly returns the hug. His head rests sweetly on top of hers like he's savoring the brief motherly affection. Mama pulls away to squeeze his face in her hands, intently staring him down.

"Don't go so long without a visit again," she demands quietly, tone brooking no arguments.

"I'm not planning to leave again."

Mama gasps and dips her head around him to look at me. "Really?"

I nod as I try in vain to hold back a grin. "He's here to stay."

Mama's entire face softens. Her eyes even go a little misty. "Love really is such a wonderful thing. You make my boy so happy. You'll have to come over to the house sometime so we can garden and gossip."

"Garden and gossip?" Trevor repeats, voice tremulous.

"Yes, Trevor. You've got so much to learn about Clay Springs now that you're one of us. Serious information sessions. We will need multiple visits." Mama kisses him on the cheek, then turns her head to regard me. "Next week, dinner, all three of us."

Then she's gone again, back to the office, and I can only grin as Trevor slowly turns to aim his gaze at me.

"She's going to make me call her 'Mom' soon, isn't she?"

I bite my lip and nod. "Definitely. Got a problem with that?"

Trevor runs shaky fingers through his hair. My heart does a deep dive and flips at the sight of him so overwhelmed. I stand before my brain has even processed the movement. Tugging Trevor into my arms, I cup the back of his head in my palm. He leans against me, giving me all his weight.

"What do you need?" I ask quietly.

"Time," Trevor replies. His fingers bite into my ribs for a moment, through my work shirt, and his shaky inhale vibrates through my chest. This man, what am I going to do with him?

"Always." I kiss him softly and wish I could both rewind a year, and fast-forward a few years from now. Time feels so caught between us as we do our best to push forward.

"What time will you be home?"

I clear my throat as he pulls out of my grip. "Probably a little after six."

"I'll be waiting." Trevor aims a devilish look at me

through his eyelashes. "Still no chance of us doing the horizontal tango?"

I laugh, deep and loud. "Not for a while."

Trevor makes an aggrieved sound. "Worth a shot."

I walk him back over to my truck, hand in hand. With one last kiss from me, he climbs into the truck, and disappears off the property in a cloud of dirt. Never before have I been so excited at the idea of leaving work. For years and years this property has been my home, been my heart's work. But now my life is driving away in my old Chevy truck, and I can't muster an ounce of worry.

CHAPTER FOURTEEN
TREVOR

An aggressive knock startles me from absentmindedly cleaning Beau's kitchen. A wince stills me at the door because the only option is the boys. And I know I'm probably in deep shit. Sure enough, Eli stands with his arms crossed, with my duffle bag dangling from his shoulder. His eyes do their best to radiate rage, but it comes off more like a little kitten that's been tossed in the tub. I've missed him so much. Jackson and Benji stand behind Eli, radiating less hostility, instead mostly radiating concern.

"You've got so much explaining to do," Eli murmurs, a clear threat in his voice.

"I am so sorry." Grabbing his shirt, I haul Eli into the house, enveloping him in a hug full of apology. "I didn't tell anyone. Just so you know."

"You should've told me. From the start," Eli grumpily mumbles into my shirt.

"Us too," Benji says from where he stands awkwardly by the front door.

Jackson tears me bodily from Eli's arms to envelop me in

one of his own warm, soft hugs. I allow myself a brief moment of comfort in his arms, leaning most of my weight against him. Benji's hand rubs up and down my back as Jackson cradles me. After enough comfort, I pull away to look around at the three of my best friends.

"It's so complicated," I admit in defeat.

Eli frowns deeply, lines appearing on his forehead. The expression is so rare to see from Eli. The man is usually sunshine and rainbows, a joy to have as a friend. I hate that I'm the reason perpetual sunshine Eli is even close to upset, even annoyed doesn't cut it for me.

"Sit down with me?" I sit on Beau's sofa and pat the space beside me.

Eli joins me with a huff, but I can already tell I'm close to forgiven. Benji folds to the floor, sky-blue eyes focused solely on me. Jackson takes up residence by the back door, looking out at the yard as he waits for my explanation.

"Start at the beginning," Eli demands.

That's such a long story. But he's right. We've all been friends for years, in close proximity, and I've never even shared about my parents. Only Claire and Beau know. Claire only knows because we were raised in the same circles in New York City. Both raised by distant, wealthy parents that thought money could erase their absence. Claire turned out normal enough, saving me from myself after my parents fell from grace.

Obviously, I had to finally tell Beau because... well. If I want to start a life here with him, then secrets aren't much of an option anymore.

"My parents are Turner and Lyla Shaw."

Eli just stares blankly at me. "Okay?"

"Those names don't ring a bell at all?"

"Are they famous?" Benji bounces to his knees, perpetual sunshine.

"Not for good reasons," I mumble sourly. "They're more infamous than anything. They're serving life in federal prison for a Ponzi scheme. They swindled a lot of innocent people out of their life savings... out of everything... and all of it just for a few mansions, some nice cars, and my private school education. I try not to think about that one too much."

Eli's nose wrinkles up in thought. "Were they bad to you?"

"Absent more than anything. Nannies raised me."

A serious, firm look gets aimed my way by Jackson. "Is Trevor your real name?"

I wince. "No."

Eli nods in understanding. "Well, lots of things make sense now. You've always been oddly paranoid about where you are, but I honestly just thought it was your anxiety. Also, one time when we were out grocery shopping, I called your name like ten times, and you never answered me. I threw a lemon at you."

Oh God, I remember that. The lemon had clocked my right cheek and Eli had apologized profusely for weeks.

"I remember that."

"So, what's this all got to do with Beau... why all the subterfuge?" Jackson asks.

"Just to be clear," I tell Jackson with a very serious look, "I have never once claimed to be intelligent."

Benji blinks rapidly. "Okay."

"I was his fake boyfriend for a wedding. Took me about twenty-four hours to fall in love with the man. Then his father died, and he asked Claire for me, but I was contracting with Nolan at the time. But we worked it out so I could come. Claire only took her cut, and I came and was a fake boyfriend for the funeral. And it hurt so much. I wasn't ready to feel that way about someone. I was still in college and my parents were causing me problems... it was all too much." I avert my gaze from Eli's sad eyes and pick at a thread on the quilt covering the back of the sofa. "So, I ran. Left him, asked him to wait for me. I didn't know if I could ever do it. But I graduated and you found your happiness and I thought... can I do it? Can I have that too? Did Beau wait for me? It's an asshole move, I admit it, but I thought if he waited for me, then it was a sign that maybe I'm not a piece of shit like my parents. Maybe there's something good inside me too that's worth being loved by someone as good as Beau Callahan."

"Oh, Trevor." Eli's tone is so heartbreaking that I have to bite my lip to stop tears from falling. "You're so worth being loved. So many people love you. I love you, and Jackson loves you, and Benji... now Beau. A lot of people love you."

"Yeah, I know. It's just... hard to remember sometimes."

"Your parents never told you they love you?"

I sniff and wipe at my nose. "Infrequently."

"Sweet Trevor," Benji whispers, heartbreak clouding his gentle face.

Benji crawls to the sofa, and envelops me in his arms, swaying back and forth on the sofa. We sit in silence for a long time with him just petting at my hair. I had missed them so much the past few months. My dearest friends. My only friends really. Now Eli and I live right across the street from each other. The world is so small and beautiful. Benji pulls away so that Eli can hug me too. I allow the affection despite not quite knowing how to accept it still.

"Colby is such a good man," I whisper into Eli's wild curls.

"Yeah," Eli admits with a soft little sigh. "He's a great man. I'm so lucky to have him."

"Maybe *Pretty Woman* isn't so far off."

Eli smacks my head. "We're both Julia Roberts in this scenario. Even with the age gap."

A moment later the back door opens to reveal a tired-looking Beau. His eyes meet mine first, then flit over to the other boys. One of those gorgeous, patented Beau smiles spreads across his face. My heart beats double time in my chest just from that single smile.

"Hey, everyone, stopping by for a visit?"

Beau slips off his shoes, then heads into his kitchen for an ice-cold water.

"Dropping off this jerk's duffle bag." Eli stands with a sigh, dusting off his tight jeans with his hands. "Colby is waiting for us in the Jeep to take us out to dinner."

"Yeah, I chatted with him for a bit outside. Maybe we can do a double date sometime?"

Eli practically beams. "I'd love that! Now, if you make Trevor anything but happy, I'll kill you. Lots of places to hide bodies out here."

Beau just chuckles as Eli pats his arm as he exits through the back. Jackson salutes Beau on his exit, while Benji gives Beau a tight hug despite them only briefly meeting the other day. A honk fills the air, before the sound of gravel kicking floats through the open back door.

"All good?" Beau asks gently.

"All good." I walk over to him in the kitchen, wrap my arms around his neck, and go up on my tiptoes to kiss the corner of his mouth. "Tired?"

"Been a long few days. I usually take Tuesday and Wednesday off, that's my weekend. You wanna do something fun with me tomorrow?"

"The answer to that question is always going to be yes."

Beau bites his lip to fight back what I'm sure would be a heart-stopping, toe-curling kind of grin. Those big strong hands that I love so much stroke up and down my back as he holds me close. He holds me like I'm something precious, something rare. My heartbeat picks up again just at that very thought. Being precious to someone like Beau is a dream come true.

"Can I just hold you tonight, sweetheart?" Beau asks softly, a hint of need in his low voice. How am I ever supposed to say no when he asks me something like that so sweetly? Saying no to Beau seems impossible, much to my perpetual enjoyment.

"'Course."

Never before have I had to worry about taking care of someone else. Not in a real-life relationship. Considering I've never had a relationship before that wasn't part of my professional boyfriend duties. Being a fake boyfriend had me taking care of other men sometimes, but my heart was never really in it. Now with Beau, there's a deep need rooted inside me that makes me *want* to take care of him. To ease his troubles, ease the weight on his strong shoulders. I feel like I can fly when he's vulnerable with me and lets me take care of him.

Which leads me to something else.

"Hey, Beau," I say as I lead him towards his bedroom.

"Hmm?"

"Do you ever like to be fucked?"

Beau's hand grips mine just a little tighter at my question. He's silent until we reach the bedroom, where he faces me head-on in front of the bed. A deep crimson blush paints his cheeks and neck, and his gaze lands firmly on me. Shyness radiates off of him, but not his normal shyness. This one is different.

"Sometimes," Beau admits quietly.

"Would you ever want me to fuck you?" I ask, reaching up to tenderly cup his jaw.

He turns his head into my palm like he always does, such a tender thing that makes my still-learning-to-love heart beat a little wilder. A slew of butterflies takes off in my chest when he affectionately kisses my palm. His hooded eyes find mine and smolder, sending a current of need through me.

"I think someday I'll need you to fuck me, sweetheart." His voice is deep and rough, like the words cost him a lot to say.

"I'll give you what you need," I promise, meaning every word.

I kiss him then because I don't know how else to follow up that sort of statement. If it was possible to pour my heart into a kiss, it would be in this one. I lick his lip so that he opens for me, and then dip into his mouth, wishing I could keep the taste of him in my own mouth even after the kiss ends.

Beau's hands grip my hips and tug me in tighter against his body. His hard cock is a line against my abdomen, and I wish that I could have him tonight, any way he'd let me. But I also want to respect his wish for us to take it a little slow, start back at the beginning. So, I pull away from him, chuckling when his mouth chases after mine.

"Slow, Beau."

He nods in the dark of his bedroom. "Right."

"Take a shower, put on some comfy clothes, and then we'll enjoy some dinner. Alright?"

Beau plods into the bathroom without a single argument. Once the sound of the shower running reaches my ears, I head out into the kitchen to scrounge up a dinner for us. In my very best dreams, I imagined a scenario much like this one. A dream where I cooked dinner for my lover, took them to bed, and woke up in their arms with a sweetness lingering between us.

And that's exactly how the evening goes. Dinner is perfectly quiet. Beau even does the dishes. Then we curl up in his bed together, his leg between my thighs, my head tucked into the warm crook of his neck. I run my finger over his eyebrows, under his eyes, over his nose, and count his eyelashes and his breathing slows. Just the shine of the moon illuminates the room as Beau slowly falls asleep with me safely inside his arms.

The very last thought as sleep tugs me into its grips is that I hope I can keep Beau forever. Keep all of this. For the first time in my life, I've found something worth fighting to keep.

CHAPTER FIFTEEN

TREVOR

Days go by with me attempting to relax while Beau goes to work. We haven't explicitly talked about the future, but it's unfurling easily before us. While the house is empty, I work on applications for graduate school. I'm not sure why I waited so long. Maybe being in Georgia after graduation was just a flyover, because I knew I'd somehow end up back here. Where I belong with Beau.

A few online-only programs appeal to me. My grades were good, and professors liked me, so I'm pretty sure I can get glowing references to help my application. But now I have to consider the proximity to this place, to Beau. For the first time in my life, I have to consider someone else. It's not as hard as I imagined it would be, to place another person's feelings or wants close to my own.

Midway through the week, Beau comes home, restless and anxious out of his skin. Most nights we spend together, just basking in the glow of each other's presence. Wanting to help him, ease whatever is worrying him, I stop him at the kitchen counter with a gentle hand on his forearm. His muscles are bunched tight as if ready for a fight. But that's not Beau, he's not a fighter. Those kind eyes ping to me, a little furrow forms between his brows.

"Wanna have a date night with me?"

Beau grimaces a little. "I'm so tired, Trevor."

"Nothing fancy." I squeeze his arm gently. "We can do it here."

After letting out a heavy breath, he nods in agreement. With a genuine smile, a rare thing for me that I only discovered once I met Beau, I shove him into his bedroom to shower and change out of his work clothes. I throw together a haphazard charcuterie board, then grab a few beers, and make my way towards the hammock in the backyard.

The hammock sways gently in the breeze under my weight. I give one fleeting thought to wondering if we'll both fit, but I end up not caring. We'll find a way. Moments later, Beau steps out onto the back porch, hair still slightly damp from his shower. He's the epitome of perfection, of strength, of everything that makes my bruised heart beat.

He nods his head towards the hammock once he stands beside me. "What's this, sweetheart?"

"Date night." I pat the hammock in clear invitation.

The hammock sways dangerously under our joined weight, but it holds, for which I'm forever grateful. He lies back against the netting and tugs me tight against the solid line of his body. He smells like his body wash, woodsy and strong, with the underlying scent of Beau that lingers on my skin after he holds me.

"Thank you," Beau murmurs softly. It's clear to me he's still not used to this, allowing someone to care for him, and that's fine because I'm still getting used to caring for him too. We'll find our way together.

"Rough day?" I rub my hand around his stomach, feeling the rise and fall from his breaths.

His fingers curl into my hair, their favorite place to find home. "Thought about my dad a lot. Lots of weight on me at the farm with the upcoming fall season. It's the first season that I'm heading alone, and I'm scared to fuck up."

"How many times have you fucked up before?" I ask, countering his worries with truth.

His fingers stutter in my hair, before a soft chuckle vibrates through his chest. "Not many times, future therapist."

"I'm not psychoanalyzing you; I swear."

"Just teasing." Beau presses a hard kiss to my forehead. "I just don't want to be a disappointment. Want to make everyone happy. The farm means so much to not just my family but everyone that lives here."

"I can't ease all your worries, but I can promise you that everyone has a lot of faith in you. And you have a great support system at the farm. It's going to be great."

Beau nods shakily against my head, his cheek stubble rubbing my hair. The breeze pushes the hammock into swaying, and the sweet smell of the gardenias, still stubbornly blooming despite the approaching season change, wafts over us. That smell will always make me think of Beau.

"I applied to a few graduate programs today. In the meantime... I need to get a job."

"No, you don't."

I sit up halfway, bracing my forearm against his strong chest. "Beau, I need a job."

He swipes his thumb across my cheek, staring deeply into my eyes. I feel unmoored by him, how deeply he can see into me.

"Why don't you take a little break for a bit. Just be here with me. You can start school when you're ready."

"I've always had a job since I left home."

Beau's mouth quirks up. "I'd like this to be your home now. One thing you'll learn about the South is that there's no rush here. Good things come with time. So, take your time figuring out your next step. If you really want a job, I can put you to work at the farm."

I grimace. "I'm not sure I'm built for manual labor."

Beau runs his hand down my back, letting his hand come to rest at the small of my back. His exploring hand is gentle, but firm, reminding me of exactly how much I enjoy his touch.

"I can teach you all you need to know about manual labor."

A laugh bubbles out of me. "Are you flirting with me?"

Red blooms across his cheeks, shattering my heart into a million pieces while simultaneously putting my fragile heart back together. "I'm always flirtin' with you."

Ignoring his blatant attempt at distraction, I cuddle deeper against his side. His arm tightens as I release a contented sigh. The setting sun disappears over the horizon, casting the yard in an orange glow. Beau's body softens beneath me, until I realize he's sound asleep.

The hammock sways in the breeze, under our heavy weight. I use this time to catalog everything I can about Beau. Dark brown hair with flecks of silver that tell me he's going to be salt and pepper in a few years. I can't wait to watch him age, to grow old with him, to love him. Lines around his eyes and mouth tell me that he's lived a happy life, despite the grief that's clouded the past few years. The wiriness of his forearms, strength of his fingers, tells me that he can hold me up no matter what threatens to take me down. Everything about Beau is perfect to me, always will be.

Beau startles awake, just as the stars blink to life above us.

"We didn't even eat the food you made," Beau points out, voice sleep soft.

"It kept. Hungry?"

Beau nods, so I carefully maneuver us in the hammock to be sitting in the hammock like a swing, then grab the tray of food. We share the meal together, picking at the food until it's halfway gone. One beer is enough for both of us, so we make our way inside once the breeze turns just a little too chilly.

Once the dishes are washed and put away, I guide Beau back towards his bedroom. The past few nights we've gotten a small tradition going. We finish our day by standing at the doorway of our rooms in our pajamas and talk about our days. It's always delightfully domestic and it always makes me feel some type of way. Some perfect type of happy.

Beau heads into his bedroom, and I head into mine. Once changed into sweatpants and a T-shirt, I lean against the doorjamb, arms crossed over my chest. When Beau opens his door, my breath lodges in my rib cage. He fills the entire doorway like usual, but something about the sight of him tonight, softened around the edges from admitting the weight he's under with the farm... it just feels like something special is happening between us.

Something so real that the idea it could slip through my fingers terrifies me.

"Alright?" Beau asks, eyes flitting between mine.

I smile warmly, emotions clogging my throat. "Perfect."

"I've got a busy few weeks at the farm." Beau runs his hands over his tired face. "But I want you here, like having you here. I just gotta get through this season, then we can settle in, figure out what kind of life you want here."

"Beau, this is exactly the life I want. There's no getting through seasons. Alright?"

Beau ducks his head for a moment, and when his gaze lifts back to mine, there's relief etched across his entire face. Relief that someone like me could want everything he has to give. Everything about my childhood, the fast cars, the money, the drugs, none of it could ever compare to the simple, quiet life that's promised for me with Beau. There's something to be said about a kind and gentle life. It's all I've ever wanted, but never realized. Not until Beau.

"Thank you."

I cross the small hallway to press a sweet kiss against his perfect mouth. "Always, handsome."

His hands wrap around me to hold my body tight against his, and I allow it, letting him take comfort from my presence. We stand together for a short while, until finally sleep comes for Beau. I watch as he heads into his room, then listen intently for the sounds of him climbing into bed. Once I'm sure he's asleep, I climb into the guest bed, and sleep comes for me with the smell of cedar and home clinging to the edges of my subconscious.

A WEEK LATER BEAU FORCES ME INTO COMFORTABLE CLOTHES one afternoon with an infectious grin that's full of mischief. I love seeing him this way. With me he's sweet, gentle, but also so silly that I can't help but fall for him a little more every day. Dressed in gym shorts, an old shirt, and one of Beau's worn-in ball caps, I feel like a totally different person. In the best sort of way.

The truck rumbles down the old asphalt roads that kick up mirages in the distance from the still-stifling Florida heat. Oak trees laden with moss line the road, cutting shadows across the road where the sun cuts through. I can't explain how some place so magically feels like home after so many years of feeling aimless. Feeling like there isn't anywhere in the world that I belong. But with Beau's hand on my thigh, country music filling the cab through the speakers, my heart settles in a way that once seemed impossible.

Beau turns down a dirt road, the truck spitting up dust around us. I fight back an indecent moan at the sight of his forearms as he handles the wheel. Bigger men haven't usually been my thing, but Beau's been exactly my type since I laid eyes on him. Big and broad, with a heart of gold, a heart that's tender for me. Apparently, that's my type. Maybe it always has been, and I just didn't know until Beau.

Surprises aren't something I have ever enjoyed. But Beau, he gets a pass, and always will, because surprises from him usually end up meaning *fun*. I expect Beau to take me to a nice dinner, maybe to a movie, but instead he aims the truck further away from town. My grin grows wider as the concrete road turns to gravel, then to clay dirt. Putting the window down, I unbuckle my seat belt, and hang my head outside.

"Be careful!" Beau shouts, his right hand painfully tight on my thigh.

"You drive so slow!" I shout back, letting the air whip through my hair.

"Precious cargo," Beau murmurs darkly under his breath. But I hear him. And I'm in love with him. So deeply, wildly in love, that my heart glows with the force of it. Hanging my torso out the window, I hold my hands out to feel the wind whip against me, all the while feeling Beau's tight grip on my thigh keeping me from floating away.

Recognition hits me. The truck comes to a crawl in a wooded area. Beau climbs out of the car to open the chain-link fence, then comes back to drive us through. He keeps his eyes off me, but I can see the smile at the edge of his lips. He can't hide that from me. The truck crawls down a tiny clay road, until finally the clearing opens up to the river that feeds into the spring. Beau looks absolutely disgruntled, so I lean back into the cab to press a kiss to his frowning mouth.

"You make me feel alive."

"You almost gave me a heart attack."

I kiss his pliant mouth again, until he opens for me, letting me sip at the sweet taste of him. "I keep you young."

Beau sighs softly against my lips. "Get out of the truck."

Well, no arguing with an order like that. The water is just as blue green as I remember. Just as calm. The cicadas aren't as loud now, but they still buzz faintly in the background. The sounds, smells, even the color of the sky comfort me like an old memory in the darkest of times. Magic is at work here in Clay Springs with Beau. A scary kind of old magic only found among the loud buzz of cicadas and Beau's gentle smile as he kisses me whole.

When I glance over at Beau, my eyes practically bug out of my head. Shirt halfway over his head, his muscled stomach shows off just for me under the bright yellow late afternoon sun. The moment his head pops through his shirt, he hastily tosses the shirt into the truck, and levels me with an absolutely devilish grin.

"Get naked, Trevor," Beau says, voice low and demanding.

An uncontrollable shiver rolls through my entire body, tip

to toe. Disobeying Beau was never an option. Clothes have never flown off me faster. A deep chuckle from Beau has my head swinging his way, only to see a flash of his perfect bare ass before he dives into the water. He breaks through the sparkling water and his hands come up to brush water from his eyes. Beau grins that wide, infectious grin at me, and I'm a total goner.

"Waitin' on you, sweetheart," Beau drawls.

The combination of the accent and the sweetheart will always be my greatest undoing. Something about the words, the tone, just *everything* goes straight to my dopamine factory. Probably everything about Beau has that effect on me. A pure shot of sunshine to my heart.

My grin is borderline painful as I run straight to the edge, jumping in with a sharp inhale. The water is just as cold as it was last summer, but the warmth of Beau makes the crystalline waves less sharp. He wraps his strong arms around me so tight that I'm forced to wrap my legs around him to keep from being squished to death. But I don't mind, not one bit. Being squished by Beau would be an amazing way to die.

"This has always been my safe place," Beau murmurs into my neck. His voice is so muffled that I can just barely make out his words. "All of us farm kids came here in the summers. We'd get up to no good, stay here until we were pruned or one of our parents came here to send us all right back home."

I place a kiss just under his ear, where he smells the sweetest. "It sounds perfect."

His hands readjust on my back, to cup my ass, pulling me flush against him. A smile fights to break free when he makes a low, soft sound of want. The sun beams bright through the branches, forcing me to blink rapidly as I look up at the small pieces of blue sky visible through the trees.

"Do you want kids?" Beau asks hesitantly.

"Not a deal breaker for me either way."

Beau sighs in relief. "I think I want them."

"They sound like a fun adventure," I admit honestly.

Beau nods against my neck, then lifts his head to meet my gaze. "Marriage?"

God, we really are doing everything backwards. Fake dating, falling in love, separation, just to find one another again and date for real. What a bunch of fools. But we're fools for each other, so maybe it's safe this time. That's a lie. No "maybe" about it. I'm safe with Beau and he's safe with me. Safe harbors in a raging storm.

I delicately rub his wiry beard with my fingers. "I'm not too interested in marriage."

"Why?" Beau kisses the tip of my thumb.

"I like the idea of marriage without the legal ramifications. All the devotion of marriage, shared bills, promises of forever... just no piece of paper."

"Sounds a lot like marriage to me," Beau points out.

He's not wrong. I sweetly kiss his nose. "Well, if that's marriage to you, then it's something I definitely want one day."

"Do you prefer to do the dishes or put them away?"

The question makes me laugh which must've been Beau's intention because his eyes crinkle with happiness at the corners. Love radiates from him. The idea makes me nervous but overjoyed at the same time.

"Put them away for sure."

Beau kisses me then as he cups my ass, tugging me closer against him until my hard cock rubs against his stomach. My moan slips from my mouth and right into his, making him tug me tighter against him. He licks into my mouth, tasting me, savoring me. I let him until I can't do anything but melt against him in a puddle of want.

"We're a perfect match," Beau whispers against my mouth.

"Because I like to put the dishes away?"

Beau nods, his forehead sliding against mine. "Best indicator of if a relationship is gonna work. Preferences for dishes."

I tighten my legs around his waist and bite my lip. "Good. Tell me more about your childhood growing up here? Tell me about your friends. About your parents. I want to know it all."

One of his big, strong hands runs up my back to cup my neck, then slowly brings me down to kiss me again, but softer this time. Just a tender press of his mouth to mine. But somehow that kiss is even better than the first. Even sweeter than sweet tea.

"I wanna know more about you too. It's a two-way street, sweetheart," Beau says once he pulls away from my mouth. And I know he's right. I have to give, to get. If I'm safe with anyone, it's Beau.

"Alright," I whisper.

"That's another great thing about this place," Beau reassures me, fingers distractedly twisting in my wet hair. "Anything we tell each other here, stays here, between us. No one else will ever know. Pretty cool, right?"

My breath hitches painfully in my chest. Annoyingly even tears form in my eyes. I don't know what I did to deserve Beau Callahan. I must've been a saint in another life. I hug him tightly, breathing in the scent of him mixed with the smell of the spring. Kind of perfect really.

"I could've been an asshole. All that money as a kid. The private schools, the nannies, the total absence of my parents, so they just threw money and expensive things at me. My first car was a Lamborghini, I mean totally obnoxious. That got taken by the feds too, by the way. All of it got taken. I had nowhere to go, nothing, even my school kicked me out. One of my former nannies took pity on me, let me stay with her, but she had a house full of kids, and that didn't last long. Just long enough for me to figure out how to get my GED. Then I worked shitty job after shitty job, couch surfed, until Claire pitched me the idea *The Boyfriend Experience*. That's my life story as an elevator pitch. Not much else to say."

I'm out of breath by the time I'm finished. Can't quite meet Beau's eyes either. His fingers leave my hair, to gently grip my chin, forcing me to meet his gaze. Those dark eyes are fathomless as they take me in, working overtime to put all my jagged-edged puzzle pieces together. In time, I know he will.

"What were you like as a kid?" Beau asks, curiosity coloring his voice.

"Quiet mostly," I admit fondly. "I loved to go to the movies. I had a nanny that took me all the time. She said that's where everyone is the same, sitting in a bad seat at the movies, with a big bag of popcorn and a soda."

"I love the movies too. Growing up, we went into the city to this fancy theater to see old movies. It was so much fun."

"I love that," I say around a small smile. "I have this pass where I can go as many times as I want in a month. That and the gym. My two favorite places."

"We show movies at the farm once a month on a big projector screen. I'll take you."

My rib cage suddenly feels just a bit too small to contain my heart. Simple as that. So Beau. So sweet. His smile goes double wide at whatever look I get in my eyes. He kisses me again, no doubt a little reward for all my honesty, then pulls away to crouch down further, until the chilly water covers our shoulders. The blaring light of the sun on my bare shoulders makes the water even colder, but I relish it as Beau tugs me even closer.

"You're beautiful," Beau says quietly, eyes twinkling in the sunlight.

"Beau." I don't know what else to say.

"It's alright, sweetheart. You're safe with me. I promise."

And then he kisses me for an endless age. By the time he gently pulls away from my mouth, I feel dazed in the best sense of the word. The emotion must show on my face because Beau lets out a delighted, warm chuckle.

"That easy?" Beau asks, fingers tangled in my hair.

"For you, yeah."

Beau chuckles again. "Hold your breath."

I obey without even asking follow-up questions. He dips us under the water. The cool water is sharp against my skin, but my skin warms as I rapidly blink under the water, taking in the sight of Beau grinning at me. His lips move under the water, bubbles floating to the surface.

I don't know what he says, but I can hope.

We swim in the crystal-blue spring for what feels like hours. A game of Marco Polo keeps us distracted for a bit, until Beau finds me, and tugs me against him to kiss the breath right out of me. Being with Beau makes me feel free. By the time we climb out of the spring, our fingers are pruned, but Beau's joyful smile makes it worth it.

Biting my lip hard, I take in Beau's naked body. Drops of water roll down his back, coming to a brief stop at the top of his perfect ass, before continuing down his legs. After throwing a towel at me, he smirks when he catches where my gaze had been.

"Checking me out?" Beau asks, tone teasing.

"Yeah, you're hot as hell. You know this already."

He hides his flush by rubbing the towel over his face. "I'm just fine."

"We're not arguing about this."

"I'm not much for arguin', sweetheart."

"What's with the sweetheart pet name?" I ask curiously while tugging on my dry clothes.

Beau eyes me as he runs fingers through his wet hair. "'Cause you've got a sweet heart."

And there promptly goes said heart. Gone. Lost to the world. Lost to Beau Callahan and his gaze that tells me everything I need to know. That I really am safe here with him.

The sound of the tailgate opening has me spinning around. In the truck bed is a mountain of blankets and pillows, along with a cooler. Confusion steals my breath for a second, before Beau's hand strokes down my arm, tugging my gaze back to him.

"Wanna sleep under the stars with me?"

"Mosquitoes," I murmur helplessly.

Beau aims a wry look at me, then pulls out a device from under the blankets. "It'll keep 'em away. Promise. I've got bracelets we can wear too that'll keep 'em away."

"I trust you."

Beau shakes his head ruefully while grabbing a cooler. "I made sandwiches for us and packed snacks."

"My romantic."

"Yours?" Beau asks gently, tone belying his confidence.

"Mine," I tell him firmly.

A beautiful flush creeps up his neck, so I kiss his cheek,

tempering whatever emotion flows through him. Toeing off my shoes, I jump into the bed of the truck with a flourish. Beau copies me by taking off his own shoes, climbing into the back alongside me. He presses me down into the comforter, arms on either side of my head. A shiver of anticipation rolls right through me.

"Tonight, I'm gonna make love to you."

Oh. My breath picks up a little and I swallow loudly. "Yeah?"

Beau nods slowly, fingers teasing at the hem of my shirt. "That alright with you?"

"What's making love entail?"

"I'm thinking I just want to suck you off, long and slow, have you tremblin'. Maybe you can suck me off too, if you're good."

"You don't want to fuck me?"

Beau laughs again. "We don't always have to fuck. You'll see. This can be even better. Want me to show you?"

"Show me," I beg, voice gruff with desire.

"Later."

Record scratch. "What?"

Beau moves to the side, lying on his back, then pulls me against him. "Let's eat and watch the stars come out, maybe slow dance to a song or two, then I'll show you what it means to be made love to."

"I'm so going to get you back."

Beau's lips dance under his beard. "I bet."

"There's something else we need to talk about." Heart pounding painfully against my ribs, I tilt my head to look up at Beau. "I stopped having sex with boyfriends a bit ago. I got tested earlier this year. Everything came back fine. All that to say if you want to... ever think about..." I trail off and tear my gaze from his, to instead stare up at the dark sky. "If you want to fuck me without a condom, then that's something we can entertain."

Beau grabs my chin, forcing my eyes back to meet his own. "Sweetheart, why did that make you nervous?"

"Not all men like it. I've never done it before, but I'd like to do it with you."

"My annual physical was a few months ago. Everything was fine for me too. If that's something you want to try, then we will. All you ever have to do is ask."

I hope this man always makes my heart soar and swoop. But there's also something else I want to discuss with him.

I draw circles against his chest, gathering courage, and using the warmth of his body to steady my nerves. A couple of deep breaths, and his hand firm against my neck, steadies me.

"Before you, I used to take the meaner johns, or should I say... the ones that like it rough."

Beau's fingers tighten ever so slightly on my neck. "Were you hurt?"

"Only when I wanted to be, mostly."

"Mostly?" Beau asks, voice dark.

"I'm fine now. But I just... I wanted to share that part of me with you. I never really liked it; I think it was another way to punish myself. Sex with you is intimate and sweet. I like it that way... you make me feel cherished."

Beau turns my head to meet his gaze. "I'll give you whatever you want. You know that, right?"

My face heats. "Yes." I press a kiss over his heart. "I like the way we are, the way we will be."

"Good," Beau says firmly.

As darkness descends on the day, we quietly eat together,

no need for talking. Our thighs and sides press tight together, like maybe if we try, we can become one person. Wouldn't be such a bad thing really. To be tied to Beau forever. The birds quiet as the forest darkens, so the sound of the river overtakes all the other sounds around us. Calm ebbs and flows over us, as if the forest and river extends their calm to us.

Silence with Beau is always comfortable. Never before have I felt no need to fill silence. Something about him just settles me, settles my sometimes too-fragile heart. Maybe that's the beauty of Beau. His presence calms all those terrible urges inside me so that I can just be myself, just be Trevor. I never thought it was possible to find someone that felt like a warm blanket out of the dryer, or the end of a summer day at the beach. But that's how Beau feels to me. His love is easy and warm.

"Thinkin' pretty loudly, sweetheart," Beau points out as we snuggle back down into the comforter.

"Thinking about you."

Beau hums thoughtfully, fingers idly playing with my hair. "Yeah?"

I tip my head to gaze softly up at him, letting every emotion coursing through me reflect on my face. His eyes sparkle even in the dying light of day. Just for me. Only ever for me. Leaning up, I sweetly glide my lips over his, just a soft press of my mouth to Beau's. Kissing Beau will never get old. The soft kisses, hungry kisses, the *give me more* kisses, all of them tilt my world on its axis.

Once the sun is long gone, and darkness surrounds us, Beau pulls out his phone to play soft country love songs. With a flush up my neck, I let him pull me out of the truck bed, to slow dance in the clay dirt. His hand finds a home at the small of my back, proprietary, claiming, tugging me as close to him as our bodies will allow.

"Dance with me," Beau demands, voice firm and low.

Wrapping my arms around his shoulders, I tangle my fingers together at the nape of his neck. An emotion I haven't felt in a long-time bubbles up inside me. Joy. Hard to explain, but being so in love, being so cared for, makes me feel so full of joy, full of stark relief. Like maybe it was worth me living just to have this moment with Beau.

A hiccuped sob almost escapes me but I roughly swallow it down. As usual, ever-observant Beau notices the fleeting emotion.

"It's alright, sweetheart. Just be with me."

Beau twirls us slowly under the stars, cheek tenderly pressed against mine. Life is so much more worth living when I accept the love around me.

Beau takes my face in the palms of his strong hands and kisses my mouth like he's starving for me. Melting against him, he holds me up, like always. He pulls away from my mouth to trail searing kisses down my neck, biting at my exposed skin with sharp teeth. Shivers roll through me from the heat of his touch. Fingers bite into the small of my back, pulling me closer against him until I feel the hot press of his clothed cock against mine. A hiss seeps out of me at just the thought of his cock, hard and waiting for me.

"Lie back," Beau orders, but his voice is tender, not demanding.

The back of my knees hits the bed of the truck. Letting myself fall back gently, Beau follows me down, so he obscures my vision of the inky night sky. Stars twinkle around him, but all I see is Beau Callahan. All the power of a thousand suns burning out millions of years ago can't even begin to match the force this man has over me. He was made for me.

I tug him down to me to kiss him, because I can't last one more moment without him. Beau shushes me through kisses, startling me into realizing pained whimpers were slipping out of my mouth. Warm hands slip under my shirt, sliding it up until we are forced to break away so Beau can pull the offending garment over my head. I blink in a daze up at Beau, head buzzing just at the nearness of him.

"Absolutely perfect," Beau murmurs as he reverently runs his hands along my ribs. "You were made for me. Weren't you?"

My lips tremble at his words. "I think so, yeah."

Beau's answering smile is earth-shattering. The force of his love makes me dizzy, all the blood rushing to my head like I've just awoken from a years-long sleep. Beau's love wakes me up. His love is healing.

My breath picks up when Beau's fingers undo the button of my jeans, pulling them slowly down my legs, until I'm left in just my boxer briefs. Kissing down my chest, my fingers clench in the blankets to stop from grabbing on to Beau. He slots himself between my thighs and rubs his beard against the tender skin of my thigh. The prickle of his beard is sharp, but perfect, giving me the edge of pain that I sometimes crave.

Beau buries his face against me, mouthing at my cock until my underwear is damp with his spit. Sparks of pleasure zip down my spine, until my toes curl against the bed of the truck where the blanket doesn't reach. The cold metal of the truck roots me to the moment so I don't float away.

"Fuck," I swear loudly as Beau finally tugs my underwear away. My cock slaps my stomach, leaving a trail of pre-cum on my skin. Beau bites his lip, eyes blown with desire, and licks my stomach with a barely restrained moan.

Survival from the onslaught of pleasure he's going to give me is probably optional.

Just when I'm wrapping my head around everything, Beau grips my cock at the base, sucking the head into his warm, perfect mouth.

"Beau!" I shout as my thighs tremble around his head. Oh, fuck. I am definitely not going to survive tonight. Just the feel of his mouth around my cock, the sight of his head dipped down to take me into his mouth, sends me hurtling towards an unfairly close orgasm.

Beau ignores me, sucking me down like he needs me to come down his throat just to stay alive. Maybe he does. The stars blink above me, bright against the inky-black sky. Everything feels so big, so real, I'm not sure I've ever felt so alive in my life.

A moan escapes me when Beau sucks me down all the way to the back of his throat, only to swallow around me. My hands fly from the blankets to grip at his short hair, finding any purchase I can. Beau only sucks me down harder, like my reaction spurs him on.

"Beau, Beau, Beau," I chant as pleasure radiates through my entire body.

His fingers dig into my hips, holding me down so I can't thrust up into his welcoming mouth. Pulling off abruptly, he sucks at the head of my cock again, before licking down my shaft to lavish kisses at the base. Fuck. He's worshiping me, this is what it's like to be wanted, to be needed. Just the thought alone shatters me into a million pieces of desire. His dark eyes stare at me, taking me apart, while simultaneously putting me back together. My chest heaves with my stuttered breaths.

"Give it to me," Beau orders, fingers a loose grip around my cock wet with his spit. "I want you to let go. Let go, Trevor. Please. You're safe."

He swallows me back down, his throat moving around me, a moan falling from his lips as if just the taste of me turns him on. Stars immediately explode behind my eyes. The stars in the sky, and supernovas behind my eyelids from the exquisite, perfect pleasure of being in Beau's mouth. Sucking me to the back of his throat, he holds me there, swallowing around me again. Thighs trembling, stars filling my vision, I come down his throat with a pained shout of ecstasy. In a daze, body floating, I blink up at the glittering sky.

Beau licks my cock clean, then slides up my body to kiss me, sharing the taste of myself on his tongue. Wrapping my arms around him, I tug him down tighter against me, until the warmth of his skin bleeds into my own. His fingers tangle in my hair, holding me close, like I'm fine china, like he's afraid to break me. But he never could. Beau could never do anything but give me joy, peace, and comfort.

"I want to taste you," I say against his mouth, breathless.

Beau chuckles, pushing the hair from my face. "Another day. Tonight was about you."

"Beau," I growl.

Beau just chuckles, totally unfazed by me. Maybe that's a good thing. Maybe I need to get used to being taken care of without owing anything back. Beau takes his shirt off, then tucks me against his body, pulling a blanket over us to keep us warm against the damp and slightly chilly air. I love the smell of his skin, even his sweat, it's sweet and earthy and comforting.

"Do you think there's life after death?" Beau asks quietly, sadness coloring his words.

"Like the Cher song?"

Beau chuckles. "I think you've got the names mixed up, but I like your intention."

I stare up at the sky, head tucked against the crook of his arm, my hand curled against his strong stomach. I rub my thumb in a circle over his skin, needing to touch him, but knowing he needs my touch too.

"I like to think there's something out there."

Beau squeezes my arm gently. "Sometimes it's nice to imagine."

"Do you think your dad's waiting for you?"

Beau hums in agreement. "He's workin' on a car, waiting for me to come home."

"What kind of car?"

Beau's fingers press hard against my spine bringing me even closer. I don't think he's going to answer me for a while. Just the sound of the heat bugs, and the gentle flow of the river filter around us. Staring up at the black night sky, the blinking stars sing a quiet song of stillness. Of hope, that I spent so long not allowing myself.

"He's working on an old truck, for you and me. One that we can drive into the sunset. His gift to us. Sounds nice, right?"

"Yeah, Beau. It sounds perfect."

Closing my eyes with a bittersweet smile, I settle more firmly against Beau. Sleep comes for me, soft and gentle. Sounds of Beau's fingers carding through my hair, wind through the trees, and the river lull me into one of the most peaceful sleeps of my entire life.

CHAPTER SIXTEEN
BEAU

Romancing Trevor is easy. Every time I make him smile, make him blush, I know this is where he belongs. With me. But sometimes that reservation lingers, like when we were still playing pretend. As if maybe he thinks he's not worth every ounce of my love.

I can only pray that time will help me solve that particular problem. He settles into my house like he's always been there. Maybe there's always been a Trevor-shaped hole in my life.

We spend my next day off wandering aimlessly around town. I show Trevor my preferred Publix, buy him some foods that he likes to keep in the house. We grab Pub Subs and eat them on the tailgate of my truck with our legs dangling over the edge. The smile he aims at me over such a simple activity is enough to send my heart into overdrive. I want to make him smile like that for the rest of my life. Even after.

This whole taking-it-slow thing is my decision, and for a good reason. Sleeping at night with him in the other room is nearly a form of torture. Sometimes I hear him get up at night to use the bathroom, his feet softly padding down the hall. Might be my imagination, but sometimes I think he pauses outside my room. I almost wish he'd just stroll right in, climb into my bed, and collapse into my waiting arms.

But he doesn't.

Because Trevor respects my wish, endearing him to me even further.

I haven't dated much in my life, always too busy with the farm. I used to think maybe there was something wrong with me because I didn't mind being single. But now maybe I was just waiting for Trevor to come along. Fate, destiny, I'm not sure what to call it. How can I explain how easily he slotted into my life like he was always made to be there?

Friday night after a long week has me dragging my feet towards the house. Trevor's waiting on the back porch for me, with a solitary beer in the loose grip of his fingers.

"Hey," Trevor calls out once he catches sight of me.

Tightness around his lips alerts me to the fact that I was right. Something's been going on.

I take the offered beer from him, but don't drink even a sip. Instead, I set it on the porch railing. Tucking my fingers into his belt loops, I tug him closer, until his face is just a few inches from mine.

"It's been a long week, sweetheart. You gonna tell me what's on your mind finally?"

Trevor lets out a weary sigh. "My parents... sometimes they ask me to come visit them. It's like they know when everything is good in my life, and they reach out." Trevor blows an annoyed raspberry. "Like they have radar for when I'm happy."

"They want you to come visit?"

"Yeah." Trevor scrubs an angry hand over his face, agitation clear through his jerky movement. I loop my fingers around his wrist and tug his hand to my chest, letting it rest over my heart. He tightens his fingers in my shirt, face thoughtful. "They ask me for money too sometimes. Usually, I give it to them."

"What worries you the most?"

A worry line appears on his forehead as he squints up at me in thought. The fear and trepidation pours off him, making me feel absolutely awful that I can't instantly solve this for him. Something inside me tells me this will be a permanent issue moving forward. So, I've got to say the right things now to lessen his worries about coming to me in the future.

"If they find out I'm with you and that your family has money... I don't know. I just worry about the power they can wield over me."

"They've got no power over you now, not when you're here with me. You know that, right?"

Trevor turns his head to the side to look out at the yard. When his gaze swings back to me, tears line his eyes. I watch on helplessly as he fights to blink them away, to hold it all in. My heart breaks for him.

"My father leaves me voicemails," Trevor admits calmly. His tone is very matter of fact, but I know Trevor by now. Hurt and anxiety radiate off of him in large, terrifying waves.

"You got one I can hear?"

Trevor nods tightly, then pulls out his phone with a trembling hand. He presses buttons on his phone screen, before finding the most recent voicemail at the top. Pressing play, he hands me the phone, still not able to meet my gaze.

"Levi," the gruff male voice comes through the phone.

"Listen, we keep calling and you don't respond. I need money in my account and so does your mother. We do the jobs they ask but we get paid pennies. If you won't give me money, then at least send some to your mother. The place she's in is a hell-hole... they have her working in the yard for God's sake. I'm afraid she'll do something stupid if we can't take care of her. You get me, son? Come on. Be good and send us each some money. You could go visit your mother too, you know. Anyway. I'll keep an eye out for the money."

Not even an *I love you* to spare. Rage overwhelms me for a second, that someone would even have a kid and then treat them this way astounds me.

"What do you want to do, Trevor?"

He angrily wipes a tear away from his cheek. "I want to not hear from them ever again. I change my phone number, and somehow, he gets it. I don't know what to do. It's so..." Trevor breaks off with an enraged sound. He clenches his fist tight for a second, then shakes it out as if he hurt himself.

Not wanting him to hurt himself, I gently tangle our fingers together, breathing a sigh of relief when he tightly squeezes my fingers. "Trevor, if you don't want to hear from them again, we can make that happen."

His nose scrunches up as he visibly wills himself to not cry. Realizing now isn't the time for fruitless words, I tug him into my arms to comfort him with my touch instead. He slumps against me in utter relief, breaths sharp as he fights against the urge to cry. My sweet Trevor. The cool air whips around us in a gentle breeze, blowing Trevor's hair into my face. I bury my nose into his hair and inhale the comforting scent of him.

After a bit, he seemingly gathers himself, tipping his head back enough to shyly gaze up at me. I swipe my thumb under his eyes to catch the lingering tears on his splotchy-from-crying skin.

"It's alright, sweetheart."

He hiccups a little. "You promise?"

I nod, because this I can guarantee. "It's okay now."

Trevor blows out a relieved breath at my reassuring words. "I trust you."

"Here's what we're gonna do." I press a hard kiss to his temple. "I've got a cousin that's a cop. I'll get with him to figure out how to get you a totally private number. One that they can't find. How's that sound?"

Trevor sharply narrows his eyes. "Is everyone here your cousin?"

"In some way or another, probably." I press another kiss to his temple, this one lingering. "Now, it's been a long week. Tomorrow night's movie night at the farm. You gonna be my date?"

"Depends on the movie."

"You'll like it. I promise."

Trevor laughs softly. "Okay."

"Okay." When I tug him inside the house for the evening, he comes easily.

Dinner is an easy stir-fry on the stovetop. We cut vegetables side by side as music softly floats from my phone. Trevor set up some playlist where we can both add songs we like to it, so it's mostly old-school country and songs that sound like they belong in an eighties cyberpunk movie. Oddly, the songs kind of blend together. Much like Trevor and me.

After dinner, Trevor cleans up the kitchen, while I start a load of our laundry. The easy domesticity of our life together reaffirms that Trevor belongs here with me. Never has someone's presence been such a blessing, so easy, so comforting.

In the middle of dropping our mixed laundry into the washer, I realize that for the first time loneliness isn't eating away at the edges of my life.

I'm not lonely when I'm with Trevor.

"Okay?" Trevor asks from the laundry room doorway.

I drop the rest of the clothes into the machine and press start before turning to face him. His eyes flick over my face, searching for signs of what's on my mind.

"I was so lonely before you," I admit before I can stop myself.

Trevor smiles, soft and slow. "Not anymore though."

"Not anymore."

"We should do a double date with Colby and Eli," Trevor announces, apropos of nothing.

He follows me down the hall towards my bedroom. "Works for me."

"Eli knows I was a fake boyfriend for you."

Turning around, Trevor stops just short of running into me with a surprised sound. My hands land on his hips, holding him still so that he can feel the lack of tension in my body. So he can know there's no danger here, not with me.

"Colby knows already," I tell him.

Trevor releases a relieved sigh, shoulders relaxing. "Good."

"I wasn't planning on telling anyone else. Is that okay?"

He waves his hand dismissively. "Totally. I just didn't want you to be taken by surprise if Eli blurted it out. Sometimes his mouth-to-brain filter doesn't work."

"Are you fine with Colby knowing?"

"Sure." Trevor presses a little closer. "As long as you're fine."

"I'm fine," I murmur just before giving Trevor a slow,

sweet kiss. When I pull away, Trevor's eyes are closed, and a blissful smile tilts his lips up.

"Are you always going to kiss me when I'm riled up?"

With a chuckle, I twirl a piece of his hair around my finger, tugging gently. "Only when you need it most. Did it work?"

"Surprisingly."

"Good."

"Can I sleep with you yet? No funny stuff, just sleeping."

I run my fingers through his hair, detangling the knots, then cup the nape of his neck in my palms. His skin is searing hot against mine, seeping into me to warm me from the outside in. Pressing a kiss to his cheek, his stubble rough against my lips, I nod slowly.

"Alright, sweetheart."

"Made your heart skip a beat?"

"You made it skip two."

"What does that earn me?"

Humming in thought, I rain kisses across his face, smiling when he laughs at my antics. "You can be the big spoon."

"A true reward," Trevor murmurs happily, a sweet smirk on his lips.

Falling asleep with Trevor pressed tight to my back is enough to convince me that maybe he should be the big spoon more often.

Saturdays are restful for most people. Never have been for

me. The farm is in between seasons for U-pick, since strawberries and blueberries are in the spring, but the fall festival starts early in Florida. Kids run around the farm in our play area, their joyful shouts following me as I do my best to work around them.

A frantic Joey hanging out of the food truck window waves me over, so I carefully steer through the crowd towards him. Pumpkins lie scattered around now that the patch is in full swing at the farm. I watch as a little kid tries to pick up one that's too heavy, his father rushing to stop him. A small smile tugs at my lips as the father carefully takes the pumpkin from the overly excited boy.

"I've got to close up. We're out of everything," Joey says in a frenzied rush once I reach the food truck.

Crap. It'll have to be fine.

"That's fine. You've been open for a few hours. The girls are still serving smoothies."

Joey hangs out the window to glance to his left. He chuckles as he looks at the forming line at the smoothie cart. The smoothies use fruit right from the farm, blueberries, strawberries, peaches, anything we grow that can be put into a blender. Not sunflowers though. Although I tried once as a kid, and it went over awfully.

A family with a few young kids grabs smoothies, then wanders off at a leisurely pace towards the pumpkins. My heart does a little skip at the sight of them, and my mind immediately wanders to Trevor. He's hanging out with Eli today, doing something that I have no clue about. Which is just fine with me. I want him to be comfortable here, feel like he's at home. Not feeling like he always has to count on me. Although, I do like him counting on me, needing me.

"I'm closing up, then. You staying for the movie tonight?"

Joey asks as he hops out of the truck, apron flapping in the breeze. He tugs the bandana off his head, letting his sweaty curls flop onto his forehead.

"Yeah," I say. "Trevor's joining me soon."

"Nice." Joey's eyes flick behind me for a brief second. Just long enough for me to trace his gaze back to Lee talking with a few parents at the edge of the property. Things between them have been odd lately, I wish one of them would open up to me about it.

"All good, Joe?"

He grunts in affirmation, then slaps my arm. "I'm going to go home, clean up, then I'll come back for movie night. Give Trevor a good, Clay Springs welcome."

"Thanks, buddy," I call out as he walks towards the employee parking lot. When I look over towards Lee, his gaze is zeroed in on Joey's back. His expression is sort of pained, but also a bit wistful. I know that look.

Lee's gaze snaps to mine and immediately averts his gaze when he notices me watching. Interesting. I'm torn from my thoughts because someone needs my help loading pumpkins into their cart. Typical farm Saturday.

By the time the early evening crowd is leaving, before the ticketed attendees arrive for the movie, I'm beat. When my truck rolls down the road, my tired heart wakes back up. Something about seeing Trevor drive my truck feels natural. He hops out, his gaze pinging around the property as he searches for me.

Waving from my position right outside the office, his gaze finally zeroes in on me. The smile that blooms across his face sends dizzying butterflies to flight in my chest. I'm so done for when it comes to him. The other door of the truck opens to reveal an excited Elijah. No sight of Colby though.

"We're a little early," Trevor admits sheepishly, as if that's a problem.

"Good." I tilt his head up with a finger under his chin to kiss him. "Hi."

His lips twitch as he fights a smile. "Hi."

"Oh, you guys are just barf city," Elijah comments from behind Trevor. "So cute though. Love it."

"Where's Colby?" I ask without tearing my gaze from Trevor.

"Work dinner," Elijah says around an annoyed sigh. "I'm third-wheeling tonight."

"There will be a lot of people here." I tangle my fingers with Trevor's. "You won't be third-wheeling. Plus, it's movie night. Those are quieter nights at the farm."

"Colby sent me with a blanket and those comfortable camping type of chairs," Elijah replies absentmindedly. He cups a hand over his eyes to look at the farm. "I can't believe this is my first time at the farm."

I frown. That can't be true. "Really?"

"Yeah. We've just been busy with other things since I came into town. Colby probably meant to bring me sooner. But you know. Life."

Trevor snorts and shoves an elbow into Elijah's ribs. "You mean you haven't come up for air until now."

Elijah bites his lip. "That too."

"Well, since y'all are here early, I can show y'all around."

"Two y'alls in one statement." Elijah pretends to fan himself, earning a chuckle from me.

"Show us around," Trevor demands softly, eyes practically sparkling. It takes every ounce of restraint inside me to not pull him to me and kiss him senseless.

Keeping our fingers tangled together, I guide Elijah and

Trevor over to the small pumpkin patch. A few families remain, but the crowd has thinned from earlier. After they've had their fill of the pumpkins, I lead them over to where the sunflower fields begin. The sun is still high enough in the sky to shine right on the flowers, so they're facing the sky, with bees buzzing around.

"God, they go on forever," Elijah says in complete awe.

"I'd almost forgotten how magical this place can be," Trevor whispers. I squeeze his fingers, so his gaze swings back to me.

"I'll remind you."

A crimson flush paints his cheeks. Trevor dips his head to avoid my gaze, but the happy smile on his lips is enough for me.

"Barf," Elijah teases, voice full of laughter. He grabs Trevor and drags him into the field of sunflowers, while simultaneously throwing his phone at me. I just narrowly catch it. "Take photos of us!"

Taking photos for people isn't my greatest gift. It's definitely more Andy's job than mine. But I bend my knees like she taught me and try to get the best angle of the beautiful boys out in the field. The sun makes it hard for me to see the screen. Best option is to just hit the capture button as many times as I can which they both seem to appreciate. They go from serious to funny to flirty in the span of seconds.

Elijah runs towards me to grab his phone. He looks through the pictures with a considering look, then smiles up at me. "Good job. Now go out there and take a photo with that gorgeous boy."

He doesn't have to tell me twice. I check behind us to make sure we're alone, save Elijah, then dip Trevor and smother him with a kiss. Trevor laughs against my mouth, and I enthusiastically swallow the taste of his happiness down. The taste of his laugh, of his joy, will always be pure heaven to me. His fingers loosely tangle in my shirt, tugging me closer even as I straighten us back to standing. When I pull away, both of our smiles are dopey. We aim our dazed gazes towards the camera, with our bodies still turned toward one another. Like our bodies are sunflowers searching for the sun, but instead finding one another.

Elijah sends a wink our way. "Those are keepers."

"What time does everything start?" Trevor asks quietly, eyes searching mine.

"Couple of hours."

Trevor bites his lip, hard enough to bruise. His gaze flicks down to my mouth for a moment, before meeting my gaze again.

"You make me happy," Trevor murmurs softly.

I let out a small chuckle. "Same, sweetheart. Wanna know tonight's movie?"

"I want to know!" Elijah shouts from where he's tenderly touching the petals of a sunflower.

Trevor chuckles and pinches my bicep. "Well?"

"One of my mama's favorite fall movies. *Practical Magic*."

Elijah practically swoons. "I love that one!"

"That is a good one," Trevor agrees before sneaking one more kiss.

We spend the next hour or so touring the farm. I shove the two of them into my truck, then take them on a tour of the back property that's not available to the outsiders. Fields of blueberries, strawberries, sunflowers, peaches, and watermelons roll beside us. Most of the berries are past season, so they're just plants now, along with the melons. Those are at their best in spring and early summer. Fall is when the farm winds down, instead focusing on events, and preparing the land for the harvest to come the next spring.

But seeing Trevor in the truck beside me, hair blowing in the wind, looking at the land in awe... well, the feelings rustling around inside me are quickly getting a name. He absorbs every ounce of information from me, eager to learn, to know about the farm that's in my blood. And that his eager attention makes the feelings inside me grow at a scarily rapid rate.

By the time we're done with the tour, people are starting to arrive early for the movie. I help Trevor and Eli get settled towards the front with the blanket and camping chairs Colby sent along with them. Once they're all set, Elijah asks for another photo, and I happily oblige. Of course, that's when Joey finds us.

Joey comes to stand beside me with a teasing smirk. "You're an Instagram boyfriend now, Beau?"

"Shut up." But I send a wink his way.

"Hey, guys." Joey waves at them both with one of his most charming grins. "This is my daughter, Savannah."

Savannah smiles shyly but waves at everyone. Eli dips down to his knees with a warm grin.

"Nice to meet you." Elijah holds out his hand. Savannah looks up at Joey in question, when Joey nods, she gently shakes Elijah's hand. "That's a strong grip you've got there."

"Thank you," Savannah says, voice still shy.

"Sit down, angel."

Folding his long legs to sit, Joey tugs Savannah down to sit beside him. He's got a band holding his black waves out of his eyes, a white T-shirt with the sleeves rolled up, and weathered jeans. Joey's always been a go-with-the-flow type of guy, a friend that I can count on. Back when I was entertaining the whole food-truck thing, Joey had basically told me he'd be running the show. No arguing with him either. It just happened.

Families join us on the slight hill where the projector screen is set up. Murmurs of voices float over us as we all settle on the blanket. It's nice to not have to work an event, to just be able to attend. Leaning back on the blanket, I pull Trevor to me until he's sitting between my legs, his back to my chest. I wrap an arm around him, tucking my face into his neck.

Trevor's fingers dance along my arm. "Pretty heavy on the PDA."

"Wanna be close to you."

"Yeah?" Trevor asks, sounding just shy of breathless.

I nuzzle behind his ear, inhaling the soft scent of him, the comfort of him. "Always wanna be close to you."

Trevor hums in agreement, then settles more deeply into my arms. He wiggles a little, until we're as close as physically possible. I bite at his neck to get him to stop wiggling. His laugh is breathy and his fingers bite into my forearm.

"Hey, Lee," Joey says, breaking me out of my Trevor-induced reverie.

Lee flushes a little at the sight of Joey, but folds to the ground beside Savannah with a sweet smile.

"Hey, bug." Lee nudges Savannah with his knee.

Her grin is blinding as she stares up at Lee. "I was named line leader for next week, Uncle Lee!"

"Oh my God, finally! Such a serious job. Are you prepared?"

Savannah nods eagerly, eyes bright. "Mostly. I think I deserve it more than Shelby. She can't keep anyone on track."

"You are the best choice." Lee nods seriously in agreement. "What's the Halloween plan for this year?"

Sitting up on her knees, she grabs Lee's face between her palms. "I want to be a werewolf, but Dad won't let me."

"Well, I'll have to wear him down," Lee says, but his words are muffled by her small hands.

"You want popcorn, Lee?" Joey asks as he stands up, brushing his hands on his jeans.

Lee shakes his head. "I'm good."

Joey skewers him with a decidedly frustrated look. "Do you *want* popcorn, Lee."

"Fine," Lee grumbles without looking at Joey.

Joey disappears towards the stand where popcorn is sold. Shoulders tense as he walks, his hands are shoved deep into his jean pockets. When I swing my gaze back to Lee, he's steadfastly ignoring my gaze, and giving Savannah all his attention.

The movie starts before I can ask Lee any leading questions. A few moments later Joey returns with multiple popcorn bags for all of us and a bottle of soda. He hands the soda to Lee without looking at him and takes a handful of popcorn for himself.

Honestly, I don't focus much on the movie. My mind stays firmly planted on the man tucked against me. Every now and then he turns his head to sweetly kiss my forearm, sending a surge of emotion so strong through me that I'm afraid it'll topple me over.

Finally, just giving up on the movie, I pay close attention to Trevor's face. His eyes are such a gorgeous shade of blue, like the color of the springs. A small scar sits at the bottom of his chin, faded with age, but I can tell it was gnarly when he first got it. One single mole rests just below his right ear. My eyes drift over his face to memorize him, memorize this perfect moment. Even though I know he'll never leave me again, just knowing his face like the back of my own hand feels like an astonishing accomplishment.

"You're missing the movie," Trevor points out, tone teasing.

"I'm not missing a thing."

Trevor turns to look at me, eyes hooded, lips slightly parted. "Yeah?"

"Can I take you home, sweetheart?" I whisper against his ear.

He shivers, the vibration rolling through his entire body. "Beau, the answer to that question is always going to be yes."

I laugh weakly against his neck. "If we leave now, we'll have to answer questions."

"My God, please leave now. You're making us sick." Joey throws a handful of popcorn at us. "I'll drive Elijah home."

I turn my questioning gaze to Elijah. "That okay?"

Elijah shrugs with a dreamy smile. "You two lovebirds get out of here. Joey will get me home safely or endure Colby's wrath."

Joey winces but laughs. "I'll definitely get you home safely."

That's all the permission I need. Standing in one fluid motion, I pull Trevor up with me, guiding him away from the movie. Multiple people try to stop us, but I don't allow it. I plow right through until we're at the truck. And I can't hold myself back any longer. I press him against the cold metal and take his mouth in a savage kiss. He opens for me, letting my tongue into his mouth to taste him.

His fingers bite into my shoulders, tugging me closer, as his lips move against mine.

I tear from his addictive mouth. "Sweetheart."

He blinks up at me in the dark. "Yeah?"

"Can I have you?" I ask quietly, fingers curling in his hair.

Trevor nods, eyes firmly on me. That's the only answer I need. I safely tuck him into the truck, even buckling him in, earning me a delighted smile from Trevor. I'll have to do that more often just to bring that sort of smile out of him. The road is dark on the drive home, but the night wind is soft as it blows through the window. I mostly keep my eyes on the road, but I can't stop from sneaking looks at him as we drive back home.

Pure happiness radiates from Trevor. The fact that I've made him that way, made him so happy, makes me want to scream with joy. If only I can make him happy for the rest of our lives.

The night is eerily similar to the last time we rushed into the house. When I made love to him. Because that is what happened last time. I was making love to him then, whether either of us could admit it or not. The air is humid, cicadas sing their lullabies, but everything between us is molasses slow. No urgency this time. Tonight isn't for rushing.

Trevor leans against me as we make our way inside under the cloak of darkness. I flip just one light on when we walk in, keeping the house warm, just bright enough to find our way to the bedroom. We take our shoes off together at the front door. I tangle my fingers with Trevor's and tug him towards the bedroom behind me.

At the foot of the bed, I kiss his sweet mouth. Tenderly, lovingly, I pour every ounce of what I feel for him into the kiss. His hair is soft between my fingers, like golden strands of pure silk. The night dips into a drowsy sensual haze as I gently shove Trevor onto the bed, then follow his body with my own. Sitting up halfway, I tug his shirt off, then kiss down his chest. His stomach caves in under the gentle glide of my lips on his skin, and he lets out a sigh full of so much want that my head spins.

His hands on my shoulders stop me at the waistband of his jeans. When I look up at him, his eyes are pleading, bright baby blues shine in the dark of the room.

"Take your shirt off too," Trevor asks breathlessly.

Smirking, I roll to my knees. His gaze travels down my chest, appreciation lighting his gaze. Tossing the shirt to the ground, I run my hands down his sides, squeeze his hips, then tug him closer to me.

"That's your one request for the night. The rest of tonight is gonna go how I want it to go. You understand?"

Trevor swallows loudly. "How do you want it to go?"

"Well," I trail off and run my fingers along the golden skin of his stomach. "First, I'm going to suck you until you're begging me to fuck you. Then I'll fuck you, in as many positions as you can handle, eating at your mouth the entire time. Only when you can't handle any more, when you've begged sweetly, will I allow you to come."

"Jesus," Trevor whispers, eyes dark and stormy. "What about you?"

"Don't you worry about me, sweetheart. I can go all night as long as I've got you on the edge. Tonight is about you."

"No." Trevor angrily shakes his head and leans up to get close to my face. "Tonight's about us."

I take his face in my palms and devour his mouth. The kiss is rough, just shy of painful, but it unlocks something inside of my heart all the same. Suddenly, the night isn't going how I thought it would. How I imagined. Trevor fights me for dominance, pushing at me until I fall to my back with my head at the end of the bed. He climbs on top of me, takes my wrists in his tight grip, and holds them over my head.

His chest heaves, his eyes blown wide with burning desire. From this close I can count his dark blond eyelashes, see the flecks of light blue around the edge of his irises. The emotion in his eyes echoes inside of me.

"You gonna be in charge tonight, sweetheart?"

Trevor nods, swallowing so hard that his throat bobs. "Can I?"

"You can have me."

Despite the inches and pounds of muscle I have on Trevor, he makes me feel small when he leans over me to take my mouth in a syrupy-sweet kiss. Like drinking lemonade in the sunflower fields in the middle of June is how his kiss makes me feel. Free and unworried.

He lets go of my wrists to kiss down my neck, biting at the tender skin there, before slowly kissing down my chest. Tongue dipping around my belly button, I tremble with need beneath him. Bottoming isn't a frequent occurrence for me, just a handful of times over the years, and every time is ranked pretty low on my list of sexual encounters. Doesn't mean I don't like to be fucked. A dildo can go a long way in that department.

My size usually makes me the easy choice to top when it comes to sex. But Trevor doesn't make me feel that way at all. I might be bigger and broader, but Trevor is just as strong as me. He works hard for his muscles, and he easily makes me feel small, in a way that I never expected to love, maybe even crave.

Once my jeans are unbuckled and halfway down my thighs, he mouths at my clothed cock, soaking my underwear. Jesus. Pleasure simmers low in my gut. Trevor's going to ruin me and I'm going to be happy about it. Thrilled. Overjoyed. Happy doesn't cut it.

My jeans fall to the floor of the bedroom in a hush of sound. When I blink back Trevor's way, he's struggling out of his jeans, swear words falling from his lips. I bite my lip to stop myself from laughing. I like knowing I've got him so caught up that he can't remain composed, that he needs me so badly he's struggling to get undressed.

He lies back over me, face close enough to kiss, but just out of reach.

"So, first on the list was sucking me until I couldn't handle it anymore, right?"

I nod and he smiles sweetly down at me. "Yeah."

"Mmm." Trevor kisses my eyebrow, making my chest tighten with desire. He rubs his clean-shaven cheek against my own bearded one. "You are so good, Beau. You deserve to be cherished and worshiped. By the time we're done, you won't remember your own name, but you'll remember mine."

A wicked smirk curls Trevor's lips up as he slowly crawls down my body. He kisses just under my belly button before sliding my underwear off without an ounce of fanfare. Before I can even steel myself for what's to come next, he takes my cock all the way to the back of his throat, choking on it, and aiming those cerulean eyes at me.

"Fuck," I mutter around a shocked gasp.

Trevor works his shoulders under my thighs so that my legs are draped over them, heels resting on his lower back. He works me over slowly, covering my cock with his spit, sending sparks of ecstasy dancing down my spine. The edge is already perilously close. My fingers twitch at my sides, aching to grip his hair, forcing him to choke on my cock until tears pour from his eyes.

But he's steering the ship tonight.

Right when I'm at the edge of bursting, he abruptly pulls off my cock. He smirks up at me, fingers digging painfully into my hips.

"That was one."

I blink rapidly in confusion until I realize what he's saying. "How many times should I prepare to be edged?"

Trevor shrugs easily, eyes still on me. "Let's see how I feel in an hour."

An hour? He's going to kill me. He takes me back into the warmth of his mouth, sucking me down, then rolls his tongue around the head of my cock. My body quakes underneath him, thighs trembling, sweat dotting every inch of my flaming skin. I throw my arm over my eyes to block the sight of him out, hoping maybe that'll help me last. But it was fruitless, because Trevor could suck me off in a dark room and I'd still be at the edge with just one touch of his lips to my cock.

"Please," I whisper as he pulls off again, leaving my cock angry and weeping.

"Please what?" Trevor asks sweetly.

"I want to come."

"There's a difference between want and need, love."

And then he takes me back into his mouth again. I lose count of how many times we repeat the same process. When he pulls off me again, I almost cry. Tears swim in my eyes. No one has ever edged me before, at least not like this. Not to the point that I feel like I'm going to crawl out of my skin if I don't come. Just on the edge of pain.

I swallow a cry and toss my forearm back over my eyes.

"Beau," Trevor whispers softly. He tugs my forearm from my eyes, forcing me to look up into his tender gaze. "You need to come?"

I nod quickly. "Please let me come. I can't... I can't do it anymore. It's too much."

Trevor nods once in understanding. "You want to come in my mouth? Or with my cock inside you?"

"Are those my only choices?"

Cocking his head to the side, he stares down at me, eyes filled with heat. His fingers affectionately brush the hair on my chest.

"You want something else?"

"I want to come in your mouth, then you fuck me after, use my body."

Trevor lets out a small rush of air. "Yeah?"

I nod just before Trevor devours my mouth. He tastes like me and him, like us. I close my eyes against the swirl of emotions inside me. The urge to cry is still there, but for different reasons than just seconds ago.

This is the man that came back for me. Even after waiting, he still came back, and he held me in one of the worst, hardest moments of my life. Trusting him to take me apart and put me back together is one of the easiest things I'll ever do. Because he'll always put me back together. Just like I have his back, he's got mine. My Trevor. My Levi. My man.

Trevor pulls away from my mouth and murmurs, "I'll get you ready while I suck you off, okay?"

Instead of answering with words, I roughly shove Trevor down my body, eliciting the most gorgeous laugh from him. Sex without laughter is miserable. Laughter in the bedroom is a level of honesty that makes it even more pleasurable for me. Always has. And Trevor's laugh lights me up inside, adding to the quaking need coursing through my veins.

He dives back down on my cock, like a man possessed. I gasp as pleasure rolls through me like a gentle wave. The pleasure ramps up when a lubed finger presses against me for entry. I bear down and an unabashed moan escapes me as his finger slips in past the resistance. By the time he's got two fingers inside me, I'm beyond sure that my orgasm is going to cause a natural event.

I try to warn him, but words won't come. All I can do is squeeze my thighs to his head, feeling his hair fall over my sweat-dampened skin, and ride out my orgasm as it takes over. Shivers wrack my entire body as he continues to swallow me down until I'm wrung completely dry. Nothing left inside me. All of it for him.

"Perfect, Beau." Trevor leans up to kiss the corner of my eye. "Now I'm going to fuck you."

My body is pleasantly loose as he gently guides me onto my stomach. Instead of positioning me onto my knees, he keeps my chest on the bed, then splays my legs out wide. The position is a little awkward, but I trust Trevor. Kisses rain down on my back as he rubs his bare cock over my hole. A moan rattles through me, just at the idea of him fucking me bare.

"Let me in," Trevor demands, voice hush quiet in the dark of the room.

A quiet moan leaves me as he slides past the first ring of muscle, giving me just a few moments to adjust before sliding the rest of the way in. His warm breath washes over my neck as he bottoms out. Every few seconds he grinds into me, forcing needy whimpers to fall from my parted lips.

"So good." Trevor nips at my ear as he grinds his cock deeper into me. Sweat drips from him and down onto my flushed skin, sending a ripple of pleasure down my spine. "You feel so good around my cock. Made for me. You know what your name means? It means handsome. Handsome and beautiful," Trevor says roughly against my cheek before sweetly gliding his lips over mine in a tease of a kiss. "The most beautiful soul on earth."

The words light me up inside, infusing me with delicious warmth. Warm with Trevor's love. Warm with his adoration. He abruptly stills inside me, panting roughly against my neck. A shiver rolls through me at the feel of him so hard inside me, his lips wet against my overheated skin. The weight of his body over me, shielding me from the world, is the most glorious thing I've ever felt.

"Fuck. I wanted to last longer but you feel so good."

"Come inside me," I beg, voice broken, hallowed out.

Trevor bites my shoulder hard with a pained groan. "Jesus."

Pushing his forehead against my cheek, Trevor barrels into me. The gentle lovemaking evaporates as he seeks his own pleasure in my lax body. He tangles his fingers with my own, thrusting one final time, trembling over my body while he comes with an almost pained gasp. Emotion overwhelms me at the feel of his cum deep inside me, adding to my already heightened emotional state. For the first time in my life, someone made love to me, to my body, and to my heart.

"Beau," Trevor says reverently.

"I love you," I admit, too wrung out to hold the words back.

Trevor gently turns my face on the bed, so he can look deeply into my eyes. His lips quirk up on one side. "I love you too. Have for a long time. Probably since the moment I walked through those airport doors and saw you standing beside the truck. My heart has been yours ever since."

"You won't leave me again, right?" I ask, heart tender and bruised.

Trevor sighs softly, dropping his forehead to my cheek. "Never again, I promise. We take care of each other now."

He pulls slowly out of me, treating me with enough tenderness to make my heart ache. I lie there quietly as he moves around the room, waiting for him to rejoin me at the bed. His hands are exceedingly gentle as he helps me up and guides me to the bathroom. The shower is small, but he somehow makes us both fit. Gently, he washes me under the hot water, placing gentle kisses along the skin he deems kiss-worthy. His fingers work at the muscles of my back until I'm a puddle in his arms. Trevor chuckles against my cheek and murmurs softly, "I've got you, Beau."

I've never believed a sentence more. He does have me; in every way a person can have someone.

By the time Trevor's got us clean, dry, and bundled back in the bed, sleep comes for me like a thief in the night. Quick and easy.

CHAPTER SEVENTEEN
TREVOR

Making love to Beau changed something between us irrevocably. The way Beau had shivered at my touch, trembled when I told him I loved him, will be burned into my memory forever. Just those simple words along with the lovemaking seemed to settle something inside of Beau that had been restless. Maybe a small part of him will always expect me to run away, but leaving Beau now would be akin to ripping my own heart out of my chest. Leaving will never be an option again.

"Ready?" Beau asks from behind me, startling me from my introspection.

Turning around, I find Beau in dark jeans, a T-shirt that hugs every beautiful inch of his chest, and camel dress shoes that I didn't even realize he owned. Keys to the Chevy dangle from his fingers as he cocks his head, trying to figure out what I'm thinking. One day I know he'll be able to look at me and just know, the very thought comforts me.

"Ready." I stride towards him, only coming to a stop once I can loop my arms around his neck. Pressing up on my toes, I kiss his forehead, then let my lips linger on his mouth just long enough to steal his breath.

"Sweetheart," Beau murmurs softly, tone heart-achingly tender.

"Aw, I got you." I drop down to the soles of my feet and send him a cheeky wink.

Beau's cheeks darken just enough to make me smile. "You could take it easy on me sometimes."

"No fun in that," I tease.

His lips quirk to the side. "Guess not. Let's go. Mama probably already has her trademark dip out and I'm sure Colby is already there eating it up."

"Not if Eli can distract him as easily as I can distract you," I sing as we make our way out to the Chevy.

Beau opens the door for me, then carefully buckles me in. If anyone else tried to care for me the way Beau does, I'd probably start a world war. But with Beau it feels too much like love to let it rile me. The night air is cool as we roll the windows down. I toss my hair up in a haphazard bun just so that I don't have a million knots by the time we arrive at our destination.

"You'll take it back down once we get to Mama's?" Beau asks loudly, over the rushing sound of the wind through the windows.

"Whatever you want, Beau."

Beau rolls his eyes, but a sweet smile twitches his lips under the dark shadow of his beard. Leaning my head against the headrest, a contented smile makes my cheeks ache. Beau parks in front of his mother's house, the one I remember from all those months ago. I was here for sadder reasons before, and tonight feels full of joy in comparison.

The beautiful sound of Eli's laughter fills the house as we make our way inside, hands tightly grasped between us. The soft murmur of voices leads us to the kitchen. Beau's hand is a steadying weight at the base of my spine. The sight that greets us is Colby devouring the dip at the table, Eli tucked against his side, with Andy at the head of the table fighting Colby for the dip. Beau's mom stands at the stove, chuckling at the antics of the adult children at the table. The atmosphere is so cozy, so warm, so *happy*, that I remind myself that this is what a home should feel like. This is family.

Eli's gaze pings to me and he grins wide. "Hi!"

I shyly wave at everyone. Beau's mom turns around, grinning when she spots me. With a cock of her head, she invites me over to join her at the stove. I head that way with a curious look over my shoulder at Beau. The man just shrugs in answer.

"Do you like chicken and dumplings?" Cindy questions, glasses slipping down her nose giving her the aura of a sweet librarian.

"Never had them."

Cindy whistles softly. "You're missing out. They're the ultimate comfort food. I always made them for the kids when they needed just a little extra love. Help me with the dumplings?"

Cindy has a way of making me feel so comfortable, even when it's something I don't understand. I help her whisk all the ingredients for dumplings in a metal bowl. Then she shows me how to spoon mix, then drop into the savory smelling thick soup. Chicken's been torn apart, vegetables look mushy, and when I eye the mixture critically, Cindy just chuckles.

"I know it looks unappealing, but I promise it tastes amazing. You're doing great with the dumplings, honey."

Butterflies take flight in my chest at her sweet praise. "Yeah?"

A soft smile turns her lips up. "Great job, I promise. How's my son treating you?"

I glance over my shoulder at Beau to find him competing with Colby for the dip on the table. Andy smacks Beau's hand and he pulls it away with a deep frown.

"I love him."

Cindy's eyes soften as our gazes meet again. "And he loves you." She slowly stirs the mixture on the stove, a contemplative look crossing her face. "When you find love so special, so true, you hold on to it as long as you can."

I clear my throat awkwardly. "I'll hold on to him as long as he'll let me."

Cindy just keeps stirring the pot, obviously not feeling the need to reply to me. With a nod of her head, she sends me back over to the table, and I stand by Beau, curving my palm around the nape of his neck. He aims a sweet smile up at me and rests his hand at the small of my back again.

Beau keeps his conversation with Colby going, but his thumb dips into the waist of my pants, carefully swiping at the warm skin he finds. The weight of his touch brings the comfort it always does, easing the bubbling nerves inside me that started simmering the moment we walked into the house.

Eli cocks his head, gaze knowing. "You love him?" Eli mouths at me.

I nod rapidly, then use my fingers to cover my smiling lips. Eli grins at me as he takes Colby's hand in his own. Colby looks down at Eli with a tender smile, eyes only for his boyfriend.

Colby wraps his arm around the back of Eli's chair. "How's life treating you in Clay Springs so far, Trevor?"

Beau's hand squeezes my hip tightly. I flick him an easy smile. "Good. Slow and sweet, two things I never knew I needed."

"I heard you've been going on runs with Eli."

I snort. "I've been going on runs and Eli tries to keep up."

"I'm trying to focus on cardiovascular health," Eli argues, a hint of a whine in his voice.

A curious smirk tilts up Colby's lips. "Aiming to run a marathon?"

Eli rolls his eyes affectionately. "Aiming to run something."

"Everything shaping up for the fall festival?" Colby asks once he can tear his gaze away from a blushing Eli.

Beau shrugs, face completely calm despite the nerves I know lie beneath. The man is a duck, calm on the surface, violently paddling under the water. "Mostly. It's always fine."

Colby's eyes drill in on Beau, studying him. I wonder if Colby can see what I see too. I've wondered the past few weeks just how deeply his family looks at him. Can they read his tells like I can? Or do they just take him at his word. Colby seemingly takes Beau at his word though, which shocks me into speaking.

"This is the first one since your dad," I point out softly. "Are you sure you're fine? Do you need extra help?"

Colby's eyes widen at my words, but Beau's gaze softens on me. I run my hand up and down his back, hoping to encourage him into sharing the reality of his situation. Beau clears his throat uncomfortably, then runs his left hand roughly along his trimmed beard.

"It's a little rougher than I expected. If you could help opening weekend, Colby, that'd be great."

Beau's words are heavy, laced with vulnerability. Love for him swirls inside me, until I feel like it could pour out of me, and right into him. Colby looks from me, then to Beau, his fingers tapping on the table. The restless tapping has Eli laying his hand over Colby's, steadying whatever emotion gripped Colby.

"Sure, Beau. Anything you ask. You know that's how it is."

Beau smiles, but it doesn't meet his eyes. "I know."

Andy's eyes meet mine and a grateful smile graces her lips. I nod at her, knowing that Beau never would've said a word without my nudging. He has a long way to go with asking for help, but I know that I'll get him there when he learns it's safe, it's okay to trust that other people want to help him. Especially the loving family surrounding this table. Maybe they took him for granted for years, but now that I'm here, that's going to change. Beau deserves to be supported.

I chance a look towards Cindy in the kitchen to find her gaze firm on me. A small thankful smile tilts her lips at the corners and tears rim the edges of her eyes. I try to smile at her in case she's upset, but the tremble of my smile feels shaky even to myself. She nods just slightly once, before turning back around to finish with dinner.

Maybe in some way we all needed one another. I needed this family, and Beau needed me to learn to ask for help. I've never been much for destiny or fate, but if it exists, then I think maybe the universe had a hand in leading me here to Beau, to these people. Belonging is the word that comes to mind. For the first time in my life, I belong somewhere. Not just somewhere, but with Beau.

While Cindy plates the food, I finally take a seat beside Beau. A smile bursts out of me when his hand rests firmly on my thigh, warm and comforting. The guys chat about the farm, catching up on things that I don't understand yet, but I know one day I will. Andy has her head in her phone, a frown marring her face.

"Everything okay, Andy?" Cindy asks as she sets a plate of food down in front of her.

"Actually," Andy says around a grimace. "I've got to go. Harper."

Beau, Colby, and Cindy all quickly tense, eyes firm on Andy.

"He's okay?" Colby follows up.

Andy stands, kisses her mom's cheek, then dips down to kiss Beau's. "Been a rough night for him."

The phrase must be code because the three of them relax from high alert. Cindy bustles around the kitchen to fill two tupperware containers full of chicken and dumplings. She returns to shove the containers into Andy's waiting arms.

"Make Harper eat this when his appetite returns."

Andy smiles softly. "Will do, Mama." Andy aims a grimace at me and Eli. "Sorry, I hate to miss this cute little double date, but I'm sure we'll have hundreds of these for years to come."

We all watch Andy leave, arms folded around the warm food containers.

"What's wrong with Harper?" I ask in a soft whisper.

Beau's contemplative for a few moments, before softly murmuring, "Harper has epilepsy. Sometimes his seizures are controlled, sometimes not. Andy and him are really close."

Cindy's gaze finally tears from the door, and she fixes her own food. I look down at my plate, weary at how the food looks, but I can't deny it smells amazing. Hard to describe. But it smells a little like how I assume home should smell. Once Cindy joins the table, she grins around at everyone.

"It's not Thanksgiving, but I wanted to say how thankful I am for all of you. It's been a rough year, but every single one of you has made it easier in one way or another." Tears rim her eyes, but she blinks them away. "Anyway, let's eat before it cools."

Beau's hand stays warm on my thigh as I grab my spoon. Everyone around the table digs in without a word, even Eli closes his eyes in bliss, so it must be good. I load my spoon up, then take a bite, and suddenly I understand why everyone is silent. It tastes like heaven on my tongue. Savory and warm and comforting. I feel like I blink, and my plate is empty.

A chuckle sounds from beside me, just before Beau stands. He goes into the kitchen, refills our plates, then plops a plate down on the table with a knowing smile. That's how I finish two entire plates of chicken and dumplings. Suddenly, I have a new favorite meal. If I had to choose one meal to eat for the rest of my life, it would probably be this one. It's not just that the food is good, but that it's made with love. My stomach and heart are full by the time I'm done with my meal.

Dinner winds down, and the boys stand side by side in the kitchen doing dishes.

Cindy fixes cups of coffee, and places creamer and sugar on the table. I add some sugar and a splash of creamer, before taking a grateful sip. Eli grins at me over his mug that says *oh, bless your heart* with a middle finger painted below the words. I snort against the rim of my mug.

"How long have you two known each other?" Cindy asks, gaze pinging between us.

"A few years," Eli says easily. "We met at our old job."

"And what job was that?" Cindy takes a sip of her coffee, not realizing the can of worms she's trying to open.

Colby and Beau both freeze, simultaneously turning to look at us over their shoulders.

With a wicked grin, I say, "We were in customer service together."

Cindy makes a contemplative sound. "Interesting."

And that's that.

After dessert of pudding pie, the four of us amble outside, stomachs full, and cheeks aching from smiling. I never thought I could have a life like this one. Never thought I deserved something like this. For so many years I punished myself for the crimes of my parents, thinking I deserved to be treated like less than to make up for their sins. The beauty of life is so easy to see when I'm focusing on *my* life, and what I want to take from it.

At this very moment, that means letting Beau buckle me into the Chevy, drive me home, and make love to me so fiercely that I feel put back together, even after he takes me apart.

CHAPTER EIGHTEEN

TREVOR

O ur feet pound the packed gravel road as we jog, drenched by sweat in the late September heat. Shadows cut across the road from the oak trees, slashing sunlight through the trees. Eli grunts beside me as he works hard to keep up.

"You're doing better than you were," I huff out.

Eli runs a hand over his sweaty forehead, pushing at the curls that have escaped from his sweatband. "You could go slower."

I chuckle. "I'm already running at half pace, half pint."

Eli tosses me an aggrieved look but doesn't reply.

We finish up our run in silence, ending up back at his and Colby's place. I quietly follow Eli up to the apartment over Colby's garage. These two are ridiculous. I've moved into Beau's house, basically living in his bedroom now too, but Colby and Eli are still trying to give the pretense of dating and living separately. My bet is that Eli will move into Colby's house before the end of October.

Whiskey greets us, tail wagging enthusiastically, as we enter the apartment. Her silliness earns a laugh out of me.

"Seriously?" I ask as Eli tosses a bottle of water at my head.

Eli skewers me with a hard look. "She likes it here with me when Colby is working. What should I do? Leave her in the big house all by herself?"

"No. You should move into the big house so you can both be over there."

Eli sucks on his teeth in thought. "It's too soon."

"My belongings are still in the guest room, but I sleep in Beau's room every night."

Shaking his head at me, Eli gives Whiskey a few pats. "You guys have been dancing around each other for over a year though. It's different. Makes sense for you."

"If that's how you get yourself to sleep at night, honey."

We toss our sweaty selves onto the small sofa in Eli's apartment. Whiskey pants down at us, tongue hanging out of her mouth as she seeks our attention. I give her a few sweet pats on her head. Comfortable silence fills the room while we come down from our run, sipping at our ice-cold waters.

"Are you coming to the start of the fall festival this weekend?" Eli asks.

I press the cold bottle of water to my neck. "Yeah, probably. If Beau asks."

"Colby's working the event, so I'll be there. Jackson and Benji were talking about trying to make the trip down. Asking if they can stay here."

"Miss them," I murmur. Whiskey tilts her head, so I give her a few gentle ear scratches. Must be a good spot because her leg starts to go, making Eli chuckle softly.

"Benji's contracting with Nolan for like a year for that

world tour. Anyway, he's been *kind of* texting about it in the group chat. It's all hush-hush, but you know how it is with Nolan."

I rub a hand over my face. I remember exactly how it was with Nolan. "I've been bad about reading our group chat. Y'all need to do updates at the end of the day for everything I miss throughout the day."

"Like a *what you missed on Glee* sort of thing?"

Such an Eli thing to suggest. "Yeah, like that."

Eli salutes me with a playful smirk. "Ready for work, sir."

We hang out for a while longer, but mostly just so I can give Whiskey more love.

She's such a good girl. How much convincing will it take for Beau to let us get a dog?

The house is quiet when I walk through the back door. Just confirming the idea of us needing a dog. Us. Warmth blooms in my stomach just from thinking of me and Beau as an us.

My phone buzzes in my pocket as I wait for the shower to heat up. Thinking it's just the group chat, I pull it out, only to be accosted with the caller ID of the number for my mother's federal prison. Suddenly, I am just so over it all. Anger so fierce, so consuming rolls through me, that with one single blink, the mirror is shattered before me.

My phone lies amongst glass in the porcelain sink of Beau's bathroom.

Fuck.

My hands tremble violently as I stare down at the scattered pieces of broken mirror around the bathroom. Oh, God. Suddenly, air can't get into my lungs. The bathroom is too small, the air too thick from the steam. I don't know how long

I stand there, just staring at my cracked reflection in the fogged bathroom mirror.

No more running away. I won't run away. There's nowhere that I can go where the sins of my parents won't follow me. Where they won't reach me. I've just got to learn to deal with this head-on. I've got to... I don't know what I need to do but it's not this. Hiding myself away under the crumbling weight of their crimes is no longer an option.

Beau finds me staring listlessly at the broken glass shards.

"What happened?" Beau asks, voice full of concern.

I take a trembling, small breath. "I got a call from the federal prison. I just..."

"Alright." Beau gently grabs my forearm, tugging me until I'm out of the bathroom scattered with dangerous glass. "I'm going to clean this up, then we're going to talk. Can you go sit on the porch?"

Nodding in agreement, I head out to the porch in a fuzzy daze. The cool night air washes over me, settling my rapidly beating heart. Running my hands through my still-sweaty hair, I turn in circles for a few moments, before settling my gaze on the patch of forest at the back of Beau's property.

"Talk to me," Beau says from where he stands at the open sliding glass door. "You wanna run?"

"No," I tell him firmly. I don't want to run. At all.

"What do you want, then?"

"I want to just... not care anymore. Not give a shit."

"I think that sort of thing takes time. You're the psychologist though."

Such a simple statement, but he's right. I cover my face with my hands and laugh because that's all I know how to do.

"Maybe I just need to tell my parents I don't want anything to do with them."

Beau nods reassuringly. "You could do that."

"It's scary."

"I bet," Beau says, taking a few careful steps closer to me. "You need to break free of them if you want a future here. You can heal with me, be safe with me, like I know I'm always safe with you. But I need to know you're doing the work here, sweetheart. You don't want me to fix everything for you, and I won't, but it hurts my heart to see you like this over a phone call."

"I know," I whisper brokenly.

"So, tell me what you want and I'll support you. We'll make it happen. Tell me what you need." Beau takes my face in his hands, sweetly swiping his thumbs under my eyes to get rid of the tears that I didn't even know had fallen. "I love you."

"Sorry about the mirror," I say in reply to his sweet love declaration.

He chuckles softly, eyes warm and intent on me. "I'm not worried about that mirror at all. When do you want to talk to them? Both at the same time, separately?"

"I think maybe I need to write them a letter. Everything with your mother... It showed me what real parents offer to their children. I think if I spell it out, maybe in some deep, hidden part of them, they'll understand."

One of Beau's eyebrows arches. "Want to do it now? No better time than the present."

I nod, unable to say the words. Beau disappears into his bedroom, returning with a legal pad and a fountain pen. "Here. Write it all out. Everything you feel, everything you want to say to give yourself peace. Then we can mail it together. How's that sound?"

I lean up on my toes to kiss his stubbled cheek. "I love you."

Beau's cheeks turn ruddy, but he doesn't reply. He just leaves me alone in the dining room to write the letter. I sit down and stare at the legal pad for a while. I'm not even sure where to start. But it's something I have to do to get my life where I want it to be. To give myself the freedom to love, to heal, to just fucking *live* my own life instead of theirs. And maybe that's all I need to say.

The pen scratches against the paper as I write my truth.

Dear Turner and Lyla,

Thank you for all the privileges you afforded me growing up. The private schools, the nice clothing, and the fancy cars. But I think I deserved more. I deserved to be loved and cherished, to be looked at as more than something you were checking off a list. I have been bearing the brunt of your crimes for the past few years, punishing myself for sins that aren't my own.

I don't think you truly understand or will ever understand how horrible your crimes were and remain. You stole livelihoods from people. I can't spend my life trying to make up for your wrongdoings and it's not fair to ask me to.

This letter is my goodbye. I will always love you, but your love isn't healthy for me anymore. Your love causes me immense pain, because it's transactional, not unconditional. I won't be sending money to your prison accounts, and I won't be visiting. Please don't try to find me, don't reach out to me. It's my turn to live my life as selfishly as I want to. I've found love and a place to start over, that is my selfish wish that I'm going to hold on to forever.

Maybe one day we'll find our way back to one another. Maybe then we can heal, but for now we need to part ways. Please respect my wishes.

Respectfully,
Levi

A tear escapes my eye, tracking heavily down my cheek. I rub the wetness away against my shoulder and sniffle to prevent the flood of tears that so badly want to come. I'm done crying over them. It feels like a closed loop, like maybe my life started the day I found Clay Springs. I will the tears away, just in time for Beau to quietly join me at the dining table.

"Feel better?" Beau asks, eyes searching mine.

"Loads." I inhale deeply, then blow it out through my nose. "I wish I had done that years ago. Didn't have the strength until you told me it was an option."

"Sometimes we don't know what we need until we're safe."

Isn't that the truth? I throw my arms around Beau's neck and kiss his sweet mouth. We kiss under the dying light of day filtering through the windows, until our lips are bruised, until I'm sure I'll remember the weight of Beau's lips when I close my eyes to go to sleep at night.

The feeling is so profound, so deep, that the urge to share it with Claire overwhelms me. She's been quiet since I returned to Clay Springs, replying to messages, but mostly staying to herself. I worry about her so much.

"I'd like to tell Claire about the letter and have her meet you."

Beau's grin is wide and gorgeous, crinkling his eyes at the corner. "No time like the present."

Biting my lip, I pull up her contact card and press Face-Time. Moments later, her sweet face fills the screen. I can already tell she's in her office, despite the majority of us now being off the market. That's the workaholic in her.

"Hi," I say softly, carefully arranging the phone to keep Beau out of the screen.

"Long time no see."

I roll my eyes. "I fell in love."

Her smile is bittersweet. "I think it was time."

"I'm cutting contact with my parents."

Her eyes soften, her smile too. That's my best friend. "I'm proud of you. Truly, Trevor. I know how hard that is, trust me, you know that I get it."

I laugh softly, fighting back tears. Too much crying lately. "I know. I'm writing them a letter, telling them how I feel. And I'm staying in Clay Springs. Indefinitely. I know we talked about me not doing escort services anymore, but I'm also done with being a fake boyfriend." I glance over at Beau and send him the sweetest smile I can muster. "I'm starting life over here. For me this time. I wish you'd come visit."

Claire sighs. "Maybe soon. I have my own... baggage."

My gaze falls on her again, taking in her messy hair, shadows under her eyes. I so wish she'd open up to me, lean on me the way she's allowed me rare moments of vulnerability with her. "You can tell me anything. I'm here for you no matter what. Always."

"I know, love. Now, can I meet your man?"

Always an expert at deflection. But I let her change the topic, knowing she's just as uncomfortable being vulnerable as I am. A product of the way we were raised, for show, not for love. I press against Beau and pull the phone further away so we both fit into the screen. Beau smiles shyly and waves, a flush blooming across his cheeks. Unable to stop myself, I kiss his stubbled cheek.

Claire sighs happily, sounding like lovestruck Eli. "Very sweet and dreamy. You'll take care of my best friend, Beau Callahan?"

"Always," Beau swears, the word holding a deeper meaning than Claire will ever know. "You're always welcome here too. Any friend of Trevor's is a friend of mine."

Her eyes sharpen, mouth twitching a little at the corners. "I'll remember that."

Beau squeezes my neck, then disappears into the bedroom, giving me and Claire a little bit of privacy. I bring the camera closer so my face takes up the entire screen.

"Are you sure you're okay? Is Davis still there?"

Claire winces slightly, but I see her clearly. "He's still here as my assistant."

"Claire..."

She shakes her head. "I'm not ready yet. One day. I love you very much. Please send me pictures constantly. Maybe enough pictures will convince me to take a vacation to come visit you."

"Alright. I love you."

Claire kisses the phone screen. "I love you too."

And then she's gone. I sit silently for a few moments, thinking over the entire interaction. I want so badly to demand she come here, tell me everything that's wrong, but that's not the way to get her here. I have to wait her out. I only hope it's not too long.

I find Beau in his bedroom, changing into comfortable clothes. I tilt my head at him curiously, and he chuckles at the sight of me. He strides over and kisses me firmly.

"I want to take you somewhere," Beau says once we pull apart.

I run my fingers through his beard. "You've got work tomorrow. We can just stay here."

"No. This is important. Come on."

He gently manhandles me into the bathroom. I've never taken a quicker shower. Beau dresses in light clothing, long cargo pants, a long-sleeve shirt, and a ball cap. Curious. I lift an eyebrow in question, but he just hands a similar outfit to me.

"Don't want to get bitten too much," Beau explains.

Mosquitos. So, we're going somewhere outside. I hurriedly dress in the clothes he gives me, then eagerly follow him out to the old truck. Angling my head awkwardly, I notice a bag in the bed, along with a few other supplies that I can't make out in the dark. The door slams behind Beau as he climbs into the truck. His hand settles on my thigh as we reach the main road, heading who knows where.

Stars blink above us due to the absence of clouds in the night sky. The air is still warm, despite it almost being October, because Florida summer lasts until November. Gravel turns to dirt as Beau turns us onto a new road. His hand squeezes my thigh to reassure me that he's got me, that I'm safe with him, but he doesn't need to do that. Because I know. I've always known.

The truck rumbles to a stop by a river, but even from this distance I can tell it's clear. Probably spring fed. Maybe we're close to our spring. The trees are sparse where the truck is parked, so there's a direct line to the gorgeous night sky.

Beau hops out of the truck, then comes around to open the door on my side. He stares at me for a few moments before tilting his head.

"Take your hair down for me?"

A warm flush spreads over me at his request. But I do as he asks. I take the tie out of my hair, letting it fall loose around my shoulders. Beau aims a pleased grin my way, before tugging me out of the car, towards the back of the truck.

Fondness swells inside me as I watch as Beau lays a pile of blankets out on the bed of the truck, then tosses a few pillows around for comfort. He aims a shy look at me over his shoulder. My sweet Beau. I hope he never makes my heart feel like it's about to take flight. I can't imagine that day. Hope I never live to see it if it ever comes.

"I thought we could stargaze for a bit, just hold one another. I want to slow dance with you first though. How's that sound?"

He somehow always knows exactly what I need, what my soul needs.

I swallow around the lump of emotion in my throat. "That sounds perfect, Beau."

He smiles awkwardly and tugs me into the safe cage of his arms. The air is humid, almost damp, but I don't care. Because being in Beau's arms makes everything else melt away. Until it's just me and him under a cloudless sky. The whole world is just us. No matter where we are, the world can be narrowed down to just Beau and me. Such a wonderful thing.

"You're so good to me," I tell him as he sways me to only the sound of the water, cicadas, and wind rustling through the trees.

"Someone has to be. Figure it ought to be me."

"Am I good to you too? I make you happy?"

Beau's eyes practically sparkle. "Sweetheart, just knowin'

you chose me makes me the happiest man in the world. Love you more than anything else in this world."

"More than the springs? More than the farm?"

It's a stupid game to play, but I just feel like teasing him. But when he aims a perfect, warm smile at me, I melt even further into his strong arms. Being weak with Beau will always be perfectly safe.

"I'd give all that up for you in a heartbeat."

I lay my head against his chest while we sway to a tuneless song. "I'd never ask you to though."

"And that's why you mean the world to me."

We dance a little longer before climbing into the bed of the truck. Beau tugs me to lie against his chest as we stare up at the sky. The stars blink down at us, as our future unfolds, big and beautiful. My future is here in Clay Springs, with Beau, with a family I'll build for myself.

SEPTEMBER ROLLS BY WITH NIGHTS SPENT BY OUR RIVER, EVENTS at the farm, and hangouts with Colby and Eli. Hard to believe I've only been in Clay Springs for a couple of weeks. Time moves so slowly here that sometimes I wonder if I really ever did have a life before. Like this is the place maybe I've always belonged. Childhood in New York City seems so distant now, almost as if it never really happened at all. In some odd way, my life began when I found Clay Springs, when I found Beau.

It took me a few days to work up the nerve to mail the letter, but I did, with Beau standing beside me at the post office as I dropped the letter into the receptacle. Such a huge step, but one that I'll always be proud of myself for taking.

Pride in myself is new, but I think it's an emotion I could get used to over time.

At the end of September Beau comes home from a Saturday at the farm surprisingly upbeat. Dropping a distracted kiss on my head, he grabs a beer from the fridge, then tosses a brand-new smartphone on the table.

"Uh."

"The phone has a private line and it's on my account with the wireless company. But my cousin Trent ensured that no one will be able to get this number. He hasn't lied to me yet." Beau leans heavily against the kitchen counter in his work jeans and work shirt. Looking a perfect picture of everything I never knew I needed in a man. "The calls should stop now. If they keep callin', tell me, I'll stop it."

"You can't fight my battles for me," I tell him softly, needing him to understand.

"That's not what I'm doin'." His southern accent comes out more when he's tired, when he's anxious, or when he's being serious. Seems he's got all three of those things going on now. "We're partners. I'm tryin' to make your life easier. Make your load a little lighter, sweetheart. A new line on my account isn't a hardship if it keeps you smilin' at me like that."

And that's apparently all he has to say on the topic because he squeezes my neck as he walks towards the bathroom for his after-work shower. For a while I just sit there, staring wordlessly at the phone. Putting up a fight seems fruitless. But I really don't want to because it's nice to be cared for by Beau. To be protected for the first time in my life.

The next twenty or so minutes are spent transferring everything on my old phone to the new one. Once it's done, I turn the old one off, then promptly throw it into the trash. Good riddance. I have no need for it anymore. Beau comes out of the shower, hair still wet, wearing only gym shorts and a faded T-shirt with a hole at the collar. My heart skips a beat just at the sight of him, and it skips another when he smiles affectionately at me, eyes crinkled at the corners.

"I love you," I tell him because I can. Because he's mine. Because hell if I'm not in this to win it now.

"Love you too, sweetheart. Now let's eat and then I kinda wanna eat you for dessert."

And that's the end of that conversation. Not that I'm mad about it.

The autumn festival starts on the bright final weekend of September. After everything with my parents, the festival is a perfect distraction. So are my two other best friends that are currently arguing like children in the back of Beau's work truck.

"No, I'm telling you for the final time, Jackson, licorice is the worst candy on earth," Benji practically snarls. His hair hangs loosely over the edge of the hairband he's wearing around his head.

"No, it's sour apple Jolly Ranchers," Jackson argues. He winks at me in the mirror as Benji tries to pummel him, only stopped by the seat belt snapping him into place.

"Sour apple is a superior flavor."

"It's disgusting. Licorice is better than sour apple."

"Are you fucking kidding me?"

"Stop arguing," Elijah orders firmly, twisting the dial of

the speakers up higher to drown us out. "We're getting along this weekend."

"Tell this nut job to stop having bad opinions on candy, then!" Benji shouts with a huff.

I have to bite my lip to stop myself from laughing at their antics. The farm comes into sight, making my heart swell just at the idea of seeing Beau soon. As if I didn't just see him this morning. He'd kissed me awake, then fucked me slowly so that I had the gentlest orgasm of my life. Then he'd grinned, showered, and left me in the wrecked bed as if it was a daily habit.

Could be a daily habit. We can make it one. The farm is still pretty quiet considering it's before opening. A worker waves me into the employee parking lot when they recognize the truck as Beau's. We all hop out of the car to look around at the farm.

"I want to take pictures with the sunflowers," Benji says dreamily. He's the most spirited of all of us. I never know where Benji might be. If he's not working a job for the agency, then he's traveling the world. Part of me always wants to keep him close because he's not much older than me, and I'm oddly protective of him. But another part of me knows Benji can always take care of himself despite his perpetually sunshiny attitude. There's something nefarious about Benji White.

Then there's Jackson. He'd kill for us if he needed to without a single question. Jackson tosses one of his trademark winks my way, then looks out over the sprawling farm.

"Show us around, then," Jackson orders, crossing his big arms across his broad chest.

Benji hits Jackson's chest. "Try to be a gentleman today."

Jackson makes a *what the fuck* face. "I'm always a goddamn gentleman."

Eli snorts. "Is it opposite day?"

"My mama raised a gentleman."

"I'd like to have words with your mama," Benji mutters under his breath. Jackson hears him though and smacks him upside the head. Which turns into play fighting in the dusty parking lot of the farm.

Which is of course how Colby finds us. He blinks rapidly as he watches his boyfriend try to stop Benji and Jackson from doing each other actual bodily harm.

"Everything alright?" Colby asks with a fearful look on his face.

"Colby!" Eli gives up on Benji and Jackson to run over to Colby. Eli lifts up on his toes to kiss Colby's smiling cheek. The smile on Colby's face just at the sight of Eli is unmatched. Joy for Eli fills me up because he deserves the devoted love of a good man. Just like I do too.

"Hi, baby." Colby kisses Eli's forehead. "It's going to be a busy day here, but I thought I'd greet you before it gets crazy. Everyone want some coffee?"

A chorus of "hell yes, please" echoes around, earning a deep chuckle from Colby. We all plod along behind Colby and Eli. Every now and then Eli turns his face up to grin at Colby and it's one of the sweetest things I've ever witnessed. I wonder if that's how I look at Beau. I bet it is.

The farm looks so different from the last few times I've been here. The pumpkin patch has triple the number of pumpkins as normal. Food trucks are lined up along the pathway leading from the parking lot. Overall, it's definitely way busier than a weekday. Which sounds about right considering everything Beau has told me to expect.

The coffee cart Colby leads us to is right beside Joey's food truck. Joey sticks his head out of the window to wave over at us with a cheery grin.

"I'd jump out and say hello, but it's going to be a crazy day. Want some muffins?"

Jackson's eyes go big. "What kind of muffins?"

"Pumpkin, blueberry, banana, chocolate banana..." Joey trails off as Jackson wanders over to the window. "Whatdya want, boss?"

"One of each."

Joey blinks down at Jackson. "For each of you?"

Jackson blinks back. "No. For me."

Joey is quiet for a beat, then helplessly shrugs his shoulders. "You got it."

A few seconds later Joey appears with a brown bag. "This has two of each flavor so the other guys can have some too. Can you share, boss?"

"Give me that bag," Benji says loudly, ripping the bag from Jackson's hands. He blinks sweetly up at Joey. "Thank you."

Joey just grins down at the two of them, like he's dealing with children. "No problem. Back to work. See you later."

Benji takes a muffin for himself, me, and Eli out of the bag, then hands the still full bag back to Jackson. A struggle ensues for a moment, but ultimately Jackson ends up with the bag, and a half-eaten pumpkin muffin before I can even blink. Jesus. They're kids. But I love them so much.

"Coffee orders, everyone?" Colby asks, just shy of a yell.

We all proceed to order our coffee. As we wait, we all look around the farm. The place is filling up now that the festival is officially open. My eyes instinctively search for Beau, but he's nowhere to be found. Colby chuckles beside me.

"He's not out here. He's in the sunflower fields making sure we have enough for all the ticketed people today. Worried we'll get picked out."

"Ah," I say stupidly.

"He'll come find you when he's done."

"He told you that?"

Colby shoots me a warm grin. "I just know my cousin. He'll find you."

Well, I can't argue with that. Beau will find me, wherever I am. It's a truth I know at the very core of me. Colby gives Eli a sweet kiss, a slap on the ass, then wanders off to help his family with the festival.

"How do I get one of these men?" Benji whines around a mouthful of muffin.

"You are always talking with your mouth full," Jackson points out, his nose wrinkled in distaste.

"Fuck off."

"Weak comeback."

"I'll show you a comeback." Benji aims a kick at his leg, but Jackson easily sidesteps it.

"Oh! It's Harper!" Eli says, sounding oddly relieved. Jackson and Benji can be so much together. We all love each other, but Jackson and Benji just rub each other the wrong way sometimes. Usually ending up arguing. I know for a fact one time they thought it was sexual tension, tried to fuck, and that did not go well. So, they're just friends that argue over every little thing. We've all accepted it.

Harper greets us with a shy wave. His service dog blinks at his feet, a vest on to designate she's working. She's a gorgeous golden retriever, with big brown eyes focused only on Harper.

Jackson pushes past me to stand beside Harper. "Want a muffin? I have one left."

Harper blinks up at Jackson, his eyes big and round. "I ate breakfast already. Thank you though."

"Oh yeah, sure," Jackson says, sounding awfully put out.

I cock my head as I take the two of them in. Harper's about my height, but stick thin, no muscle on him. But his long auburn waves, bright green eyes, and smattering of freckles makes him seem sweet. From my interactions with him when I was a fake boyfriend, he's anything but though. More like a sour patch kid than anything. That boy has a sharp tongue and want for trouble.

Harper looks away toward the crowd, but Jackson's gaze stays firmly on Harper. I've never seen Jackson look at someone with so much longing before. His eyes trace Harper's face, deep want written all over his own lovestruck face. Oh, sweet Jackson. Our gazes collide and Jackson just shrugs, then he makes a helpless gesture towards Harper with one hand.

"Hey, Harper, isn't there a pie-eating contest? I bet Jackson could win it."

Harper's gaze pings back to Jackson. His eyes slide from the top of Jackson's head all the way down to his feet, before lifting back up to meet Jackson's hooded gaze.

"Yeah, maybe."

Well, that was a bust. Harper looks away again and I grimace, making my own helpless gesture back to Jackson. I'm not going to be able to help with this one. That's all on Jackson. A frustrated sigh escapes Jackson, but it goes unnoticed by an oblivious Harper.

"What's going on?" Eli murmurs out of the side of his mouth.

"We're witnessing a very bad mating dance. Jackson is like one of those birds that bring all the colorful fauna to the other bird only to be denied."

Eli grimaces in sympathy. "Ouch. Harper seems totally disinterested."

Seems like it, yeah, but I don't believe it. I'll have to play matchmaker later. We wander aimlessly around the festival for a while, sipping at our coffees. Half the time is spent taking photos of Benji around the farm for his social media accounts that have more followers than I could even imagine having. A shudder passes through me at even the idea.

And then my eyes land on Beau cutting through the crowd, eyes firmly set on me.

Even in a crowd of people the man can easily find me like he's got a homing beacon on me. Like maybe his heart will always be able to easily find my own. Two souls intertwined. The idea is so lovely and nice that I can't help but smile as he approaches. He grins back, eyes half hidden by the ball cap on his head.

"Happy to see me?" he asks softly.

"Always."

He kisses me softly, smelling like sweat, the earth, and pure fucking sunshine. Looping arms around his neck, I kiss him again, just to lay claim to him. His hands land on my hips, tugging me closer, before he pulls away from me with a delighted chuckle.

"My mama isn't far behind," Beau whispers in a rush, warning in his voice.

"She can't see us kiss?"

"Not the way I wanna kiss you, sweetheart." Beau presses a kiss to my temple, and begrudgingly pulls away from me.

Cindy comes around the corner, all messy hair, rain

boots, and intention. Her grin grows even wider at the sight of me. I still haven't done that dinner with her, and this is a good reminder for us to do that.

"Look at all you boys. Harper, your mama is in the office looking for you."

The words seem to be code, because Harper's face pinches, and he wanders off with his dog in tow. Jackson stares longingly after him. I think maybe he won't do anything, before he swears "oh hell" and runs after Harper.

"Aw," Cindy whispers with a hand over her heart. "Another love match."

Benji snorts and looks sheepishly away when Cindy glowers at him. "I have to get back to the office, but Beau told me you were here, and I wanted to say hey. Reminding you of that dinner. You owe me a couple of them, honey. Beau been treating you alright?"

"Beau's perfect."

Cindy grins at me and winks. "Don't I know it. Y'all be good. Take a pumpkin on the house."

And then she's gone, like a twister touching down and taking back off. Benji and Eli skip off towards the pumpkins. I start to follow, but Beau's grip on my wrist halts me.

"Come see the sunflowers with me?"

I grin up at him. "Of course."

He leads me towards the sunflower fields with a heavy hand at the small of my back. Families are scattered around, laughing in joy as they pick sunflowers. But Beau leads me towards one of the plots not being picked. Noise disappears the further we go, until he cuts through a path to lead me into the field. I trust him though, because this man knows these fields like the back of his hands. Like he knows me.

His hand is firm on mine, thumb caressing the tender skin on top of my knuckles. Sun pours down on us, but the air is crisp considering summer is slowly giving up her grips. Beau comes to a stand amongst the sunflowers.

"I wanna tell you something."

"Alright."

Beau nervously licks his lips. He pushes his ball cap up on his head a little, so I can see his eyes better.

"I've got this crazy idea," Beau confesses.

"I love crazy ideas."

Beau chuckles but sends me a worried smile. "I think maybe we could build you an office one day, in the middle of a sunflower field. You can have clients here. See them inside, or out in nature. What do you think about that?"

The force of Beau almost knocks me over. This perfect man. I'm just barely thinking about the future, but he's already got it halfway planned out. I could assume it's our difference in age, but I really don't think that's it. I think it's just the difference between Beau and me. I worry about the now, and he worries about the then. Makes us kind of perfect for one another.

"I think that sounds perfect."

Beau smiles shyly. "Yeah?"

"I think coming to work, surrounded by sunflowers to help people, only to return home to you... sounds like a dream come true."

"You'll always come home to me," Beau says gruffly.

"Always," I reassure him.

And then Beau tenderly tugs me into his arms, kissing me with all the urgency of a man that knows his future is held tightly in the cage of his arms. The kiss goes on and on, until

I'm reassured of one single thing. Love is a gentle man that holds my battered heart safely in the palm of his hand. *For keeps*, I think, in the middle of the warm sunflower field. Beau's elated smile widens against my lips, and I know without a doubt that I'm home.

The fall season is finally over at the farm. Spring, summer, and fall are always the roughest seasons for me. Worn ragged by hard work, I use winter to decompress, to work the earth, to spend time with Trevor.

Time passes a little differently now.

I quietly leave the front office behind with a kiss to Mama's brow. Then I start the thirty-minute trek to Trevor's office. We'd built the small office a year ago, after he'd graduated with his clinical hours under his belt. A small little office at the edge of the property is all Trevor wanted. Colby, Lee, Joey, Jackson, and I had planted rows of sunflowers around it before painting it a bright baby blue. Happy is the only vibe we wanted Trevor's workplace to give off. I think we succeeded.

For the past year, Trevor has been seeing clients in the small office. People drive thirty minutes from the city to spend an hour with him. He's young, but he's building a client base. And I'm so damn proud of him. It doesn't hurt that he's within my reach. Close enough that we can get lunch together most days throughout the week. Close enough that my heart longs for him even though we're only a short walking distance from each other.

Short for me, too long for Trevor. He usually hops in the classic Ford I surprised him with for graduation that we rebuilt together. Trevor still drives my truck sometimes. Usually just when he wants to really get me going. Which is a lot. Everything about Trevor gets me going and it only gets better with time.

The walk clears my mind of the cobwebs of the day. By the time I reach the small office, everything feels so much lighter than it had just moments before. I knock on the door and kick the dirt off my shoes before entering.

"Sweetheart?" I call out.

Trevor's head peeks out from the office. His hair is longer now, held up most days with a hair tie to stay professional. One look from me has him chuckling and tugging his hair down without a single argument. His hair cascades down his back as his chuckles echo around the office.

"Hey, handsome." Trevor grabs his workbag, then slowly makes his way down the hallway. He presses a soft kiss to my cheek, smelling like lemon, sunshine, and sweetness.

"Ready to go home?"

"Are we walking or taking my truck?"

"Let's take your truck. Been a long day."

Trevor winks at me, then leads us out to his truck. Tossing his bag into the bed, he slowly climbs into the cab. "I got an interesting call today."

I roll the window down as Trevor pulls out of the property, heading towards our home. The ring on his finger catches the light just right, sending a spray of refracted twinkles to the ceiling. A sight that'll always make my heart go a million happy beats a minute. I vividly recall the day we exchanged vows and rings by the spring on a hot summer day. No one else, just us. That day was grander than a wedding ever could be for me. No paper necessary for us. Just the sweet promise of forever.

"Yeah?"

"From the social worker assigned to us." Trevor keeps his eyes on the road. But his jaw firms up as his hair blows in the whip of wind through the window. By the look on his face, I assume it's bad news.

Working on getting approved to foster, then adopt, for the past year has been an arduous process. It was one of the first things Trevor wanted to do once he finally earned his graduate degree. Kids. He'd been mostly uncaring about the idea when we first got together. But watching Colby and Eli become parents softened him. Made him realize maybe it was something he really wanted after all.

And I always just want what Trevor wants,

"What'd she say?"

Trevor parks the car in front of the house, eyes firmly out of the windshield. His fingers anxiously tighten and then loosen on the wheel.

"There's a little girl they think is a good fit for us. They want us to meet her. Her name is Rose."

"Rose," I repeat softly, hope swirling inside me.

Trevor's gaze finally swings towards me, revealing tears welled up in his eyes. "Rose."

"How old is she?"

"Two years old." Trevor pulls his phone out, fumbles with it for a second, then hands it over to me. A picture of a little girl with a riot of blonde curls, bright blue eyes, and a wicked smirk stares up at me. Oh, my heart.

"She's ours."

Trevor clears his throat. "She can be."

"No, Trevor. I'm telling you. She's ours. That's our little girl."

Trevor holds back a pained noise, maybe a cry. "Yeah, I think so too."

"When can we see her? When can we bring her home?"

"We can see her this weekend. If it goes well, then we can bring her home in a few weeks."

"Where is she now? Is she safe? Is she okay?"

Trevor wipes away a lone tear. He leans over to press a kiss to my unruly beard. "She's safe with another foster family right now. But they were temporary, they're hoping we can be more permanent."

"We're so permanent. Beyond permanent. Forever."

Trevor laughs, a tinkling perfect laugh. The laugh that's worked its way into my bones, to become a part of me. Suddenly, I can't hold it in anymore. I tug him to me in the truck, until he has to crawl over the gearshift to sit in my lap. I tangle my fingers in his hair and stare unblinking up at him.

"Are you happy?"

"Beau, I've been happy since the first time you kissed me. You can stop asking now."

I kiss him, just a firm press of lips. "I'll never stop asking. Your happiness is my life's greatest mission, don't ya know."

Trevor tenderly runs his thumb over my bottom lip. His gaze is fathomless, looking into the deepest parts of me. "I love you."

"Love you more."

Tugging him to me, I kiss him in the warm cab of the truck until he's boneless against me. Until everything but the taste of Trevor is burned from my mouth. Just Trevor, Trevor,

Trevor. That's all I want for the rest of my life. This life is ours, and I'm going to make it something beautiful, something perfect.

And I know Trevor is going to do the same for me.

Life is so beautiful when we let it be.

The End

WANT MORE TREVOR AND BEAU? **DOWNLOAD THEIR BONUS epilogue** to find out how Trevor got that nice ring on his finger.

Jackson and Harper are coming in early 2025. No pre-order for now, but follow me on Instagram to be the first to know when they'll be released.

Thank you so much for reading. If you've made it this far please consider leaving a review on Amazon, Goodreads, or wherever you review. Reviews help indie authors like me more than you can ever know.

ACKNOWLEDGMENTS

First and foremost, I must thank every gentle southern man that has been a quiet presence in my life. Beau is for you.

Thank you to my husband and daughter for being patient through all the late nights and early mornings writing. When the writing bug hits me you both understand without a single argument. I can't thank you enough.

Thank you to every small town in Florida that has welcomed me home.

To Amber, Lexi, and Devin who read this countless times, every *single* version and told me it wasn't hot dog barf... even when I thought it was. This one's for y'all.

To Donatella, I guess will see who wins the bet, huh?

To Hannah, your friendship bolsters me. I can never thank you enough.

To Gabi, thanks for being my forever hype girl.

To Amanda and Jenni... thanks for holding my hand!

To JJ, I'll learn to be better with the delete button. Promise.

To every person that was excited for Trevor and Beau just from their little glimmer in The Husband Experience. To every ARC reviewer. To every excited reader that treats me with kindness and joy. This book is a little bit for you too.

ABOUT THE AUTHOR

Maya spends most of her time imagining happily ever afters for the characters that live in her head. If she's not plotting how to heal broken hearts for her characters then she's spending time with her devoted husband and precocious daughter. She loves baking competitions, listening to the same song on repeat for months, and discussing the latest pop culture event in a group chat with her best friends.